D0065762

SAMMY TWO SHOES

SAMMY TWO SHOES

Phillip DePoy

**SEVERN
HOUSE**

First world edition published in Great Britain and the USA in 2021
by Severn House, an imprint of Canongate Books Ltd,
14 High Street, Edinburgh EH1 1TE.

Trade paperback edition first published in Great Britain and the USA in 2022
by Severn House, an imprint of Canongate Books Ltd.

severnhouse.com

British Library Cataloguing-in-Publication Data
A CIP catalogue record for this title is available from the British Library.

ISBN-13: 978-0-7278-5066-9 (cased)
ISBN-13: 978-1-78029-813-9 (trade paper)
ISBN-13: 978-1-4483-0551-3 (e-book)

All Severn House titles are printed on acid-free paper.

Typeset by Palimpsest Book Production Ltd.,
Falkirk, Stirlingshire, Scotland.
Printed and bound in Great Britain by
TJ Books, Padstow, Cornwall.

ONE

Sometimes I really missed New York.

I loved my little town in Florida. Good seafood, a couple of great friends; a girl at the donut shop who didn't mind spending time with me. But when's the last time some total stranger told me to go screw myself? Or a hooker grabbed my arm and coughed in my face? Or I had a great pastrami on rye? These were the things that you'd miss when you've been away from New York for too long.

And I'd been away too long.

I knew I'd have to slip into town without too much notice. I'd have to be careful. I mean, I still had an outstanding warrant. But it was nearly five years old. What kind of cop was going to be looking out for a dinky car thief with five-year-old paper on him? And anyway the hubbub had been in Brooklyn, so maybe I would just stick to Manhattan.

My good old '57 T-bird convertible had made the trip before. If I took a couple of back roads I knew about, I could really open up the engine. It was nothing to go a hundred and twenty miles per hour on one particular two-lane blacktop across the Florida–Georgia line.

So I packed up my three best suits, a week's worth of everything else, and stole out of town after midnight like I was on the lam. I figured I could make it there in twenty hours.

In the bad old days, of course, I would have relied on coke and whites. But I was a responsible citizen now and would have to make it on a thermos full of espresso and an overwhelming desire for a slice at Ray's. Any Ray's.

So, that's how I happened to be in Reno Sweeney's on a Thursday evening, having a good old-fashioned negroni and waiting for Blossom Dearie to start.

Blossom had been a primary cause of my trip, as it happened.

The barber shop in my little Florida hideaway of Fry's Bay was more sophisticated than I might have imagined when I first arrived there. In the magazine rack I could always find that week's edition of the *New Yorker*.

Sitting at the barber shop in the sweltering heat despite the window air-conditioner, I had often delighted in scanning the 'Nightlife' section, daydreaming of The Village Vanguard or Birdland. But on the recent Tuesday morning I happened across the announcement that Blossom Dearie would be appearing at Reno Sweeney's to record a live album for her own Daffodil label, and Bob Dorough would be her guest artist.

I loved Blossom, but Bob Dorough was a demigod. Miles Davis had called Dorough his favorite vocalist. Bob Dorough, a skinny white kid from *Arkansas*. In my opinion, Bob's version of 'Baltimore Oriole' was the perfect vocal iteration of Miles's cool school.

So the fact that I could see the both of them in a tidy little club like Reno Sweeney's – well, it was too much to pass up. Along with the aforementioned Ray's and the pastrami and everything.

So, to continue at Reno Sweeney's, my negroni arrived and the bartender said, before he even set it down, 'On the house.'

I stared at him. He shrugged and was gone.

I thought, 'Who am I to pass up *le negroni gratis*?' And I sipped.

A couple of minutes later a cheese plate appeared along with a second negroni.

'For you,' the bartender said.

I shook my head. 'I didn't order it.'

He smiled. 'You think I don't know who you are? You're Foggy Moscowitz. If it wasn't for Blossom, I'd make the door guy give you back the cover charge. Anyway. Welcome home.'

And once again, he was gone.

I began to understand. Modesty kept me from overstating it, but I was a kind of hoodlum hero in certain parts of the city. And in a way I didn't like.

To be brief, I stole a car. It was what I did when I lived in Brooklyn. Only the particular car in question had a kid in the back seat, a kid of which I had been unaware. Didn't make a peep. I only knew about it when the mother started screaming and running down the street after me. It was the worst night of my life.

The mother had a heart attack or something. She died chasing the car. She was an addict visiting her wealthy upper-class drug connection. The connection was also the father. So when the mother died from running down the street with too much skag in her system, and the father denied even knowing about the baby, the little tyke got placed in the system and I got gone. All the way to Florida.

The reason I got free cheese that night at Reno Sweeney's was what happened after that. After that I sent money every week from Florida to New York so that the kid would be taken care of. I set up a good adoption, I started a college fund, and I opened a bank account in its name. All anonymous.

But the thing about *anonymous* in the petty underworld is that it almost always equals *notorious*, which can turn into *famous* pretty quickly.

I had money to send the nipper because I had a gig working – and this is how I knew that God had a sense of humor – with Florida Child Protective Services. Look up the definition of *irony* and there I'll be.

Anyway, word got around. My old cronies in crime started spreading the scurrilous rumor that I was some kind of good guy. I'd mostly avoided encountering such an uncomfortable ethos by being in Florida, where no one knew about my old life.

But there I was that night: at Reno Sweeney's on West 13th Street. In *Manhattan*.

So what could I do? I drank the negroni, and several more. I ate the cheese. All long before Blossom was supposed to appear, because I'd gotten there plenty early in order to get a seat.

And then it happened. I was suddenly and inexplicably accosted by Sammy Two Shoes. Apparently, some busboy told some delivery guy, and, like a bolt of lightning, everybody knew I was in town.

And Sammy wasn't just anybody. We grew up together in the streets. We pitched pennies, stole hubcaps, got shot at. The kind of thing that makes you somebody's brother, even though I hadn't seen him in five years.

He sat down beside me before I even knew he was in the club. That's how much of my New York savvy I'd lost over the course of my time in Florida, that a guy with a gun could get that close to me without my even noticing. So, you know. Damn.

'Give my friend another,' he said just as I saw him sit beside me.

The bartender had already made another, and he set it down right in front of me, and then vanished.

I swiveled at the same time. 'Sammy?'

'Hello, Foggy,' he answered.

He didn't seem surprised to see me. He didn't ask me what I'd been doing for the number of years since he'd seen me. He didn't ask me why I was in town. Instead of any preamble or small talk, he just sighed.

'Foggy,' he said, 'I'm in love with a woman who's in love with the theatre. And here she is.'

He pointed to the woman sitting beside him. She was a knockout, about five foot six, white-blond hair, eyes greener than money; dressed in junk-shop chic.

Sammy was wearing one of his old favorite suits, the double-breasted salt and pepper with the lapels too wide for his skinny frame. If you asked me.

'Her name is Phoebe Peabody, and she's what you call a stage manager, which, far as I can figure, is the person in charge. When the director goes on to another project and the producer is busy complaining about audience numbers, the stage manager has to keep the whole thing on its feet. Say hi.'

'Hello, Phoebe,' I said.

'Hiya,' she said right back, sweet as you please.

'I told her about you already, Foggy,' Sammy went on. 'Phoebe's in trouble, and I know you can help. Because I always considered you something of a buttinsky. At least that's what your aunt Shayna used to call it. I call it helping out a friend. In this case.'

All I could think of to say, under the circumstances, was, 'Um.'

'You gotta do it, Foggy,' Sammy said plaintively. 'See, somebody wants Phoebe dead.'

I guess I had gotten a little too used to the pace of things in small-town Florida. The speed with which things were happening in the city turned my mind around just a little bit. I'm in town for an hour and already everybody knows where I'm drinking, and old friends gnaw their way out of the woodwork to cop a favor? For a *girlfriend*? Seriously, if it hadn't been for Blossom and Bob, I might have just finished my last negroni and made a beeline south.

I should have done that. But before I could gather my wits, Sammy laid his giant paw on my forearm.

'Now, you gotta understand,' Sammy said to me very softly, 'I been kinda keeping my relationship with Phoebe on, you know, the sly.'

'Because you don't want your new flame to get hip to your old crowd,' I assumed. 'Actors and hoodlums maybe don't mix. And vice versa.'

'Exactly.' He nodded. 'I don't want her and criminals to get into any sort of *cahoots* type of situation.'

'Right,' I told him. 'So why risk it with me?'

'Right. Exactly. That's where you come in,' he said. 'She don't know you and you ain't on the wrong side of Johnny Law no more. Am I right or am I right?'

'I suppose I'm as close to being an upright citizen as I've ever been,' I agreed.

'OK, that's settled.' He turned to Phoebe. 'So, tell him.'

'Right.' She leaned on the bar. 'The trouble is named Emory. She's in the show.'

'Which, alone, is trouble enough,' Sammy interrupted. 'Actors.'

'They're all trouble,' Phoebe agreed, 'but Emory more than most.'

'Show him the latest,' Sammy said to Phoebe.

Phoebe produced a note and put it on the bar beside my negroni.

It said, 'How now? A rat? Dead, for a ducat, dead!'

I looked up from the note. 'What's a ducat?'

'It's from *Hamlet*,' Sammy told me. 'That's the show Phoebe is running.'

'It's an all-girl cast,' Phoebe added, a little wearily. 'The director had a *concept*. It's set in a women's prison.'

I finished my drink. 'Sounds just terrible. How can I help?'

'Razz this Emory character,' Sammy snapped. 'Get her to stop leaving Phoebe notes like this. You know, put the freeze in her knees.'

'Why don't you do it?' I asked Sammy.

'I'm Phoebe's boyfriend,' he told me, like I was an idiot. 'If I hassle the help, Phoebe gets blamed. Actor gossip. Suddenly Phoebe's got no work. It's a big mess. *You* gotta do it.'

'What makes you think,' I asked Sammy, 'that I'd be the sort of person to rile some poor actor just for leaving a note?'

'Tell him,' Sammy said to Phoebe.

'It's not just a note,' Phoebe said. 'Emory wants to kill me.'

'Why would she want to do that?' I asked. 'I just met you and I already like you.'

'I'm replacing her in the show,' Phoebe said. 'I'm tossing her out.'

'Why?' I asked her.

Heavy sigh. 'She's always late. She doesn't know her lines. She's missed two performances altogether. And we've only been open for a week!'

'Tell her about Nan,' Sammy prodded.

'Oh yeah!' Phoebe said. 'Emory *already* tried to kill Nan!'

'Nan is what you call an *understudy*,' Sammy told me.

Sammy began to explain what an understudy was, but I stopped him. It wasn't an unfamiliar term.

'The understudy's taking over?' I said to Phoebe.

'Tomorrow.' Phoebe nodded. 'And Emory, she's out for blood.'

'Blood? Well, they say actors *are* a high-strung lot,' I observed, nodding.

'The thing is, Nan's understudying *every* role,' Phoebe told me. 'She's the only substitute we got. I can't have anything happen to her.'

I locked eyes with Phoebe. 'Isn't it just possible that it's all talk? I mean: theatre, right?'

Phoebe shook her head. 'Emory went to Nan's apartment last night and fired a gun into the poor kid's door. Five bullets. It was just lucky Nan was in the bathroom.'

'This understudy,' I asked, 'she knew it was definitely Emory?'

'Emory was screaming, "I'm Ophelia! Not you!"'

'That's the part this Emory dame's got, see?' Sammy filled in. 'Ophelia. She's Hamlet's girlfriend.'

Phoebe looked at Sammy with love in her eyes, or something like it. 'He's seen the show seven times.'

He nodded, staring back. 'I think I almost got the hang of it.'

I stood up, mostly to get away from the mooning.

'Look,' I told them both, 'I've had people shoot at my door. More than once. It's just a way to blow off steam. You're making too much out of this.'

'But that's *our* world, Foggy,' Sammy entreated. 'Normal people don't participate in that kind of a deal, i.e. shooting at innocent doors.'

I sighed. 'You just want me to talk to this Emory?'

'Just set her straight,' Sammy agreed. 'You can be nice *and* threatening. I seen you do it.'

'OK.' I shook my head. 'Where can I find her?'

'The show starts at eight,' Sammy said instantly. 'Let's go.'

'Now?' I looked over at the stage. 'No. I gotta hear Blossom. And *Bob Dorough* is sitting in.'

'But . . .' was all Phoebe could get out.

Anyone could see why it was a tough decision for me: save a theatre type or listen to Blossom Dearie. On the one hand, they say that theatre people are almost like real human beings. On the other hand, what if I missed Bob Dorough?

In the end, Sammy prevailed upon my better instincts by saying, 'Come on, man, I'm in *love*.'

Sammy Two Shoes in love was indeed a rare monster, and I couldn't ignore it. So I downed my last negroni and off to the little theatre I went. If I'd known what was going to happen, I would have handcuffed myself to the bar stool in Reno Sweeney's and had about ten more negronis.

TWO

The theatre, if you could call it that, was on Cornelia Street, not far from where Caffe Cino used to be. Really just a storefront with folding chairs and coffee can lights. When we walked in, the place was deserted, dark, and depressing.

'I'll show you the dressing room,' Phoebe told me. 'That's where the trouble always is.'

She took me down a hall to a medium-sized concrete closet that would have made a neat slaughterhouse. Along the walls there were tables, and on them cheap mirrors were propped up. Every chair had a name Scotch-taped to the back. We stopped at the one that said *Understudy*. There was a dead rat on her hand mirror. Fresh.

'Are you seeing what I have to deal with?' Phoebe complained, more calmly than I would have. 'This is too much! The understudy's scared to come in, audiences *hate* the play, the director's in Philadelphia, and the actors haven't been paid since the second week of rehearsal. Now I gotta deal with a dead *rat*!'

With that she picked up the poor thing by its tail and marched out of the room.

Sammy appeared in the doorway of the dressing room.

'Is she the coolest thing you ever saw?' he asked me.

'Like a daiquiri,' I told him. 'So this rat motif is a thing, then?'

'What's a *motif*?'

'Doesn't matter.' I sighed. 'When do the actors show up? I mean, I guess I'm meeting this Emory?'

'Any time now,' he said.

I went to the chair that said *Ophelia* where Emory was likely to sit. Unlike all the other places, it was neat as a pin. Makeup lined up, notepad with a pencil in the spiral, an opened bottle of water. The pencil in the notepad was a mechanical, larger than most, very sturdy.

Before I could examine it further, I heard voices coming down the hall. Sammy stepped aside and three younger women stormed in. They came to a silent halt when they saw me.

'Oh, good,' one said, squinting. 'Another stage-door Casanova.'

'That's Foggy,' Sammy protested, then lowered his voice. 'He's here to help. You know. With Emory.'

They all remained frozen solid.

One whispered, 'Is she here?'

I shook my head.

They seemed relieved and a kind of general hubbub resumed. But when each got to her assigned seat, a weird silence settled into the cramped little room once again. More actors came in, all very quietly, like they were intruding on a funeral service.

Within five minutes the entire cast was there and seated at her station. Except for Emory.

Polonius sat back in her chair and gave me the once-over.

'You really gonna help us with Emory?' she asked me.

'I'll do my best,' I said.

'Good,' she said. 'She scares me.'

'I'm about to punch her in her face,' Claudius mumbled, putting on her wig.

Gertrude shrugged. 'I wouldn't mind if she got hit by a cab.'

Phoebe stuck her head in and said, 'Supposed to be half-hour, everybody. But we're holding for Emory.'

'Half-hour?' I asked Hamlet.

'We're *supposed* to start the show in half an hour,' she explained. 'But since Emory's not here . . .'

She trailed off and fussed with her shirt. I resumed my examination of Emory's things. Neat as a pin except, I noticed, for the hand mirror. It was just like the one at the understudy's place, only there wasn't a rat on it. There were smudges and streaks of white powder. It was right beside her notepad. A quick glance around told me that nobody else had a pad and pencil.

'Why does Emory have a notepad here?' I asked out loud.

Hamlet answered without turning to face me. 'She makes a big deal of taking notes after every show.'

'Notes about what?' I asked.

Hamlet shrugged. 'Acting notes, like we get in rehearsal?'

So, I opened the pad. The notes were all printed in capital letters.

HAMLET LEFT OUT THREE WORDS IN 'TO BE OR NOT TO BE' SPEECH.

GERTRUDE CALLED ME A COW BACKSTAGE.

POLONIUS STINKS.

They were all like that. All bad. Just as I was flipping the last page, I heard an angry voice behind me.

'I got here before anybody, Phoebe!' she was screaming. 'I was here for an hour, then I got the jitters and – and went out for a walk, and – hey! What the hell are you doing?'

I turned to see the kid: red-faced, skinny, dressed in black, eyes wild, standing next to Phoebe. Her hand was reaching into her bulky purse.

'Are you Emory?' I began.

But the hand came out of the purse with a can of Mace in it.

I didn't mean to smack her. It was instinct. Someone on the street pulls a gun, I don't think about it. My hand just does what it does.

In this case, my hand whacked Emory on the ear and then knocked the Mace out of her hand. Unfortunately, the Mace responded by crashing down on to Emory's dirty hand mirror. The mirror did the only thing it could do under the circumstances. It shattered into a million pieces.

Mayhem ensued.

Apparently, actors are a superstitious lot. You can't say 'good luck.' You can't whistle in a dressing room. You can't say the word *Macbeth* even though it's the title of a perfectly good play. All of which I learned right after the Mace hit the glass. A broken mirror was, according to the general consensus of the assembled, the *Titanic*, the Hindenburg, and Pearl Harbor rolled into one.

It took Phoebe a full ten minutes to calm everyone down.

Emory was shaking and her face was the color of a fire engine.

'I want this person in *jail*! He was touching my stuff and then he slapped me! Who is he?' She went on like that for a while, talking so fast that no one else could get in a word.

I just figured to let her run out of steam, but when that didn't happen, I spoke right up.

'I agree,' I said to Phoebe, pointing at Emory. 'I want the cops here. This person assaulted me with a can of Mace, which is considered a weapon by the State of New York and can only be used for self-defense. Any other use is going to result in criminal charges against her.'

Emory stammered, but no actual English words came out.

'Did anyone see this person assault me with this weapon?' I asked everyone.

Without hesitation every other cast member raised a hand.

I nodded. 'Then, yes, let's call the cops.'

'He was touching my stuff!' Emory screamed.

Phoebe shook her head. 'Doesn't really merit Mace, does it?'

Emory sputtered, shoved Hamlet's chair, and kicked the shards of mirror around for a minute, but in the end, it was showtime. Even Emory knew that.

So they all went to the stage, and I found a seat out front. There were plenty of them available.

I watched the entire show; seemed to last about a day and a half. Many of the performers got some of the lines right. I was especially impressed with Emory's ability to make every single one of her lines last longer than Hamlet's entire speeches. And when she's got a speech about a bunch of flowers in her hand because her father died and she's nuts at that point, every flower took about ten minutes.

'Here's rose . . . mar . . . mary. For. (Breath. Sob. Sniff. Cough. Sigh.) For . . . re . . . re . . . remembrance.' Followed by lots of crying. And not the dainty stuff. The Lucille Ball full-on wailing.

I shifted in my chair a lot and, for some reason, was put in mind of those animals who chew their own limbs off to get out of traps.

When it was over, the audience, all fifteen of them, left very quickly and without the applause that sometimes follows a theatrical endeavor.

I stood up and tried to thaw the numbness in my brain, waiting to have more words with Emory, when there was a scream from the dressing room.

Phoebe shot out of the lighting booth and flew backstage. I saw Sammy follow her; he'd been watching from the wings because Phoebe had banned him from the booth.

By the time I got there, everyone was staring at one particular actor, and all the dressing-room lights were on, so it wasn't hard to see the blood coming from Emory's neck. She was face down on the table in front of her. The mechanical pencil from her spiral notepad was stuck in her jugular. I knew she was dead before I went to feel for a pulse.

I looked up at Phoebe.

'Right. So, call the cops.'

She hesitated. 'Um.'

'Right now,' I insisted. 'And nobody leaves. I mean it.'

Sammy spoke softly to Phoebe. 'He's right, sugar. Foggy don't call the cops unless it's absolutely necessary. And, I mean, you got a dead actor here, so . . .'

For some reason that seemed to convince her, and the call was made from the telephone in the booth after Phoebe herded the rest of the cast into the theatre and they all sat down. Not a peep. Silent as the grave.

Sammy and I stood in the hallway outside the dressing room.

Sammy was itchy. 'Um, Fog, I gotta say I've had some extremely uncomfortable encounters with the police in my lifetime. And, unless I'm wrong, you still got an outstanding warrant on you from five years ago, right? I mean, I understand your telling Phoebe that nobody should leave. But is it smart to hang around and give the police some kind of excuse to abuse our civil rights?'

A moment's reflection convinced me that he had a point. We both made convenient targets for the average New York policeman.

So, by the time the cops showed, Sammy and I were gone.

I went back to Reno Sweeney's; walked in just in time to hear Bob Dorough and Blossom sing 'Two Sleepy People.' It was fantastic.

I don't know where Sammy went.

THREE

Next morning I awoke to the sound of banging on my hotel door. I'd taken a room at the Benjamin on East 50th rather than stay with my mother and my aunt Shayna in Brooklyn. My intention was to slip into the city, eat real food, maybe see a show, and return with all due speed to Florida before I got arrested on the outstanding warrant. I hadn't figured it would take longer than a couple of days to quench my New York jones. But I also hadn't figured on my old friend Sammy falling in love and getting me mixed up in a Manhattan theatre homicide. Some poet said the best laid plans of mice and men often go kerflooey. I didn't know how the mice were feeling, but brother was he right about me.

I always liked the Benjamin. Put up around 1927 when they called it the Beverly. Got a Neo-Romanesque edifice by the famous architect Emery Roth. So famous that it inspired Georgia O'Keeffe to take a break from painting suggestive flowers and do a portrait of the building called *New York – Night*.

None of which quelled my anxiety that someone was pounding on my door like the place was on fire. This always makes me nervous, because it can't be good that someone is that agitated before noon.

So, I stumbled to the door in my underwear, my .44 in hand, stood to one side, and said, very gently, 'Who is it?'

'It's Sammy! You gotta help me. Phoebe's in jail!'

I sighed and opened the door. He flew in, same suit as the night before.

'You might have expected that,' I told him. 'The cops nabbed the person standing closest to the body. That would have been you and me if we'd stayed there.'

'I don't care,' Sammy said. 'You gotta get her off because we both know she didn't do it. She was in the booth for the whole show!'

'How did you know where to find me?' I asked him.

'Foggy!' he shouted.

By which I assumed he meant that he didn't want to take the time to explain his methods. He just wanted me to help.

'Now, Sammy,' I said, lowering my pistol, 'the cops in this general neighborhood are overworked and underpaid and plus which people are very often tossing slugs of lead their way. You and I have no idea what it's like to be a cop in the neighborhood of a theatre where an all-woman *Hamlet* would play.'

'My opinion is that they might not be completely committed to their work,' Sammy responded. 'Because it is a lazy thing indeed to arrest the person who called in the crime!'

'Agreed, agreed,' I said soothingly. 'How about if you give me a minute to put on pants and then I'll buy you a nice breakfast, after which we can explore our options.'

He grudgingly agreed to pants, but he really didn't want to take the time for breakfast. We compromised. I put on my Florida seersucker suit, because it was a warm day, and a skinny tie, because I always want to look my best, and then we went out to the street. A single left turn found a diner, and I ate while he watched and fretted.

I was on my third cup of coffee before he blew up.

'Now!' he demanded, standing up.

Sammy's a big sort of person, about six-six, shoulders like he had on football pads, and a jawbone the shape of a boomerang. When he stood up and shouted, the rest of the diner went quiet.

I slugged back the rest of my coffee, left a twenty on the table, and stood up.

'Right,' I agreed at length. 'Where to, then?'

'Scene,' he snapped impatiently, 'of the crime!'

It was a bit of a walk, but the day was pleasant, and I was digging everything about a city street-side stroll. Pigeons, bums, bankers, models, students, Latvians, Chinese, barefoot wonders, and thousand-dollar-a-shoe stockbrokers – all in the first block. Jesus, I missed New York.

When we finally arrived at the theatre, it was locked, of course, but that wasn't a problem. I could pop a lock like falling off a log, as they say in the swamps of Florida. The problem was the time of day. Lots of people walking by. No privacy in which to convince the front door to open.

Sammy was antsy.

'I can't stick around here, Foggy,' he whispered. 'I got an allergy to cops. Look.'

He held out his hand. Hives.

'An actual allergic reaction,' I noted.

'Doctor says it's nerves,' he told me. 'I gotta go see Phoebe. But look, you go to the booth. Phoebe's got a contact sheet for all the actors there somewhere. Name, character name, address, telephone number. Cool?'

'That's why you wanted me to come here?'

'Yes! Christ! Let me go see Phoebe!'

'Right,' I assured him. 'Tell Phoebe not to worry. I know she didn't do it and I'll find out who did.'

He didn't seem relieved. 'I'm gonna find out how much her bail is, and pop her out, then.'

And he was off without another word.

I thought about telling him that there wouldn't have been a bail hearing yet, and since she was in for murder, there was no chance of getting her out before the hearing. But the big guy was so low that I just let him go on his fool's errand. Because he was a fool in love, which, in my experience, is a person for whom logic is only an irritant.

So I watched him walk away and then I wandered around the building to the back alley. It was much less crowded although a lot more disgusting. And, as it turned out, the back door wasn't locked.

And when I opened it, I heard people talking inside.

Someone said, 'Couldn't have happened to a nicer girl.'

'Is that Hamlet?' I called out.

Silence.

I eased in the door, took a few steps.

'It's me, the guy from last night.'

Still no answer.

I made it to the dressing-room door.

The little room was full. All the actors were packing up their things.

'You guys going somewhere?' I asked.

They all glared.

'No show tonight?' I stood in the doorway. 'I thought you had an understudy.'

'Cops closed us down,' Polonius told me.

'Look, man,' Hamlet said. 'Did you do this?'

'Close your show?' I smiled. 'I'm not a cop.'

'Stab Emory with her own pencil,' Hamlet snapped. 'I mean, you said last night you were going to help with the situation, but this was a little severe, don't you think?'

'Me? Why would I stab an actor? I'm not a theatre critic.'

'What are you doing here then?' Gertrude mumbled, brushing the last of her stuff into a large paper shopping bag.

'Phoebe's in jail,' I said. 'And I don't think she did anything to deserve it.'

'So you're here to help get Phoebe out?' Hamlet sounded doubtful.

I nodded.

Skepticism reigned, but at least they didn't ask me to leave.

'I would have thought this would be, like, a crime scene,' I ventured.

'When I got here,' Hamlet explained, 'the police were packing up. Case closed. Crime solved. Phoebe was standing next to the body, so Phoebe did it, I guess. That's cops for you.'

We agreed about the cops in this particular instance, and I spent the next twenty minutes talking with the actors. It wasn't especially interesting and mostly useless. Hamlet hated Emory the worst. The scenes they had together were a nightmare, apparently. Emory changed Ophelia's lines in such a way as to make Hamlet look stupid. But everyone in the cast had it out for Emory, so there really wasn't a shortage of suspects. As they all finished packing up and started to filter out, I asked the big question.

'So, who did kill Emory?'

Sometimes you could ask a question like that and throw everyone off balance. Sometimes a person off balance will say things that she wouldn't ordinarily admit.

But not these kids. All they did was look at each other.

I stared down at Emory's place at the dressing table. It was messy: broken glass from the mirror, dried blood from the actor, bottle of water knocked over on its side.

'I heard she had a boyfriend she cheated on,' Polonius suggested after a minute. 'She complained about him a couple of nights.'

'It wasn't one of us,' Gertrude told me. 'Actors only *want* to kill other actors; they don't ever really do it.'

'I had a girlfriend in college,' Claudius said, 'who put cayenne pepper in my face powder once.'

Everyone stared at her.

'What about this Nan, the understudy?' I asked.

'She wasn't here last night,' Hamlet said.

'She wasn't called,' Polonius said. 'Phoebe would only call her if she was needed, right?'

'She was scared of Emory,' Gertrude whispered. 'Emory shot up her apartment.'

'I had a girlfriend once who shot at me,' Claudius volunteered.

Everyone stared at *her*.

I looked around the room. My impression was that none of these people could kill anything stronger than a bottle of Chardonnay. But I didn't really know the theatre world. Who knows what lurks in the heart of an actor in an all-female *Hamlet* set in a prison?

'I'm leaving now,' Hamlet said without moving, clearly expecting me to object.

All I did was wave goodbye.

Everyone else took that as a cue and split with relative haste.

As soon as they were all out, I took a good look at Emory's place. Most of her stuff was gone, including the spiral notepad and the pencil, of course, but also most of her makeup and some of the bits of costume. I was certain that the police had taken everything that mattered, but I thought it was still worth a good close look.

I was staring at all the bits of broken mirror when I suddenly had an idea about *when* Emory might have been killed. Her place was the tidiest one of all the actor spots when I'd first seen it. Emory was neat. She would have cleaned up the bits of mirror if she'd had the chance. And the thing about her character, Ophelia, is that she jumps in a river and drowns before the play's over.

Which said to me that Emory, the actor, would have had time to tidy up when she came off. Long before the curtain call. She had to have been killed sometime between then and during the last scene of the play, when everybody in the whole thing is on stage for the final slaughter scene. Besides Ophelia, the characters *not* on stage, because they were already dead or gone, were Polonius, Rosencrantz, and Guildenstern.

Then, of course, there was Nan, the understudy, who could have showed up, snuck in the back door right when she knew Emory would be there, and given Emory a note she couldn't ignore.

I thought that's where I'd start. So I found my way to the booth in the dark and flipped on a little lamp beside what I assumed was the lighting board. There was a prompt book, a couple of candy bar wrappers, lots of tissues, and, eventually, a contact sheet.

Top of the list: *Nan Breen, Understudy*.

FOUR

L ess than an hour later, I knocked on Nan's door. It had five
bullet holes in it.
'Who is it?' someone asked; the voice was jittery.
'I'm sort of a friend of Phoebe's,' I told her.
'What do you want?'
'Did you hear about Emory?' I asked her softly.
Silence. Maybe she hadn't heard.
Then the lock clicked, and the door cracked. Nan peered out.
'I heard.' She stood there, tissue in hand, sniffling.
'Then you may also have heard that they arrested Phoebe,' I
went on.
'Yeah,' Nan said. 'Phoebe didn't do it.'
The door opened all the way.
Nan was a manic pixie: five-foot-nothing, close-cropped hair,
dark blue eyes. She was wearing a T-shirt that said 'To be or
. . . line?' and no shoes.
'The police came to see you?' I asked, still standing in the
hall.
She shook her head. 'Gossip's like lightning in the theatre
world.'
'May I come in?' I asked.
She thought about it.
Her apartment reminded me of one of the downsides of
Manhattan living. I could see from the hallway that it was only
one room and a bathroom. There was a kitchenette stuck in one
corner and a rusted radiator taking up almost as much space as
her futon. She had a poster of a window where she wished a
window would be. The other posters, all over the walls, were
nature scenes, like the woods in autumn and a snow-capped
mountain. There was Mozart on the stereo. Papageno from *The
Magic Flute.* There was a pleasant smell of coffee in the air.
She decided that she wouldn't let me in. She just wiped her
nose and swallowed.

'Your place is smaller than my hotel room,' I said, looking around.

'If I'd been in this room when Emory came over the other night and shot up the place,' Nan told me, 'I'd be lying here dead.'

'Emory was scary,' I agreed.

'How can I help you?' she asked, standing at the door like a guard. 'Or really, how can I help Phoebe? I like her.'

'Me too, far as I can tell.'

She gave me a quick once-over. 'You've got to be a friend of that Sammy character, her new boyfriend. What is he, like, some kind of smalltime hood?'

'Did you kill Emory?' I asked calmly.

Sometimes a thing like that worked, as I was saying. You might catch a person off guard, and their face could tell you everything.

Nan's eyes widened. 'Me?'

'She tried to shoot you through this door. That's what we call a motive in the killing game. Did you go to the theatre last night?'

'God, no,' she assured me. 'I was at Tap-A-Keg down the block. From around seven until, like, after midnight. They know me there. Ask anybody.'

'I'll do that.'

She looked like she was telling the truth, but she was an actor, so, yes, I was going to check.

'Jesus,' she muttered, shaking her head. 'Emory's dead.'

'Right,' I said. 'Can you go through a few things with me?'

'Such as?'

'In the last scene, when Hamlet kills everybody,' I began, 'some characters aren't on stage anymore because they're dead or gone, right?'

She thought about it a little longer than we both felt comfortable with, and then she finally stood aside to let me in.

'Those *characters* aren't on stage, but the *actors* are,' she told me. 'They fill out the court. Everyone's on stage for the last scene, in different costumes. You want espresso? I got a machine.'

I shook my head. 'So nobody would be in the dressing room?'

She bit her lower lip. 'Well, nobody's *supposed* to be. But most of the time Emory didn't come back on after Ophelia's dead. She told me at a rehearsal that her performance would make too strong an impression, and she'd be recognized if she came back on stage. She said it would spoil the show. I always assumed she meant "more than it was already spoiled," right? I mean, you saw the show?'

'Right. But nobody else would have been back in the dressing room during the final scene. Except Emory.'

'No. Everybody else is always on stage at the end as far as I know. Why? Is that important?' She sat at a little two-top table near the kitchenette, sipped from a demitasse cup, and pointed. 'Sit?'

I sat.

'If Emory was killed during the last scene,' I said, 'then we have a dozen witnesses who can clear Phoebe. She was in the booth and it was obvious to me that the actors could all see her there from the stage.'

'Not to mention the light cues and the sound cues,' Nan agreed. 'Phoebe was the only one in the booth, and I assume all that happened in the final scene.'

'Now you mention it, there were plenty of lights changing, especially when Horatio sang Hamlet to his rest.'

'It was actually flights of angels that did the singing,' she corrected me, 'but, yes.'

'And, anyway,' I went on, 'there's no way to get from the booth to the dressing room without everybody in the audience seeing.'

'Because the booth is right there at the back of the audience.' She nodded. 'And no way Phoebe could have slipped out of the booth, out the front door, around the back, stabbed Emory, and gotten back to the booth without everyone seeing her *and* missing a *bunch* of cues! Hey, you're not as dumb as you look!'

'Thanks.'

'You solved the case!' She smiled in a very appealing way.

'No. This line of examination doesn't tell me who killed Emory,' I said. 'But it does tell me that Phoebe *didn't* do it, and that's all I really care about at the moment. So, thanks for your help.'

I stood.

'That's it?'

'Well, Phoebe didn't do it, and you didn't do it,' I told her, 'so now I figure I gotta go talk with the other cast members, don't you think?'

'Oh,' she said slowly. 'Like, you're a private investigator!'

'Something like that,' I said.

'Cool.' She stood and saw me to the door.

'Tell them I sent you when you go to Tap-A-Keg,' she encouraged me. 'They can be a little standoffish with strangers, but they love me there.'

I smiled. 'And I can see why.'

What I didn't say was that I had no intention of actually letting her off the hook. Her or any of the other actors. Because if it was true that Emory hung out back in the dressing room for the last scene instead of going on, then everyone would be aware of that. It would be the ideal time for someone to slip in, ice her, and be back on stage or out the back door before anyone could notice. Very dramatic, and very opportune. I couldn't see any of these actors murdering anything other than Shakespeare's language, but I had to be sure.

So, I bid goodbye to Nan, but I went directly to Tap-A-Keg.

FIVE

Tap-A-Keg was five doors south of Nan's apartment building on the same block. I pushed open the door into the familiar smell of fried onions and spilled beer. When my eyes adjusted to the relatively low light, I could see everyone in the place giving me the once-over. In absolute silence.

I closed the door behind me and headed for a bar stool. The place was more or less like a thousand other neighborhood bars in Manhattan. Ten tables, same number of booths, tall wall of booze behind a short bartender. Red neon in the window, unlit candles on the tables, maybe fifteen guys in the joint before noon on a weekday. I'd been in the place before, only it was in Brooklyn, and on a Sunday.

I sat. 'Dark draft?'

Not a move or a peep.

'Nan sent me on ahead,' I went on.

Everybody relaxed.

'Can't remember the last time we saw a guy with a suit in the place,' the bartender said, pulling a beer glass from under the bar. 'You gotta be one of Phoebe's *theatre* buddies.'

He said *theatre* like it might have been catching.

I smiled. 'Not me. Nan's in a little bit of trouble and she asked me to help.'

A couple of the guys at the bar nodded. They wanted to let me know they were wise.

'Who told you to help Nan?' one of them asked, only a little belligerently.

'Allie Tannenbaum,' I shot back without a split-second hesitation.

I might as well have fired a gun. One guy at a table actually ducked a little.

'Tick-Tock.' The bartender nodded, referring to Allie's hitman moniker.

Now, in reality it had been years since I'd seen Tick-Tock. As a teen, I'd had a sort of Dutch uncle by the name of Red Levine, may he rest in peace, and Red had introduced me to Tick-Tock. Their idea was that they were grooming me for some kind of position in their organization, but I never got any farther than boosting cars in Brooklyn before my fatal incident and subsequent lamming to Florida.

Still, if you knew anything about the Jewish mob, you knew Red. And if you were really wise, you were a little afraid at the mere mention of his name. Because Red and Tick-Tock had been members of the Combination, which was the real name for what the press called *Murder, Inc.*, a very professional association of Hebrew hitmen. Men I grew up under when I lived in Brooklyn. So.

'Yeah,' I said, 'my uncle Red Levine introduced me to Mr Tannenbaum a number of years ago. I try to help out when I can.'

All relatively true, although not remotely germane to the current situation. But it had the desired effect. To wit, there was a lot more deference in the room than there had been a few moments previously.

Jesus, I missed New York. Where else can you mention an obscure hitman and garner some serious respect?

'Nan's in some kind of trouble, you said,' the bartender said, setting down a dark beer in front of me.

'One of the actors in the show for which she is the understudy,' I said carefully, staring at my beer, 'is dead, and Nan's a suspect.'

Nobody moved.

'You guys seen her lately?' I asked.

Nobody spoke.

I hoisted my beer. 'She told me she was in here last night.'

'Oh,' the bartender said, like he'd gotten a sudden electric shock. 'She was. She was sitting right there, in that stool.'

Several others nodded instantly.

'All night?' I asked.

Everyone in the place nodded. It was a little creepy.

A guy in a booth cleared his throat and said, weakly, 'Nan's connected with Tick-Tock?'

I tossed back another slug of beer. 'Not exactly. But, I mean, who do you think runs Broadway? Our people, right?'

Eyebrows lifted. Whether they were thinking that hitmen ran the theatre or Jews were ultimately in control didn't really matter to me. I was thinking about how differently these guys were going to treat Nan from then on, and it made me smile.

That is, if Nan didn't zotz Emory. If she did, they probably wouldn't be seeing much of her, what with her subsequent arrest and jail time and all.

'Well,' I said. 'She's alibied, courtesy of you guys, so that's that. Thanks, gentlemen. What's the tab?'

The bartender shook his head. 'It could not *be* more on the house. Anything for Nan.'

That was genuine. He really cared about her.

I stood up. 'Nan's got good friends. I'm glad of that.'

Table guy ventured, 'She's the only girl who comes in regular. She's, like, a little sister to most of us. You know?'

Once again, I was reminded of a bar just like that one, only in Brooklyn, where I'd been a kid, maybe nine, and all the guys in the place, drunk or sober, took care of me, watched out for me, wouldn't let anything happen to me.

So I said, 'I do know. It's a good feeling.'

'Like family,' table guy said, 'only without all the fighting.'

And that, of all things, made me lonesome for my mother and my aunt, damn it. Looked like I was going to be in New York longer than I'd planned, and I didn't see how I could stay there any longer without going to Brooklyn to see them.

But I put that out of my mind as best I could for the moment, waved to all and sundry in the joint, and popped back out to the morning street, headed toward Hamlet.

SIX

amlet's address was Central Park West. Apparently, Hamlet's parents were loaded. They weren't home, but Hamlet was, along with some sort of little dog that yapped and snapped when she opened the door.

Hamlet was hungover and dressed in a floor-length kimono. She sported long blonde hair that had been hiding under a short black wig for the show. Her skin was tea-cup delicate and pore-less. And her eyes looked like a red roadmap.

'What do *you* want?' she snapped in almost the same register as the dog.

'Phoebe.' I wanted to see if she knew what had happened, to see if Nan was right about theatre gossip.

'Oh.' She rubbed her head, then she screamed at the dog.

The dog shot off like a cannonball into another part of the house and a blessed silence reigned.

'I can't *believe* they closed the show,' she muttered. 'When am I gonna get another chance to play Hamlet?'

'Let's talk about Emory,' I said.

'Why?' She tried to focus her eyes.

'I thought you'd want to,' I said, somewhat disingenuously. 'She's dead. Somebody killed her. That's the reason the show got shut down.'

'No.' Hamlet shook her head slowly. 'That's just an excuse. The show stank up half of Manhattan. Critics hated it. Audiences agreed. I'm never going to get work again. Come on in.'

She headed for a large white sofa in a room flooded with sunlight and left it to me to close the door.

She collapsed on to the sofa like Camille and let out a sigh that could have cracked the world in two.

'I thought you were pretty good,' I told her, but mostly because I'd heard that actors responded well to compliments.

Hamlet lifted her head and looked me in the eye. 'Really? Did you really think so?'

'You're the best female Hamlet I ever saw.'

'Well.' She smiled. 'Have a seat, then.'

I came to rest in an overstuffed leather chair.

'Emory was a pain in the ass,' I prompted.

'There's not an actor in the cast who wouldn't have minded sticking that pencil *somewhere*,' Hamlet agreed, 'but actors *complain*. They don't kill people.'

'John Wilkes Booth was an actor.'

'I don't know his work. Was he in anything that I might have seen recently?'

I moved on.

'Right,' I said. 'You were on stage for the last scene.'

'Yes.' She blinked. 'I kill a bunch of people and then I get killed.'

'I remember,' I told her. 'You couldn't possibly have gotten off stage to stab Emory, so you're one of the only people I can be certain *couldn't* kill Emory. But who could have? Any thoughts?'

She took a second.

'Polonius stays in the shadows,' Hamlet said, 'because she's supposed to be dead, so, of course, she couldn't let anyone in the audience get a look at her face. She could have slipped away. Same for Rosencrantz and Guildenstern. Everyone else is kind of prominent.'

'Because they end up slaughtered on the stage.' I nodded. 'Mostly by you.'

'Why are you doing this?' she asked. 'Why are you trying to get Phoebe out of jail?'

'Because she didn't do it.' Simple.

'No, but, I mean,' she went on, 'what's your motivation?'

'Oh.' I smiled. 'Sammy Two Shoes is my friend, and he's in love with Phoebe.'

'That's the hoodlum boyfriend? His name is Sammy *Two Shoes*?'

'Yes.'

'And that's all there is to it?' She squinted. 'You're helping a *friend*? Honor among thieves.'

She didn't know how right she was, and I was in a mood to oblige her curiosity.

'A number of years ago, a cop was whacking me with a club one night.' I explained further, 'Sammy kicked the cop in the head. Another time, when I got shot, he took me to a guy and got me patched up. And also, when my mother was sick, Sammy brought her soup. And when I was in jail once, Sammy bailed me out. Should I go on?'

'I'd rather you didn't,' Hamlet said, holding her head like it might fall off. 'I have come to realize that my limit is eleven martinis.'

'I understand. What else can you tell me about the three actors who might have slipped away to pop Emory?'

'Emory hated Polonius,' Hamlet told me. 'Every night there was some complaint about how Polonius didn't understand the relationship with Ophelia.'

I nodded. 'I saw one of the things Emory wrote about Polonius in that little spiral notepad that Emory kept.'

She snapped upright.

'I *hated* that book!'

She'd mustered a good bit of venom for the statement. Would it have been possible that she'd hired someone to ice Emory? She certainly had access to the dough.

'Emory wasn't especially nice to you in it,' I commiserated.

'No.' She fell back on to the sofa. 'No, she wasn't.'

'How about Rosencrantz and Guildenstern?' I said, deliberately changing the subject.

'Oh. Well. With them it might have been more personal. They're dating, and I think Rosencrantz used to go out with Emory. So.'

'Jealousy is always a good motive for murder, they say.'

'Your problem is,' she said, nodding, 'that everybody hated Emory. I mean, if you're asking me, my money would be on Nan. If somebody shot up my door, I'd be the worst kind of mad.'

'The worst kind of mad?' I asked.

'You know, *scared*-mad. The kind where you're not thinking, you're just reacting.'

'Oh.' As it happened, I did know scared-mad. Like when a cop was beating you with his club and you're pretty sure you're going to die.

'Anything else?' she asked, holding her head like it was a delicate pumpkin.

'Not really,' I told her. 'You're the only person besides Phoebe that I'm certain didn't kill Emory.'

'Funny,' she mused. 'Scholars for hundreds of years have debated about whether Ophelia was dead because of Hamlet. And now, here we are.'

'It's a complex problem,' I ventured. 'But Ophelia iced herself because her boyfriend killed her father.'

She glanced up at me. 'Look who paid attention to the play.'

'The thing is, though, killing someone isn't always as straight-forward as lots of people think. You get all churned up in your guts about something, and sometimes it's something that the victim doesn't even know about or remember. But the killer is riled, and maybe it has more to do with what's on the inside than anything the victim did or didn't do, see?'

She stared. 'I did an episode of *Adam-12* about a year ago. I was Girl in Miniskirt.'

I got the impression she was trying to explain to me that she somehow knew what I was talking about. And maybe it was the fact that she had money and lived in an apartment as big as the White House or the fact that she was more concerned with her acting career than the death of a fellow traveler, no matter what that traveler had been like in life, but I felt like giving her the scoop.

'My father was a hitman for what they sometimes call Murder, Inc. He got rubbed out when I was a kid, and I grew up with mobsters, murderers, and mugs. I make with the allit-eration so that you'll know I'm not stupid. And I understand more about killing people than anyone you'll ever meet. So, please.'

She swallowed and sat up. 'I didn't have anything to do with Emory being dead.'

'You probably didn't.' I turned toward the door. 'But I gotta do my work, right?'

'You should go see Rosencrantz and Guildenstern.'

I nodded. 'You know there's a great new play called *Rosencrantz and Guildenstern are Dead*. I just read about it, in the *New Yorker*, I think.'

She blinked. 'Is there a part for me in it?'

SEVEN

According to Phoebe's contact sheet, Rosencrantz and Guildenstern lived together in a one-room place at the edge of Spanish Harlem. It was one of the neighborhoods I'd never seen. It wasn't rough where they were, exactly, but you couldn't have called it an upscale block.

So I wasn't surprised when Guildenstern flung the door open and demanded, 'What?'

Through the open door I could see that the place was a wreck. Piles of clothes on the floor, no bathroom door, dozens of takeout containers everywhere. Guildenstern had come to the door in her underwear. Rosencrantz appeared to be asleep on the mattress on the floor. The blinds were drawn against the sunlight, exacerbating the atmosphere of chaos and gloom.

'*What?*' Guildenstern snapped again.

'I was at the theatre last night,' I said quickly. 'Phoebe's been arrested for killing Emory and I don't think she did it.'

Rosencrantz rolled over in bed. She wasn't wearing a top and there was a gun in her hand. It was too dark to be sure, but it looked like a .38 Special.

I stood very still.

'It would go like this when I call the cops,' Rosencrantz told me, cold as an ice pick. '"There was a strange man at the door, Officer. He menaced my roommate and tried to force his way in. You don't know what it's like to be a young girl in this part of town. Poor young girl. We were terrified."'

I nodded. 'It's a plausible speech.'

'So maybe you should get lost,' Guildenstern suggested.

'Don't you want to help Phoebe?' I asked. 'Because you know she didn't kill Emory.'

'I don't really know anything,' Guildenstern answered belligerently.

'The cops know what they're doing,' Rosencrantz added.

'Just let me ask you one question,' I said. 'During the last scene, when everybody on stage gets killed, did you see anyone slip out? Because I think that's when Emory was killed. During the last scene.'

Rosencrantz lowered her gun. 'Oh.'

'So whoever left the stage,' I suggested, 'might be the culprit, as they sometimes say in the mystery books.'

'OK.' Rosencrantz set the gun down on the mattress. 'Polonius always splits when Gertrude dies. She's dressed as a courtly lady, right, and she makes like it's too much to see the queen dead. She, like, flees.'

Guildenstern agreed. 'That's right. She flees.'

Rosencrantz nodded. 'She actually just goes out in the back alley for a smoke. She's got a real nicotine problem.'

Guildenstern shrugged. 'It's a *real* problem.'

'You both stayed on stage for the whole scene,' I said.

'Of course,' Rosencrantz said, a little offended. 'You can't just walk out of a scene. It's not professional.'

'It isn't professional at all,' Guildenstern echoed.

'So you think it's possible that Polonius could have killed Emory?'

'Fuck.' Rosencrantz yawned. 'Anyone in the five boroughs *could* have killed Emory. I don't think there was a single person in the theatre world who didn't hate her.'

I hesitated, but I had to say, 'Um, you didn't always feel that way about Emory, though, right?'

Rosencrantz glared. 'You are referring to the rumor that we used to date, me and Emory.'

'I heard that you two were an item.'

'Were. *Were* an item,' Guildenstern said.

'Maybe *you* hated Emory more than the others,' I said to Guildenstern.

'Why would she?' Rosencrantz objected defensively.

'Emory was jealous of me.' Guildenstern shrugged. 'I wasn't jealous of her. She lost. I won.'

'I have come to believe that matters of the heart are never really that simple,' I told them both.

For a second, we were frozen, all three of us. I was prepared to dodge a bullet, and Guildenstern was still blocking the door. But after that second, Rosencrantz got up out of bed.

'You want some coffee?' she asked me. 'We got a French press. It's really good coffee. You can skimp on a lot of things, but not caffeine.'

'It's good,' Guildenstern assured me.

I wasn't that interested in coffee, but I did want to talk with them a little more, so I nodded, and Guildenstern stepped aside.

Once I was in, the place looked even worse. The bathroom door was leaning up against the wall, splintered at the hinges. The toilet was running. The lamp beside the mattress had no shade.

There was a little café table. Two chairs. Rosencrantz didn't bother to put on a top and I maintained a scrupulously intense eye contact.

'You figure Emory was jealous of you two?' I asked Rosencrantz.

Guildenstern turned on a hot plate and poured water into a pan from a jug of bottle spring water. Rosencrantz sat down at the table and offered me the other chair with a nod of her head.

'Emory was one of those people who's mad all the time,' she told me.

'Mad about what?' I asked.

'The usual. Her career wasn't moving like she wanted. New York was too hard to live in. The deli put too much mustard on her pastrami.'

'I hate that,' Guildenstern said absently, staring at the pot on the hot plate. 'Too much mustard.'

'Not to mention that she hated being with me,' Rosencrantz went on. 'She thought she was supposed to be with a guy.'

'Then why was she with you?' I asked.

'Right?' Rosencrantz agreed. 'I mean, we argued about it all the time. I told her to just leave if she felt that way. Plenty of fish, you know?'

'I know.'

'But the thing was,' she went on with her voice lowered, 'she was into S&M. So that the fact that she didn't want to be with a woman, and I was, like, forcing her to do stuff, it was kind of a thing for her.'

'Forcing her.' I blinked.

'Nothing too weird,' Rosencrantz assured me. 'She liked to be tied up.'

'She was bi,' Guildenstern volunteered, still staring into the as-yet un-boiled water.

'You know what you call a bi woman?' Rosencrantz asked me.

'A lesbian who just doesn't want to admit it,' I said.

She laughed. 'Exactly. What makes you so smart? You know a lot of lesbians?'

'I used to know a lot of strippers.'

She nodded. 'Same thing.'

'A *lot* of the time,' Guildenstern added.

'But you and Emory broke up eventually,' I said, attempting to steer the conversation back closer to the point of my visit.

'Six months ago,' she said. 'The day I met Beth.'

Beth was, I gathered, Guildenstern's real name. A quick glance down at Phoebe's sheet confirmed it.

'We were in the chorus of *Guys and Dolls*,' Guildenstern said, smiling sweetly.

The water had apparently boiled, and she was pouring it into the French press.

'The seven thousandth revival of fucking *Guys and Dolls*,' Rosencrantz said wearily.

'It was in Newark,' Guildenstern admitted, 'but it wasn't bad.'

'I met her on a Tuesday at ten in the morning,' Rosencrantz began, staring at her beloved, 'and I was in love by lunch break. Went home that night and told Emory to move out.'

'She was mad?' I asked.

'Tell the truth,' Rosencrantz said, 'I think she was relieved. You know, the whole not-really-sure thing. About being with a woman, you know?'

'Right.'

'But she sure was jealous when the two of us showed up holding hands at the first *Hamlet* rehearsal,' Guildenstern said. 'Made a big stink.'

'In what way?' I asked.

'Told the director she couldn't work with us,' Guildenstern said.

Rosencrantz grinned. 'The director turned to Nan and said, "Looks like you got a part after all." That changed Emory's tune, and she deigned to go on as Ophelia.'

'Nan was upset that she wouldn't get to play the part,' I assumed.

'Not really,' Guildenstern said quickly.

'Nan has a sort of reputation as a professional understudy,' Rosencrantz told me. 'It's a good gig if you navigate it just right. You get a little money for zero work.'

'She told me that she hadn't bothered to memorize anybody's lines,' Guildenstern said. 'What was the point, really? The show sucked. It was never going to run long enough for her to have to take over for anybody. So she goes to that stupid Tap-A-Keg every night and the show pays for her drinks.'

'Tap-A-Keg?' I asked innocently.

'Her home away from home. She took us all there on opening night. It's a real neighborhood bar. Same locals on the same stools, night after night. We really gave them a jolt.'

'I think she was kind of panicked when Phoebe said she was going to fire Emory,' Rosencrantz said.

'She wasn't prepared,' Guildenstern agreed.

Guildenstern pushed down the plunger on the French press.

'I guess you're familiar with the play *Rosencrantz and Guildenstern Are Dead*,' I ventured.

'Only the greatest play written in the twentieth century,' Rosencrantz told me. 'How in the world would you know about it? You don't strike me as a theatre guy.'

'Never saw it,' I admitted, 'but I read a lot, and sometimes I'll read a play if I'm having trouble sleeping. Why couldn't that be next for you guys?'

'An all-female *Rosencrantz and Guildenstern Are Dead*!' Guildenstern said.

She poured the coffee and then sat on Rosencrantz's lap. We had a jolly conversation about theatre, which mostly consisted of their telling me about all the roles they'd played and how good or bad the shows had been. Turns out the only thing actors like better than acting is talking about acting.

In the end I finished my coffee and apologized for bothering them.

Because it's always a good idea to apologize to a person with a gun.

EIGHT

Next stop, Polonius, who lived in a sort of a dorm room at Tisch with three other students. She was tall and weighed in at about ninety-five pounds. Stringy blond hair, bloodshot eyes, she came to the door in a large mechanic's shirt that said 'Ralph' on it, wearing it like a dress.

'You're that guy who saw the show last night,' she mumbled. 'The nosy one in the dressing room.'

'Right,' I said.

'What do you want? I'm not like Phoebe. I don't date stage-door Johnnies.'

I smiled. 'Not here for a date, and the name is Foggy.'

'Foggy? What kind of a name is that?'

'It's a nick. Got it when I was a kid and it stuck.'

She looked me in the eye. 'Foggy because you can't think straight, or Foggy because you hide inside ephemeral weather?'

I stared back. 'Can I come in? I'm trying to get Phoebe out of jail.'

'Phoebe's in jail? What for?'

So theatre gossip had its limits.

'Cops think she's the one who stabbed Emory,' I explained.

Polonius shook her head. 'I love Phoebe. She would never kill anybody who was in one of her shows. She's a professional.'

'So can I come in?' I repeated.

She stepped aside. The roommates were all at a table having breakfast. At a little after noon. Didn't give me a second look.

Polonius sat down on the sofa next to the door. I joined her. She lit a cigarette and closed her eyes when she inhaled.

'*I* didn't kill Emory, if that's what you want to know.'

'Why would you think that's what I want to know?' I asked her.

'Because I hated Emory. She hated me. She made notes about me in that stupid book of hers. I think I probably said, "I could kill you" to her maybe three times a week.'

'And you did leave the stage during the last scene,' I said. 'I'm pretty sure that's when Emory was stabbed.'

'I went out for a smoke,' she complained. 'I do it every show. Ask anybody. If I go more than a half-hour without, I get itchy. I left the stage, zoomed out the back, smoked in the alley, and was back in time for final bows. Sue me.'

'Sue you? You're an actor. How much money could I get?'

'Good point.' She smiled. 'How come you want to get Phoebe out of jail?'

'She didn't do it.'

'Agreed,' she said, 'but what do you care?'

'Her new beau is my old friend,' I told her.

'Of course. You and Sammy are kind of cut from the same cloth. I could tell that last night. Brooklyn?'

'Exactly.'

'I'm good with accents.'

'I don't have an accent,' I objected.

'You've been living in Florida for a few years, but you haven't completely shed the speech patterns of your native habitat.'

'I'm impressed,' I said. 'How did you know it was Florida? Florida doesn't have an accent.'

'No, but I know clothes. And you, my friend, are wearing a type of seersucker that you can only get in Florida. That cut, that number of buttons on the sleeve, and that particular shade. So I guessed. And I guessed right, I see.'

My eyes widened. 'That's phenomenal. I *did* get this suit in Florida. You *do* know clothes.'

She shrugged one shoulder. 'I model.'

Hence the weight, or absence thereof, I assumed.

'I guess you're asking me about this because your pal Sammy saw me swoop out in a hurry during the last scene last night.'

'He was standing in the wings,' I told her.

'Can't miss that salt-and-pepper suit with the oversized lapels.'

'But it was actually Rosencrantz who told me you always ducked the last scene for a smoke. Or Guildenstern – one or the other.'

'That's the joke,' she said.

'Joke?'

'Hamlet gets them confused in the play.' She stabbed her smoke out on a plate on the coffee table and lit another one from a pack she had in her shirt pocket. 'But Polonius is the *foggy* one, right?'

'Ha,' I said flatly.

'You know,' she observed, taking a deep drag, 'Emory was always complaining about some ex of hers. Maybe that's something. You know, in the murder arena.'

'Boy or girl?' I asked.

She smiled big. 'I see you're wise to Emory's predilections. And now that you mention it, she never specified as to the gender of her complaint. I mean, I guess it could have been Rosencrantz, right? You know they were an item before.'

'I know,' I assured her. 'It's funny how you all refer to each other by the character name instead of the actor name.'

'Who keeps track of actors' names?' she asked. 'I never worked with any of these people before, and I probably never will again. That's the lonely thing about being an actor, you know. You're closer than family on a show, and then when the show's over, you may never see any of them again for the rest of your life.'

I nodded. 'I guess you could say that *Foggy* was my character name. Very few people know my given name.'

'What is it?' she asked.

'I'd rather not say. Look. You seem to be a little more on the ball than some of the other actors. You have an opinion about who killed Emory?'

She shook her head. 'I was out in the alley. Nobody came in while I was there. And nobody else left the stage. And nobody could get to the dressing room while the show was going on. I mean, maybe she stabbed herself. She was miserable enough.'

'Sad?'

'No, I mean she was a miserable human being, and not a very good actor. You know she only got this gig because she boinked the director. Repeatedly.'

I sat back. 'No kidding.'

'No kidding,' she assured me.

'Maybe I should talk to this director?' I wondered.

'She's in Philadelphia,' Polonius told me. 'Left town right after the dress rehearsal, didn't even come to opening night. That's how much confidence she had in the show.'

'So, Philadelphia is a pretty good alibi,' I said.

'I guess you could check with the theatre there, see if she really left town or just abandoned us poor sailors.'

'What theatre in Philadelphia?' I asked.

'Hedgerow,' she told me. 'I think it's the oldest resident theatre company in America. I'd *kill* for a gig there. Pardon the expression.'

I nodded. 'I'll check it out. Anything else?'

'Tell Phoebe I'm rooting for her,' she said.

I stood. She made it to her feet to see me out.

'Your friend Sammy wasn't in the wings, by the way,' she said as she opened the door. 'When I dashed into the alley for a smoke, he was in the dressing room.'

NINE

I found Sammy at Izzy's Deli. I wasn't sure it would still be a hangout for him, what with the ensuing years, but there he was, at the same old table, staring down at his crème soda. He hadn't touched his bagel.

He looked up and saw me. All he did was nod, like he'd been waiting there for me. I guess he could tell by my face that I was troubled.

'Polonius saw you in the dressing room, Sam,' I said right away. 'She told me, just as I was eliminating all the actors as suspects. Only now I've got a new suspect, and he's ignoring a perfectly good bagel.'

Before I could sit down, he said softly, 'The cops are gonna find my prints on the pencil that was in Emory's neck.'

'Because you put the pencil there, right?' I asked, just as softly.

He shrugged.

'I only wanted to help Phoebe,' he said softly. 'That Emory, she was a nightmare. I didn't mean to ice her. I only wanted to scare her.'

'You couldn't think of some better way to do that?' I complained, taking my seat. 'Other than stabbing her in the neck with her own *pencil*?'

'It was handy.' He shrugged.

'That wasn't my question,' I began. 'You came to *me* for help with Phoebe. Why didn't you just let me take care of it? This does *not* add up. What's the matter with you?'

'I . . .' he began, but he couldn't seem to go on.

'What happened between you and Emory that could have made you—'

He held up his left hand, took one bite of his bagel, and stood up. 'Let's go.'

'Where do you think we're going?' I asked him.

'I figure you wanna take me to the cops,' he told me, 'now that you're an upstanding citizen.'

'I'm not taking you to the cops,' I assured him. 'I'm just going to tell them what I know. Except I'm going to leave out your name, and you're going to blow town.'

'I can't do that,' he began. 'I'm in love with Phoebe.'

'How do you think she's going to react to the news that you killed somebody?' I asked. 'You were nervous about even *introducing* her to your hoodlum friends. Her world's all make-believe and play-acting. Your world is . . . you know.'

He nodded. He did know.

'So.' He stared out the window. 'You tell the boys in blue that you know who done it, as they say in the movies, and Phoebe gets out.'

'Meanwhile,' I added, 'you abscond.'

'Like you did,' he said, but it wasn't an accusation, it was an agreement.

'Like I did.'

He finally looked me in the eye. 'Why are you doing this, Foggy? I ain't seen you in a good while, and plus you went straight. You got good. People, like, admire you. If it gets out that you let the killer go, what's gonna happen to your rep?'

'One, I don't care about my *rep*,' I began. 'And two, you're my friend.'

'We were friends once,' he allowed, 'but it was a fair number of years ago.'

'I'm supposed to forget that you saved my life?' I asked him. 'I'm supposed to ignore the fact that you took soup to my mother when I couldn't? *That* would be more likely to sour my rep than anything else, don't you think? People would say, "What kind of a weasel is this Moscowitz character? He turned in a pal!"'

He smiled. 'You just said you didn't care about your rep.'

'Come on.' I fished a twenty out of my pocket and tossed it on to the table. 'I'll figure something out. I just don't know what. Yet.'

He lifted his eyebrows about as far as they would go. 'I guess you could call your aunt Shayna.'

Now, my aunt Shayna was one of the ten most loving women in the world. A hug from her was better than a gin martini. And do *not* get me started on her brisket.

By Shayna had also, in her youth, been the bookkeeper for the Combination, a collection of the most professional hitmen on the planet. Everybody said that Shayna dated Allie 'Tick-Tock' Tannenbaum, one of their guys, when he lived in Brooklyn, but she denied it. Like taking the Fifth.

They also said that Allie and my father had worked on hits together once or twice. I never knew my father, but he was a legend in our neighborhood – mine and Sammy's.

And Shayna, sweet, short, round little bundle of love that she was, also was still connected. So when Sammy said her name, I understood what that meant.

'Right,' I told him softly. 'I guess I could call my aunt Shayna.'

But I couldn't just show up. I'd have to explain that I'd been in the city long enough to see Blossom Dearie and get involved with a murder. In a theatre, no less. That was going to take some finesse.

So I did it this way. I took Sammy with me back to the Benjamin and while he watched *Happy Days* on television, I called Brooklyn.

My mother picked up the phone and before she could say *hello*, I said, 'I'm in town.'

She paused. 'Are you in trouble?'

'No,' I assured her. 'Blossom Dearie is playing at Reno Sweeney's.'

'You're calling me from Reno Sweeney's?'

'No. Look. Where's Shayna?'

'Shayna?' my mother asked. 'She's in the living room watching *Happy Days*. Why?'

'You remember my old pal with the two shoes?'

'Oh. Yes. I remember him. Why?' She was wise. She knew that if I didn't say his name on the phone, she shouldn't either. And the fact that I wouldn't use his name told her a lot. Like, for instance, that some switchboard operators at some hotels like to listen in.

'Well, I ran into him,' I told her, 'at Reno Sweeney's, you know, and it's old times and so forth, and we were wondering if we could come visit you and Shayna. For old times' sake.'

'Oh.' Again, she got it. 'The good old days. Yeah. Got it.'

My mother and I weren't as emotionally connected as Shayna and I were, but my mother could read my mind since I was three, and it always impressed me.

'So, shall we say, like, within the hour, if we can get a cab right away?'

'You're taking a cab? What are you, suddenly Mr Moneybags? The subway's not good enough?'

'It's good enough,' I said, smiling, 'it's just not fast enough. My friend is on his way out of town and doesn't have much time.'

'And he's in a hurry to see your aunt Shayna before he goes,' she said.

'Yes. You know how close they are.'

They weren't close as far as I knew.

'I understand completely,' she said. 'Shayna and I will put together a little something right away, so you can sit down and eat the minute you get here.'

'That sounds perfect. We'll see you as soon as we can.'

'Shayna!' my mother hollered and hung up the phone.

My smile only got bigger and I hung up too. 'Man, my mother is on the ball.'

Sammy turned my way. 'Why do you say that?'

'We just spoke in some sort of arcane code that we were making up as we went along, and I think she'll have something for us by the time we get there.'

'Something for us?'

'I think they'll have a plan for your lam as soon as we get there.'

He stood up right away and clicked off the television. We were down on the street in under five.

The traffic was a little heavy, but we still made it from the Benjamin to the apartment in Brooklyn where I grew up in about forty minutes.

I hadn't seen the old neighborhood in a while. It was funny to see the things that had changed, and the things that hadn't.

It was a quiet afternoon, a little cloudy, not too hot.

When you walk down a street where you grew up, you're not just walking down a street right then, you're also walking down the street ten years ago. Twenty. The place where the old broken-down Chevy used to sit. The stoop where Mrs Linden sat alternately talking to herself and yelling at her cat. Which had been dead for a couple of years. The store at the end of the block that used to be a flower shop, but you couldn't tell what it was now.

We stopped in front of the building where I grew up, and I looked up at the window where I knew my mother would be watching. I knew if there was any kind of trouble, she'd give me some kind of high sign, and Sammy and I would walk on to the whatever-it-was store.

But there was nothing. So I looked at Sammy.

'I feel weird,' I told him. 'I didn't expect to.'

'You been gone,' he said, very sympathetically. 'When you left you were basically a loveable car thief. You're back and you're a local legend. That's a complicated thing to live up to.'

'I guess.' I stared up at the window. 'But it's more like I don't know how to behave around my mother and my aunt anymore. I've been an adult in the extremis for a number of years now. But the second I walk into that living room, I'm a kid again.'

'And it will always be that way,' he told me. 'My name is Samuel, and many people call me that now. But what do you call me?'

I smiled. 'Sammy Two Shoes.'

He smiled back. 'There you go. And the fact is I like that you call me that. I like that there's a part of me pitching pennies on the curb with you. In this way, I am forever young.'

'My least favorite Bob Dylan song,' I assured him, and then started up the stairs.

My mother greeted me at the door with tears in her eyes, and then she jabbed my upper arm with a pretty tough knuckle or two.

'You come into town to see Blossom Dearie and you don't call me?' she demanded.

'I didn't want to get you in trouble,' I explained. 'I've still got paper . . .'

'Oh, it's all right to avoid me when it's musical,' she continued to object, 'but when it's murder you don't mind?'

I started to answer, and then rethought it. 'Sammy's in trouble.'

She turned her love light on. 'Hello, Samuel.'

She reached up and patted his cheek.

She had put on a good dress for our visit. And real shoes. Under most circumstances, she would have been in a nice kimono and a pair of expensive Japanese slippers. But a visit from the long-lost son *and* his old pal Samuel, that merited a smattering of dress-up.

Shayna was nowhere to be seen.

My mother beckoned. 'I made kugel.'

And with that, we headed for the kitchen.

I missed a lot about New York, and Brooklyn, and the neighborhood, and the street, and the old apartment, but more than everything else put together, I missed that kitchen.

It was nothing special in the traditional sense, I guess. A sink, a stove, a table, some chairs, dishes and towels and pale-blue cabinets. But the kitchen was where most of the memories lived. I had to steer myself away from the ghosts entirely, or I would have been lost in reminiscence and where would that get Sammy?

My mother sensed my dilemma and took charge.

'I would like to spend a week catching up,' she said to me, 'and after that another week just cajoling you until you invited me to visit you in Florida.'

'Visit me in *Florida*?' I grinned. 'You haven't left this *block* since 1966.'

'True enough,' she agreed, 'but you could at least invite me!'

'Ah, well then,' I said. 'Please. Mother. Come visit me in Fry's Bay.'

'With my knees, a trip like that?' she railed. 'Are you trying to kill me?'

I shook my head. 'All right, now that that's over with . . .'

She sat down at the kitchen table without the kugel. 'Was that so hard?'

'But to the point . . .' I prompted.

'Right.' She patted the top of the table. 'Sit, sit.'

We did.

'The first thought was to send Sammy to your place in Florida,' she began, 'because we figured, Shayna and I, that the chumps and beach-heads wouldn't know oneΔ50 Brooklyn lamister from another. But Shayna pointed out that Sammy is taller than you, and his shoulders are twice the size of yours. This much differential even a Baptist would notice.'

'Well, also,' I began, 'I have friends there who know me, like, *really* well.'

'So we discarded that idea,' she rushed along. 'Then I thought Canada. But after a second, I remembered what a bruhaha you had down your way with the Canuck crowd a while back. So we settled on Atlanta.'

She folded her arms, sat back, and smiled in a very contented way.

Sammy and I looked at each other.

'Atlanta?' I finally asked.

'We know a guy.' That appeared to be all she wanted to say on the subject.

Sammy squinted. 'I don't wanna go to Atlanta. I mean, for starters, what would I eat down there?'

'Who's the guy?' I asked her. 'The guy you know.'

'Mike, but I don't like to say his last name,' she whispered, 'because he's a millionaire on account of the porno peep machines down there.'

'How in the world would you and Shayna know anybody associated with the world of pornography?' I asked her, trying to stifle a grin.

'This guy, Mike,' she allowed, 'is connected to a guy who knows a guy who works for a friend here in New York.'

'What friend in New York?'

'Her name is Candice, but she goes by Candida,' my mother said, avoiding eye contact.

I knew who she meant. Candida was a genuine artist, and a true feminist. Her newest career was as a performer in what were sometimes known as adult *art* films, but her commitment to a more honest assessment of sexual behaviors was, to me, revolutionary. In short, I admired her.

'So Candice knows, however circuitously, a guy in Atlanta,' I concluded. 'And you've done the vetting. It's safe for Sammy.'

She nodded once. 'Even got him a job.'

'What's the job?' Sammy piped up.

My mother rolled her eyes. 'Does it matter? It's legit, low profile, minimum wage, and easily lost in the system.'

'When do I leave?' he said.

'You already left,' she told him and handed him a bus ticket.

I stopped wondering a long time ago how my mother and Shayna could do the things they do. I just accepted it as a part of life.

Sammy took the ticket and stared at it. 'Well.'

'Foggy is not gonna know the specifics,' my mother went on. 'So when he goes to the cops, he can be more or less honest when he says he doesn't know where you are.'

Sammy nodded. He looked like he was going to say something, first to my mother, then to me, but in the end, he just turned around and left the kitchen. A second later we heard the front door open and close, and Sammy Two Shoes was gone.

As soon as the door closed, Shayna appeared. After the hugging and the kissing and the what-the-hell-are-you-doing-in-town, we all sat down.

'I didn't want to come in while Samuel was here,' Shayna told me, 'so I could honestly say to the cops that I hadn't seen him in a couple of years. The best lies are the ones that are true.'

So *that's* where I got that idea.

My mother weighed in. 'I'm better at the "I'm an old woman, what do I know" schtick. I can run a cop around in circles. It's fun.'

I smiled at them both. Nobody stood a chance against these two.

'So.' My aunt Shayna patted my hand. 'You missed New York.'

I sighed.

My mother cut a huge piece of kugel and slid it toward me across the pink linoleum tabletop.

'I was gonna come see you,' I began, 'after I heard Blossom.'

'But you're staying at the Benjamin,' Shayna said, looking down.

I started to protest, then I started to ask her how she knew, but in the end, I just said, 'Yes.'

My mother said, 'As my old friend Damon Runyon used to say, "A story goes with it."'

I don't know if she actually knew Runyon or not, but she certainly wanted to hear the story, so I told her. Starting with sitting in the barber chair and reading about Blossom in the *New Yorker* and ending with figuring out that Sammy killed an actor.

They both sat in silence for a moment, and then my aunt Shayna smacked me on the back of my head. Not hard, but serious.

'How in the hell could you think Samuel would do a thing like that?' she demanded. 'He's not a maniac. He's a nice boy with a few bad habits. Period.'

'And not *one* of those habits includes anything like killing anybody,' my mother added. 'Even an actor.'

'I think you'd agree that your mother and I know a thing or two about killers,' Shayna went on. 'Samuel's not the type. Not even.'

'Look,' I said to them both, 'he did it. He shoved a pencil in a girl's neck. He told me so. And he said it in a way that made me believe him.'

'And what way was that?' my aunt asked, sitting back in her chair and folding her arms.

'He said the cops were going to find his prints on the pencil. He said he did it for his girl, this Phoebe. Speaking of which, I have to go get her out of jail.'

I stood.

Shayna looked at my mother. 'Prints.'

My mother nodded. 'There's more to the story.'

'There probably is,' I agreed. 'But if the cops *do* find Sammy's prints on the pencil, he'll be gone from us a very long time, right?'

'Sammy who?' my mother said.

'I haven't seen the boy in years,' Shayna added softly.

TEN

Cornelia Street, where the murder took place, was in the Sixth Precinct. The precinct house for that area was on West 10th Street. Seemed like the best place to start. It had been maybe eighteen hours since she'd been arrested, so she might have been taken to Central Booking at the nearest court-house for arraignment, and maybe that had already happened too. But it had been a long time since I'd been through all that, and my memory was a little fuzzy about the details, because, who wants to remember?

So, another cab to the Precinct House, a bit of wandering around, and then an encounter with Sergeant Weiss. His desk was tidy; he was not. He'd had chicken soup for lunch. I could tell because there was a lot of it on his shirt, including noodles, and he smelled like a bay leaf.

I sat down and he looked up.

'What?' he wanted to know.

I showed him my Child Protective Services investigator's license. It was a risk, but it had my full name on it, and nobody but family knew what *that* was. He might have recognized 'Foggy' but never *Fyvush*.

'Florida Child Protective.' He gave me the once-over and shook his head.

'I'm investigating a possible child abduction, and someone named Phoebe Peabody has information that can help me,' I told him, using my official law enforcement voice, 'but I discover that you guys arrested her.'

'Never heard of her.'

'Then point to someone who knows dick about what happens in this precinct,' I said, 'because you guys arrested her for murder, like, yesterday.'

He squinted. 'The theatre thing.'

'So I'm told.'

He looked back down at the work on his desk. 'Took her to Centre Street.'

'Was that so hard?' I stood up.

'Might have already been arraigned,' he said, not looking up.

'But she wouldn't get bail on a murder charge no matter what her plea was,' I suggested, 'and she couldn't have been moved yet, right?'

He tilted his head. 'Probably not. She's gonna tell you about some kid that got grabbed in *Florida?*'

'I hope so.'

He'd already lost interest.

I'd never been to the Centre Street Courthouse. And when I got there, I was confronted by the statue of a giant marble woman sitting on a stack of books, or something. And there were very tall columns. All very disorienting to me after a couple of years in Florida getting used to flat buildings, seagulls, and a lot of the color pink.

I managed to keep it together long enough to find a desk sergeant who knew what from what.

'You're talking about the theatre kid,' he said. 'Heard some of the guys laughing about it.'

His voice was husky, and his hair was thin. He was teetering on the brink of retirement and diabetes. His tone said he didn't care, but his eyes disagreed.

'Phoebe Peabody is her name,' I told him.

'You got paper?'

I shook my head. 'You have to understand the rubes in my little town. The kid that I'm looking for, the one who got snatched, she's a Seminole, and the locals don't care.'

'But you take it more serious.' He stared into my eyes like he was looking for the Hope Diamond. Or, anyway, some kind of hope.

'I'm more serious about my job than you can possibly imagine,' I said, and I meant it.

He could tell. 'You're not from Florida, though.'

'I'm from Brooklyn. I live in Florida now. The weather's nice.'

'So they tell me,' he said. 'But see, you're not her lawyer, and you've got no paper, and I'm off in, like, five minutes.'

'Is she still here in the building?' I asked him. 'Can you at least tell me that?'

'Far as I know.'

That was all he was going to give me. I stood there for a second to be sure, and then I launched myself away from his desk, trying to figure what to do.

What I *should* have done was leave it alone. Let the cops find Sammy's prints. Let justice take its course and Phoebe would be out in no time all on her own. What I *should* have done is go back to the Benjamin, take a shower, and get myself over to Reno Sweeney's for Blossom's second night. And *then* what I should have done was take myself back to Florida where I should have stayed in the first place.

But I hadn't gone more than five steps away from the sergeant when I heard him say, 'Hey, Florida!'

I turned around.

He pointed. 'I think that's the PD who's handling the theatre kid's case.'

I looked to where he was pointing, and she looked like a public defender. She was six feet tall. Her hair was the color of night and cut short. She was wearing those round-framed metal glasses like John Lennon wore. Her suit was as crisp and clean as it was plain and inexpensive.

I only hesitated for a heartbeat, and then headed her way.

'Sorry,' I said as soon as I got close enough, 'are you Phoebe Peabody's lawyer?'

She was startled. 'Who?'

'Theatre kid,' I went on. 'Death by pencil.'

'Oh. Jesus. Yeah.'

I showed my badge. Sometimes it impressed people.

'I'm Moscowitz with Child Protective Services in Florida. Do you have three seconds?'

She adjusted her glasses with the hand that wasn't holding an overstuffed briefcase.

'I can give you two if you walk with me,' she said.

We walked.

'I'll be brief. Make sure the cops find all the fingerprints on the pencil because some of them belong to Samuel Cohen.'

'Who?'

'Samuel Cohen. He's the person who put the pencil in the dead actor's neck. Not Phoebe Peabody. So maybe you could nudge the cops, like, in that direction. You know, find out who's actually guilty, let the innocent go free. That sort of thing.'

The lawyer stopped walking. 'How would you know a thing like this? What's it got to do with Florida Child Protective? What are you doing in New York? Who *are* you?'

Yeah. I was going to have to answer all those questions. But first I had to find out what kind of a person this lawyer was.

'I think I just told you who I am,' I said. 'Showed you a badge and everything. It's your turn.'

She adjusted her glasses, shook her head, and then her shoulders drifted about two inches south.

'Helen Baker, Public Defender's Office, home of the most overworked lawyers in the fifty states. What makes you think this Cohen guy is guilty?'

'He told me so. And he said they'd find his prints on the murder weapon.'

'Uh huh.' She appeared to doubt my story. 'You Phoebe's boyfriend?'

'Not even a little bit,' I assured Ms Baker. 'I just happened to be at the show when the victim was killed. The all-female *Hamlet*. Set in a women's prison.'

'Sounds terrible.'

'It was. Nevertheless.'

'So the story I heard you tell Sergeant Weiss about some lost little lamb from Florida was bullshit.' She stared. 'As much bullshit as your current "I just happened to be there" routine.'

'I work for Child Protective Services in Fry's Bay, Florida,' I began, 'but I grew up in Brooklyn, and sometimes I miss the city. So I came up . . . Jesus, it was only yesterday. Long drive. Just wanted to get away from all the sand in my shoes, like, for a few days. Take in a show, have a real slice, look at a pigeon.'

Why not give her the full information? Wasn't the truth a complete defense under the law?

'And the show you decided to see was lesbian *Hamlet*?' She laughed, but it wasn't the jolly sort.

'It wasn't . . . the show that I came up to see was Blossom Dearie at Reno Sweeney's.'

Her face changed. 'With Bob Dorough? I read about that.'

'He sat in,' I confirmed. '"Two Sleepy People" never sounded so good.'

'Damn it.' She set her briefcase down. 'I *love* Blossom. Last time I saw her was at the Algonquin.'

I nodded. 'Saw Bucky Pizzarelli there. Kind of a while back.'

'OK, Mister . . . what was your name?

'Moscowitz.'

'Mr Moscowitz. How the hell did you get from Blossom to *Hamlet*?'

I told her the story in five sentences. All of it, but with a low percentage of detail. And I left out the part about my mother and my aunt helping Sammy get gone, of course.

'Uh huh,' she said, 'and how is it that your friend Sammy knew you were in town at all, let alone at Reno Sweeney's?'

OK, I may have left that part out. She was, after all, an officer of the court, and I really didn't want her to get me nabbed for an old transgression. Such as escaping a police vehicle and absconding to Florida.

So I said, 'Weird coincidence, believe me or don't. A bus boy who works at Reno Sweeney's was a mutual pal back in the younger days and gave Sammy a call to instigate some sort of reunion. I haven't been back to the city for a number of years and my return was, apparently, what passed for news among the easily amused.'

She sipped a breath but didn't say anything for a minute. 'All right, I completely don't believe most of this, but if it might get the kid off, I'll suggest a thorough fingerprint check with this Samuel Cohen.'

'His prints will be on file,' I assured her.

'As long as I'm at it,' she went on, 'I'll maybe get the full battery of tests, just so there aren't a lot of questions about all this specifically. I get the impression that you'd rather not answer a lot of specific questions.'

'I don't see how they could have any bearing on your particular case with Phoebe Peabody.'

'So.' She picked up her briefcase. 'What else did Blossom sing?'

'Well,' I told her, 'of course there was "I'm Hip" and "Lush Life".'

She laughed. 'I hate that I missed it.'

'You work too much,' I said.

'You got a card or something?'

'A card?' My turn to laugh. 'I work in a tiny little burg on a bay, I can't afford stationery, and everybody knows me. I'm that Jew from Brooklyn.'

'So how am I supposed to get in touch if I need to?'

'Why would you need to?' I asked.

'Like when the police want to ask about Samuel Cohen, for example,' she insisted.

I wondered should I tell her or not.

Then: 'I'm staying at the Benjamin on East 50th.'

She nodded, then reached into her pocket and got a card, handed it over. 'Or you call me.'

Then she hoisted up her briefcase and was gone.

ELEVEN

Now, everybody knows that the very first place to have the name *Ray's Pizza* on a sign was opened in 1959 on Prince Street in Manhattan. After that, it's a matter of opinion. But listen, wars have been fought on lesser grounds than which one is the real Ray's. So all I decided when I left the courthouse was that I would go to the *nearest* Ray's.

I walked about twenty minutes north up Hudson Street then 9th Avenue until I got to Famous Original Ray's on 9th. I got one slice, but it wasn't enough, so I got two more, which was too much. I had planned to walk back to the Benjamin, but the seventy pounds of pizza in my stomach told me it was a bad idea. So I grabbed a cab and almost fell asleep before we got to the hotel.

I'm not saying that I had a dark night of the soul when I was trying to take a nap once I got to my room. But it was a pretty overcast afternoon at the Benjamin. What was I doing in New York? Was it really about good pizza and bad streets? And I owned every record Bob Dorough ever made. Even the imports.

So was it really worth driving over a thousand miles to hear him sing two songs?

As I lay there tossing and turning in my second-best suit, I was riddled with regrets and second thoughts. Mostly about pizza, but a little about the whole trip in general. Like maybe the Angel of Karma had whispered into my ear, enticed me back to the city of my sins. I was there to pay a debt or right a wrong or some other such metaphysical malarkey.

The room grew dark as the afternoon turned into evening. I wasn't going to sleep, but I didn't feel like getting up.

So I nearly jumped out the window when the phone rang.

I grabbed it before it could ring again.

'Yes?' I snapped.

'Moscowitz?' said a female voice.

'Who is this?' I asked.

'It's Helen Baker.'

'Who?' I sat up.

'The lawyer. For Phoebe Peabody.'

'Right.' I rubbed my forehead. 'Right. What can I do for you?'

'You can meet me in the bar downstairs at your hotel.'

'I can?' I looked at my watch. It had somehow gotten to be nearly seven o'clock.

'I'm buying,' she insisted.

'Oh.' I stood up. 'In that case, when?'

'I'm down here now.'

'Ah. Well, then, I'll be right there.'

A quick comb through the hair and a straightening of the tie, and I was out the door and down the elevator.

The place was crowded, pleasantly noisy, still the after-work crowd. Helen Baker was, indeed, at the bar, taking up three seats with her coat, her stuff, and herself. I joined her.

The bartender appeared instantly.

'Gin and tonic, please,' I mumbled, 'and could you make it a half and half, I've got a stomach.'

He seemed to understand. And then he vanished.

'And?' I prompted Ms Baker.

'I have a pal who's a coroner.' That's all. She seemed to be upset about something.

'And?' I repeated.

'And she told me that . . . Would you be surprised to learn that the pencil in the dead actor's neck was not, in fact, the proximate cause of her death?'

'Hold on.' I focused. 'What was?'

'Hydrogen cyanide.'

'No.' I laughed. 'This isn't an Agatha Christie novel.'

'Hydrogen cyanide,' she repeated. 'It was in her stomach. Not a whole lot, but apparently enough to kill her. She swallowed it down, and she was probably dead in a couple of minutes.'

'But the pencil,' I began.

'Your boy Samuel Cohen's prints were on the pencil,' she interrupted, 'along with the victim's. But since the victim actually died from the cyanide, Sammy Two Shoes is off the hook for the murder, sort of. They don't really know *what* to charge him with. They do wonder why he bothered to stab her when she was probably already dead from the aforementioned poison. All of which, thanks very much, does not, in fact, get Phoebe Peabody *off* the hook. The cops figure she could have put the cyanide in the water bottle before the show even started. Her lighting booth alibi doesn't matter. So she's staying in jail and my job just got a lot harder.'

The bartender chose that moment to deliver my G and T.

I stared down at it. 'So you did not invite me here to thank me for helping you. You invited me here to berate me. Or worse.'

She nodded. 'Worse. You're going to help me get Phoebe off. I did a little checking up on you. You're some kind of a genius detective down there in Florida.'

'Not even remotely,' I insisted, picking up my drink.

'Well, your work here in New York doesn't exactly support that theory,' she agreed, 'but the people I talked to in Florida all sang your praises. To the tune of "Amazing Grace."'

'I don't have any singing friends. You talked to the wrong class of person.'

'Your bosses at Child Protective,' she said, 'some guys at the FBI, and someone with the unlikely name of Betty Mae Tiger Jumper.'

'Only woman to ever be chief of the Florida Seminoles.' I smiled. 'She's a remarkable person. Supernatural, in fact. But I don't really know her.'

'You're not getting out of this,' Baker snapped. 'You're highly esteemed and that's that!'

'A scurrilous lie,' I told her, 'but I'm not trying to get out of anything. I'll help Phoebe because I promised I would. And by the way, how did you know he was called "Sammy Two Shoes"?'

'His rap sheet,' she answered. 'Which is the proverbial mile long. Also known as Spider Cohen.'

I shook my head. 'That was a joke from when . . . Sammy and I went to the Newport Folk Festival when we were teenagers and he fell in love with Spider John Koerner. So when we got back to Brooklyn, he made everyone call him Spider Cohen for about six weeks until he fell in love with Bob Dylan, at which point all bets were off.'

'Good story, but my point is: where is he?'

'I don't know.'

'He's a material witness at the very least, you have to tell me where he is.'

'I really don't know,' I insisted, and silently thanked my mother for not telling me where she was sending Sammy.

'Well, find him, Mr Fancy Detective. And when you're not doing that, figure out who poisoned Emory Taylor. And how. And why.'

I downed my drink. 'Anything else? Want me to take a crack at a unified field theory?'

She sat back and snarled. 'Look at you, knowing science stuff. But no, just fetch me the real perpetrator, and make it snappy.'

She slapped down a check on the bar top in front of me. Right next to my empty glass.

'This hires you as my legally authorized operative. I registered you as my investigator. I know you have a P.I. license in Florida; I fixed the paperwork for the State of New York. It's not entirely legit until all the paperwork is done, but it gets you working, like, now. Tonight. Also, here's your New York City card.'

I stared at the card. 'I was thinking of going back to Florida tomorrow.'

She slid off the bar stool. 'If you've found the killer by then, be my guest. Otherwise . . .'

She grabbed her briefcase and her coat.

'I don't have to do this, you know,' I said.

'I know,' she agreed, 'but you'll do it anyway. Because you're a good guy.'

I didn't want to argue with her, even though *that* wasn't true.

What I couldn't figure out was why she hadn't brought up my outstanding warrant. Because if she'd checked up on me enough to talk to Betty, she'd also run me through the system enough to find it. I didn't want that over my head.

'Ms Baker,' I said just as she was about to leave, 'you probably know I've got paper from a couple of years back. Isn't that going to be kind of a problem for you in this whole business?'

She sighed. 'I did find an arrest warrant in *Brooklyn* in my search, but it was for a Fiver Moskovitz. With a *k* and a *v*. That's not you, is it?'

'What?'

'They got your name wrong, genius. Both names, actually. The warrant is useless. Besides, it was only for stealing a car. Geez.' And with that, she was gone.

I couldn't say what I looked like then, because there wasn't a mirror anywhere around, but was almost certain that the word *stupefied* would have described it. Years of worrying about the long arm of the law were slowly melting away.

Turned out there had never really been anything to worry about at all, because the brain attached to said long arm, it didn't know how to spell.

TWELVE

After Ms Baker left, I availed myself of five or thirteen more gin and tonics. Gins and tonic. What's the plural? Doesn't matter. What mattered was figuring out my next move.

My choices were as follows. Go back to Florida. Go to Atlanta. Go to Brooklyn. Go to bed.

I chose option D. I went upstairs and fell on to the bed, seersucker suit and all, and dropped down a deep dark hole until the crack of dawn the next day.

When dawn shoved its way through the hotel blinds, I tried to sit up, but it didn't take. I rolled away from the window, but the sun was very insistent.

I examined my suit from my prone position, and it was obvious that it needed a cleaner. Or maybe a mortician.

So.

Up. Shower. Shave. Shake.

I had to shake myself a couple of times to focus. And it took all that focus to call room service and get eggs, bacon, cheese, and wheat toast, with two pots of coffee. I had to say it three times. Yes. Two pots of coffee. Good.

And then all I could do was sit there in the very white bathrobe provided by the hotel and wait for the rescue.

Which came eventually. Could have been ten minutes, could have been a month. No idea. The point was, there was a knock on the door. Then there was a guy. Then there were two pots of coffee and the heaven of scrambled eggs.

I doubled what was on the ticket for a tip, and the guy stared at it for a minute before he said, 'Anything else?'

'Is there a dry-cleaner nearby?' I asked him, pouring my first cup.

'We can clean that suit here on the premises, Mr Moscowitz, if you like.'

He was staring at what had once been my lovely seersucker suit, now in ruins on the floor.

'You can?' I sipped.

'Have it back to you by early evening.' He scooped it up.

He was gone before I finished that first sip of coffee.

The breakfast was every bit as invigorating as the shower had been, and by 8:30 I was dressed in my best dark blue suit and my favorite black tie, looking very much like a mortician myself. Seemed appropriate. I was going to have to do something about a corpse.

By 9:15 I was tapping softly on my mother's apartment door. That particular Brooklyn neighborhood was always an early riser. Plenty of people in the streets, lots of hustle to go along with the bustle.

I could see the peephole in the door darken a split second before the door flew open.

Shayna stood there beaming in her red bathrobe, curlers in her hair.

My aunt Shayna had looked the same to me since I was five. She'd taken to putting henna in her hair and she always had a ginger candy in her mouth. For health reasons, she said, without any other explanation.

'Hello, kiddo,' she said. 'I knew you couldn't stay away.'

Then there was a lot of hugging and face patting.

'Your mother's still asleep,' Shayna said softly. 'She was up all hours with a migraine.'

'Oh.' I guess I didn't know that my mother had migraines.

'Coffee?' she offered.

'Already had too much,' I said, eyeing the hallway bathroom. 'Be right back.'

I went into the bathroom; Shayna went to the kitchen.

Within moments we were sitting at the kitchen table and she was staring at her cup. She knew I was there for a reason and she was just waiting until I told her what it was.

'So,' I began, 'there's new information. It's a little convoluted, but it comes down to something important. Sammy didn't do it.'

'He didn't stab the actor?'

'No,' I said, 'he did that. But I think the actor was already dead at that point. Poison.'

She smiled. 'Poisoned actor in a dressing room. What is this, an Agatha Christie?'

'That's what *I* said,' I told her.

'So why did Sammy feel the need to poke a pencil in the poor thing?'

'That's what I'd like to know,' I said.

She lifted her head. 'Oh. You want me to tell you where he is. So you can ask him.'

'Well, for one thing, he's innocent so he didn't have to abscond,' I said. 'And for another thing, the cops would like an answer to the question you just posed, to wit, why jab somebody who's already dead?'

'How did you find out about all this?' she asked.

'Got it from the public defender lawyer person who's on Phoebe's case.'

'Phoebe?'

'The stage manager person that Sammy's in love with, the one who's in jail for the crime she didn't commit,' I said. 'Like we told you.'

'Didn't remember her name.' She nodded. 'But look, if I tell you where he is, you can't say you don't know where he is anymore.'

'Right,' I said. 'I already got off the hook once by not knowing where he was, so thanks for that. But at this point, I think I have to get him back here.'

'Well, you can't just call him and get him on a plane,' she said. 'You're going to have to go down there to Atlanta and get him.'

'Why?'

'Where he's staying, they got no phone. And it's not even an address, strictly speaking. It's very, like, sequestered. Like a monastery, this place. No phone calls, no letters, no visitors unless you know the right things to say. I mean, I thought you wanted him safe and sound.'

'I did. I do. Only, now I have to get him back. So.'

She stared back at her coffee. I could almost hear the gears in her head grinding. After what seemed like ten hours, she nodded.

'Got it.' She reached into the pocket of her robe and produced a small spiral notebook and a pencil.

I'd seen that notebook, or others like it, a hundred times when I was young. They should all have been in some kind of safe deposit box because of all the highly prosecutable information in them. But I knew for a fact that they were in a dozen-or-so shoe boxes underneath her bed. Wrapped with a big rubber band. Half the hoodlum element in Brooklyn could probably be put away forever by what was in those boxes.

She scribbled a few lines on a sheet and ripped it out, slid it across the tabletop in my direction.

I looked down at it. 'Dickson Place, off 11th, ask for Benetta McKinnon. Say that Tree is your friend.'

Maybe that's why her notebooks were safe where they were. Maybe everything in them was that vague.

'No address?' I asked.

She shook her head.

'Who's *Tree*?' I asked. 'Is that a person?'

'Tree is a well-respected member of the Atlanta Outlaws, kind of a Hell's Angels type of organization.'

'And I'm supposed to be his friend?'

'Well.' She laughed. 'You certainly don't want to be his enemy.'

'OK, but, I mean, what if they check with Tree and he's never heard of me?'

'He has,' she assured me.

'He has?' I stared.

She patted my face again. 'You don't seem to realize that your rep is gargantuan.'

In the first place, I never heard my aunt use the word *gargantuan*, and in the second place, it was about as inaccurate a description of my reputation as you could get, in my opinion.

'You think that *Tree* has heard *anything* about me?'

'I know he has because I let it be known that you were righteous.' She sat back. 'All over town. The town, in this case, being Atlanta.'

And I knew the look on her face. It was also something I'd seen plenty of times before. It said that she had hidden depths, connections beyond connections, and influence in circles where angels feared to tread. I believed all of that.

So I said, 'Right, I'm on the next plane to Atlanta.'

I stood up.

'You're not going to say hello to your mother?' she asked me.

I looked in the direction of my mother's bedroom. 'Should I? I mean, what with the migraine and all.'

'I can't tell her that you were here and didn't pop in to see her,' Shayna said firmly.

I nodded and headed down the hall.

I tapped very gently on the door. 'Um, Mother?'

There was a beat of silence and then a hearty, 'Foggy?'

I poked my head in. 'Shayna said you had a bad headache, but I wanted to say hello anyway. Is that OK?'

'OK?' She sat up. 'Get in here.'

The room was dim. What little light there was came in through the closed blinds. Otherwise, it was as it had always been: neat as a pin, minimally furnished, a little stuffy, and smelling of lavender.

She patted the bed and I sat down.

'I guess you're going back to Florida now,' she began. 'You came to say goodbye?'

'No,' I said.

'Look, Fyvush,' she said softly, 'maybe I wasn't the greatest mother in the world. And maybe your father was gone too soon, and it made me too lonely to take care of you so good. And maybe you like Shayna better than me. Who could blame you? But none of that matters, really. What matters is that you're a person. You're a person who does good things. Helping children. I want you to know that. I want you to know that I know that.'

I shifted on the bed. 'I really just came in to check on your migraine. I'm coming back. Like, soon. You're talking to me like I'm never going to see you again. But you should realize by now, you don't get rid of me so easy, right?'

'Oh.' She looked around like she'd lost something for a second. 'OK, then. Can you do something about these blinds? They're closed, but it's still too much light.'

I stood. 'Yeah. You have to close them going up instead of going down, it makes it darker.'

I made the adjustment, and the room was almost black.

'Oh, my God.' She sighed. 'That's so much better.'

'Good. So. See you in a couple of days.'

I turned and headed out. Just as I was about to close the door behind me, I heard her say, 'While you're in Atlanta, you should stop by the art museum. I hear they got a Monet down there that'll knock your socks off.'

All I could do was laugh. I tried to do it quietly, but I'm sure she heard me.

THIRTEEN

I couldn't get a flight to Atlanta until the next day, and to make matters worse, it was rough. Some kind of storm over the Carolinas. I hadn't brought any luggage because I didn't think I'd be in Atlanta more than a couple of hours. I'd go get Sammy, tell him the news, and we'd be right back at the airport.

The Atlanta airport was named after a guy called William B. Hartsfield, who was the longest-serving governor in the state of Georgia. Sounded like a great honor to have a busy airport named after you, until you heard that the Atlanta Zoo also named a big gorilla *Willy B* after the guy. I guess politics is a rough game.

The airport was huge and crazy. Must have taken me a half-hour to find my way out and into a cab. Then the cab ride into town was weird. Wasn't right, somehow. I couldn't explain it except that it was nothing like a cab in New York. The driver had no idea where Dickson Place was. He knew 11th Street, so we just drove up and down it until we hit Dickson, second time by. The sign was turned funny.

Dickson Place was a one-block dead-end street in midtown, or more like a cul-de-sac, really. It had a median, and maybe there had been grass in it once, maybe even plants. But it was scrawny and sad that day. The whole area had probably once been nice. But it had a look of *former* glory. Maybe it was hippies, maybe it was white flight, but something had given the whole area an aspect of quasi-abandonment.

Before the driver let me out, I had to pay him a ridiculous amount of money. And he wouldn't wait; took off the second he got my cash.

The sky was overcast, and it was humid like you wouldn't believe. It was nearing sunset. There was no one out, no one on the street. Desolation Row. After I stood there for a while, sweating, I considered just calling out Sammy's name until something happened.

Just as I was about to start throwing rocks, an older woman

in a quilted housecoat came out of one of the little row houses
with a sack of garbage to put in the can at her curb. She was
about a hundred yards away.

I waved. She stared.

'I'm looking for Benetta McKinnon,' I called out.

She set down her garbage. 'Passed away.'

'Oh.'

She pointed across the street from where she lived to an
up-and-down duplex.

'That was her place,' she said. 'Top's for rent now, bottom's
got hooligans.'

'Hooligans,' I said.

'How'd you know Benetta?' she asked.

'Friend of my mother's,' I said. 'How about you?'

The woman smiled. 'She was a cut-up in her day. A flapper.'

'You knew her that long ago?'

'My sister,' the woman said, and then she started coughing.
Sounded bad. She headed back indoors without another word.

I headed for the hooligans' door.

There was loud music coming from the place, a song called
'Play that Funky Music, White Boy.' I had to bang for a while.

When the door opened it was clear that the *hooligans* were,
in fact, *junkies*. The guy who came to the door had the look. He
was sweaty, losing his teeth and his hair, and didn't care that I
saw a dozen needle marks in his left arm. His T-shirt was smeared
with food and his short pants were about to fall down.

'What?' That's all he said.

'My friend Tree told me to stop by.'

He blinked. Then he turned into the darkened room. 'Turn
down the goddam music, man!'

It took a second, but the music softened.

'Say it again,' he went on, squinting. 'What about Tree?'

'Tree told me to come here,' I said firmly. 'I want to visit my
friend. New arrival. Upstairs from you.'

That was a guess on my part, but I was fairly sure I'd put
together Shayna's clues appropriately.

The guy looked me over. 'Yeah, you're from out of town.'

He shook his head, hiked up his shorts, and disappeared into
the room, left the door open. The DJ on the radio asked us all

if we believed in miracles, and then a song called 'You Sexy Thing' came on. Apparently, the singer *did* believe.

After a very long moment of enduring disco torture, Dr Short Pants appeared again with a key.

'Don't nobody know about this guy upstairs,' he told me, barely above a whisper. 'But if Tree said . . .'

He handed me the key. It was a padlock key. I started to ask, but he closed the door in my face.

The stairs were right there, so I took them. Two doors at the top, no light. One door was slightly ajar, and when I peeked in it looked like attic storage. The other door had a padlock on it. I knocked. Seemed more polite than just using the key, although if the door was padlocked from the outside, there wasn't much chance that Sammy was there. Unless the junkies had locked him in.

I knocked again and then put my ear to the door. Not a sound. So I used the key, popped the lock; cracked the door.

'Sammy?' I said softly.

Nothing.

I went in. Three rooms. I stepped into the living room. There was an antique wicker sofa with red velvet cushions and a neat old Persian rug on the hardwood floor. To the left I could see the kitchen, a white stove, and a wooden table with bentwood chairs. To the right there was a small bedroom with a wrought-iron single bed and another door which was probably the bathroom. The place was neat as a pin, and I felt the sudden presence of Benetta McKinnon appreciating the fact that someone had kept her rooms so tidy.

But that thought evaporated when I heard a low growling coming up the stairs and Dr Short Pants appeared in the doorway with a baseball bat in his hands and a deranged look on his face.

No words; he just lunged. Once again, old instincts took over. I kicked the guy right in his short pants. Really hard. Twice.

When he went to his knees making a squeaky sound, I snatched the bat away from him and bopped him, just once, on the back of the head.

Seconds later two other denizens of the apartment below appeared. One of them had a gun. The other one had a fried chicken leg.

The one with the gun had wild eyes, and he wasn't wearing a shirt. He had maybe a dozen needle marks on his stomach and plenty more on both arms. The guy with the chicken looked sleepy.

'Sorry about your friend,' I began.

'You don't know Tree,' the guy with the gun announced.

'What makes you think that?' I asked.

Chicken leg glanced down at the unconscious Dr Short Pants. 'He said.'

'Plus, you dress like a queer,' Gun guy snorted. 'Tree don't know no queers.'

I shook my head. 'My suit isn't fashionable enough to be seen on any self-respecting gay man that I know. But it's good enough for a cop.'

I swung the bat backhanded, like a tennis racket, and knocked the gun out of the guy's hand. It flew up, dented the ceiling, and cracked down on the hardwood floor just a few feet from the entrance to the kitchen.

The guy yowled like I'd chopped his hand off. Chicken leg just froze, staring.

Then he said, 'Cop?'

I whipped out my Child Protective badge and then put it away really quickly. They were too far gone to have seen what it really was, and too experienced with law enforcement to give me any more trouble.

'Come on in,' I beckoned. 'Have a seat on the sofa.'

They did, in kind of a daze.

I backed up, picked up the gun and put it in my suit coat pocket.

'There was really no need for all of this,' I explained to them. 'I'm friends with the guy who is currently staying in this apartment. I came here from New York to see him. It's important.'

Neither guy on the sofa said a word. Dr Short Pants groaned.

'Do you know where he is?' I asked.

'Who?' Chicken leg peeped.

'The guy who's staying here,' I said, maybe a little impatiently.

'Oh.' Chicken leg looked at Gun guy. 'Do we know where he is?'

'Yesterday around four o'clock,' Gun guy said, blinking like a strobe light, 'he made a big bowl of yogurt and honey and brought it down to us. It's so good.'

It made sense that Sammy had figured out how to make friends with his junkie watchdogs. Stood to reason. All the junkies I knew were partial to sweets, and yogurt's good for the digestion.

'My nuts,' Dr Short Pants moaned.

I was beginning to see that it might be a bit more difficult to extract information from these boys than I might have thought. I backed away again and leaned the baseball bat against the wall.

'All I want to know . . .' I began again.

'Tree's gonna kick your ice,' Gun guy muttered.

Took me a full three seconds to get that *ice* was *ass*.

'Nice accent,' I told him. 'I guess you're a Georgia boy.'

'Valdosta,' he told me.

I didn't know what that was, and I didn't care.

'Well, Georgia boy,' I said. 'I already told the guy on the floor that Tree and I are friends.'

Gun guy laughed. 'Guess we'll see about that.'

He looked sideways at Chicken leg. Chicken leg looked down, a little smile on his face and said, 'Any minute now.'

'Tree's coming here,' I surmised.

'It's rent day,' Chicken leg told me.

'Tree collects the rent?' I looked around. 'I thought he was with that biker gang, the Outlaws.'

Chicken leg looked lost for a second. Then he repeated, 'It's rent day.'

Once again, I realized the futility of trying to get any real information out of these guys, and that reminder came just as I heard someone else coming up the stairs. I put my hand in the pocket with the gun, and then I heard the voice.

'Y'all up there?'

It was the deepest human voice I'd ever heard. And it was followed by a vision. Suddenly standing in the doorway was Goliath. Goliath in jeans, and a T-shirt with a leather vest over it. And boots the size of a medium dog.

He was stooped over because he was at least seven feet tall, and the door frame had been built for people under six.

The boys on the sofa were looking down. The guy on the floor pretended to be unconscious.

'Um,' the giant said.

'I'm Foggy Moscowitz,' I told him steadily. 'Shayna says hello.'

He grinned. 'Shayna!'

He made his way through the door. It wasn't easy.

'I was just up here waiting for Sammy Two Shoes when these locals paid me a visit,' I went on.

He nodded. 'Yeah, that sounds right. Boys? Git.'

All three of the boys jumped like they'd been electrocuted and scrambled, a little like cartoons, past the giant and out the door.

'May I call you Tree?' I asked.

He shrugged. 'Everybody else does, little buddy. How you know Shayna?'

Little buddy. Right. I was extremely happy to be this guy's little buddy.

'She's my aunt.'

'No shit!' He nodded.

'How about you?'

'Oh. Um. Business, I guess. Shayna knows Candice. Candida. Candida is associated, occasionally, with associates of mine. I never actually met her. Shayna, I mean. She's, like, a ball of fire, right?'

'She is,' I confirmed.

'I *love* talking to her on the phone.' He nodded again. 'So, Shayna's your aunt, which means your mama was married to one badass Jew in Brooklyn.'

How did he know that?

'That's what they tell me,' I said. 'I never really knew him.'

'Yeah. You got a nice rep yourself, though. Saving little kids. I like that. You're like that guy . . . you ever read that book *Catcher in the Rye*?'

I was about to say something stupid, like, 'Everybody's read *Catcher in the Rye*,' when Sammy appeared at the top of the stairs with a Colt Python in his hand. He was wearing the salt and pepper suit. He looked even more out of place than I did, which was an accomplishment.

Now, the Colt Python was a six-shooter and a popular gun in the movies. It made a nice first impression.

Tree just stared at it, smiling.

'Hey, Sammy,' I said, before anything got out of hand.

Sammy lowered the gun. 'I heard voices in my apartment. Sorry. Hello, Tree. Hi, Foggy. What the hell are you doing here? I'm busy.'

I was in a hurry to get back to the city, so I abbreviated.

'OK, this is the thing,' I began. 'You didn't kill anybody. Emory was already dead when you stabbed her with the pencil.'

'Jesus.' Tree squinted. 'I *gotta* hear that story.'

'Maybe another time.' Sammy put his gun away and looked at me with a lot of pain in his eyes. 'What about Phoebe?'

'That's another thing,' I said. 'You really ought to come back to New York, like, immediately, because Phoebe's lawyer said so. See . . .'

'He's not going anywhere,' Tree interrupted calmly. 'He's got work here.'

I nodded. 'Right, but, see, that *work*, it was just a ruse.'

'A what?' Tree asked me, still very sedately.

'The work, whatever it was, only existed to support Sammy while he was here in Atlanta. Something Shayna set up, right? But since he's going back to New York . . .'

'He's not going back to New York, or anywhere else, until he finishes his work here. I mean, I can see that from your point of view, his work may have been a *ruse*. But from my point of view, I don't care. He's got a job to do and until he does it, he stays here. Me and Shayna had a deal. That's the end of the story, like.'

I took in a long breath. It was clear Tree meant business. And even if I *was* his little buddy, I had the impression that he wouldn't hesitate to knock me into next week if I went up against him. The guy was a tank. A tank with a howitzer in each hand. Also, his implacable demeanor scared me. I knew guys in Brooklyn who had the same gestalt: cooler than a bushel of cucumbers because they knew they could kill you with one finger. No fear, no scruples, no remorse. In other words, by the time I let out my breath, I knew Tree was right. Sammy wasn't going anywhere until Tree said so.

'So, Sammy,' I announced amiably, 'what's the job, and how can I help?'

'There you go,' Tree said happily.

'No,' said Sammy. 'Foggy's out of that world. He's legit in the extreme, and *I'm* not gonna mess that up. He just came down here to get me, which was nice of him and I'll thank him for that later. But he'd be out of his mind to get involved with this.'

'Yeah, I know,' Tree said reasonably, 'but, you know, if he *wants* to . . .'

'Maybe you could both stop talking about me like I'm not here,' I interrupted, 'and, Sammy, maybe you could let me make up my own mind about my own mind, right?'

'You don't understand, Foggy,' Sammy began.

'What's the job, Tree?' I insisted.

'OK.' Tree settled. 'How can I put this? A guy owes another guy some money, a lot of money, and the first guy has, like, split.'

'And you wanted Sammy to find the guy who owes the money so that he can pay the other guy,' I said.

'Well, OK, the *other guy* is me. But the problem is that I'm, like, up to my ass in another situation, you know? I don't have time to run all over town looking for some pissant welcher. Shayna says give this Sammy guy a job, so that's the job.'

'Find the welcher,' I concluded.

'Right.' Tree nodded. 'I already gave Sammy the name and, like, the places he's likely to be. It's an easy gig.'

'There.' I turned to Sammy. 'How hard can that be? Especially if the two of us are working on it together.'

Sammy groaned like an old door hinge, but after that, he nodded.

'What's the welcher's name?' I asked.

'Denny Bennet,' Sammy said, resigned.

'Works in one of Mike's adult peep show stores on Cheshire Bridge,' Tree added. 'Mike, Shayna's friend. Sammy's boss. My boss.'

I nodded.

'You got a car?' I asked Sammy.

He shook his head. 'But I know how to get there on the bus.'

'The *bus*?' I looked at Tree.

Tree shrugged. 'I offered him a sweet little Harley. SR-750. Just come out.'

'I'm gonna ride a motorcycle?' Sammy asked me.

'Doesn't seem like the kind of thing either one of us would do,' I agreed. 'Which way to the nearest bus stop?'

Tree smiled and made his way out the door. I took a last look around Sammy's digs.

'Nice place,' I told him.

He agreed. 'When the guys downstairs are asleep, I feel like I'm at my grandma's.'

I was out the door and halfway down the stairs before I thought to ask Sammy, 'How do you know how to get to this adult entertainment place on the bus?'

'Tree told me,' Sammy said, 'right after I wouldn't get on his motorcycle.'

'OK,' I said, 'let's go nab the poor slob who owes Tree money.'

'The original job I was offered,' Sammy explained as we walked up Dickson Place, 'was working the counter at the bookstore where this Denny guy also works. But I asked Tree if he had something a little less sedentary. Hence, nabbing the welcher.'

'Ah.' I'd wondered why Shayna had set Sammy up as a debt collector. But she hadn't. She'd set him up in sales. And Sammy wasn't much of a salesman.

FOURTEEN

The so-called 'bookstore' on the upscale-sounding Cheshire Bridge was one of the most depressing places I'd ever been. And I'd been in trailers owned by child abusers. And deserted Seminole villages where hundreds of people had been murdered in their sleep. And jail. That store in Atlanta had them all beat in the first three seconds. Low light, black walls, sticky floors, stale air, and porn. It was an overcast sunset outside; inside it was midnight in the unfinished corner of creation. Florescent lights didn't help the gloom, and they blinked off and back on every once in a while.

There were only two customers. One was a pimply kid in a bowling shirt, the other was an older man in a cheap suit, who walked with a limp.

At the back of the store there was a door that said *Peep Shows! 25¢!*

Behind the counter was a beer belly attached to a bald smoking machine. The guy had one burning in the ash tray and another dangling from his lips. He was wearing a T-shirt that said 'What?' on it, and the shirt didn't even *try* to cover his belly button.

He looked up from the book he was reading. 'Hey, you're Tree's new guy. He told me you were too good to work here.'

'Is this the guy?' I asked Sammy. 'Is this Denny?'

Couldn't be that easy, could it?

'This is Blay,' Sammy said, shaking his head. 'Tree told me about him.'

Blay glanced my way. 'And?'

'Gotta see Denny Bennet,' Sammy said softly.

'You and me both,' Blay snapped. 'He's supposed to be working tonight.'

'But he didn't show,' Sammy surmised.

'Do you *see* him here?' Blay was irritated.

'OK,' Sammy told him, 'I'm gonna need his address or his phone number or something.'

'Why?'

'Tree said,' Sammy answered, even softer.

Blay glanced up at the surveillance camera that was pointed his way. Then he slapped his book face-down on the counter and swiveled off his chair. I looked down at his book. It was *Nausea* by Sartre. When he came back, he had a torn piece of paper that he handed to Sammy without a word.

I couldn't help myself. 'You're reading Sartre,' I said to him, but I sounded more surprised than I'd intended to.

He paused, then grabbed some ferocious eye contact.

'I taught World Literature at Georgia State University for eleven years,' he growled, 'until they found out I was *also* working with the local branch of the Weathermen.'

'The radical left guys?'

He nodded. 'We were going to blow up the Muzak center here in Atlanta.'

I blinked. 'Why?'

'Because having to listen to that crap all day in an office,' he explained, 'is cruel and unusual punishment, and it was driving the straights crazy. We were going to do it for the workers, man.'

I nodded slowly because I didn't disagree.

'And I've read *Nausea* about a hundred times,' he concluded.

'A hundred times.' I tried to sound impressed instead of sad.

He looked back down at the book. 'Just keeps getting funnier every time I read it.'

'One of my favorite lines of all time comes from that book,' I said, thinking I might impress the guy, for some reason. 'Sartre says, "I do *not* think, therefore I am a *moustache*."'

He didn't look up. 'The only perfect refutation of Descartes.'

'Can we go?' Sammy said to me.

I stared at Blay for another second, going over the concept of judging a book by its cover, but in Blay's case it seemed like too complicated an issue.

'Yeah.' I headed for the door.

Standing outside, watching the cars on Cheshire Bridge, Sammy stared down at the note he'd gotten from Blay.

'What does it say?' I asked him.

'Cheshire Motor Inn,' he told me, pocketing the piece of paper.

We looked up and down the street, and after a few minutes I saw the sign maybe a quarter of a mile away going west.

We walked by three more adult bookstores and two massage parlors until we came to The Colonnade, a crowded restaurant next to the Cheshire Motor Inn. There was a line just to get into the waiting room of the restaurant, but the motel looked nearly deserted.

'Why don't you let me take a crack at this,' I told Sammy.

We got to the check-in at the motel, a little eight by ten room with beige walls and an indoor/outdoor rug. There was a young woman lounging behind the counter watching television.

I zipped up and flashed my badge. She stared, sighed, and stood up slowly.

She was in her twenties, wearing a blue tank top and white shorts with flip-flops. Her hair was in a ponytail and her eyes were framed by clotted mascara.

'How may I help you?' She wore a name pin that said *Cheryl* on it, and she had the most southern accent I'd ever heard. It took me a second to decipher it.

'I need to know what room Denny Bennet is in, please,' I said. She tilted her head. '*Please?*'

'And thank you,' I added. 'Cheryl.'

She gave me the once-over. 'You are *not* a policeman.'

'I'm an investigator for Child Protective Services,' I said quickly, 'and I need to know what room Denny Bennet is in.'

'Child *what*?' Cheryl said.

Sammy stepped up to the counter and showed the kid his Colt. 'Denny Bennet. Now.'

Cheryl stared at Sammy's gun with an impressive degree of composure. She blinked once, then looked down at something behind the counter.

When she looked back up, it was right into Sammy's eyes. 'I've just mashed the little silent alarm here. It's a whole lot of cops over next door at the Colonnade? They love me. Whole bunch right there in the waiting room. I'd be surprised if it took more than two minutes for about a hundred of them to be here. If you walk out right now, I'll tell my friends that it was a homeless man in here making threats, and you two can be on your way. Or stay right here, that little pistol in your hand, and get all shot up by some trigger-happy lawman.'

I turned to Sammy. 'Didn't I *just* say to let me handle this? Put that gun away and mind your manners.'

'Here they come,' she sang out, glancing in the direction of the Colonnade.

I looked. Maybe ten cops were headed our way.

Sammy put away his gun.

'Denny Bennet is a bad person,' I announced.

'And your friend has a gun,' Cheryl countered. 'That he *threatened* me with.'

'Damn it, Sammy,' I muttered.

'We gotta go,' Sammy said, watching the cops come our way. Then glanced at the kid. 'Sorry.'

I was already out the door. I walked slowly toward the rooms of the motel so the cops would think I'd just checked in if they saw me.

It was a fairly typical motel arrangement. One-story rooms attached side by side, in a single row, a blacktop parking lot.

Sammy sidled up to me. 'What are you doing?'

'Trying not to get arrested, trying to find Denny Bennet, and trying to get the hell out of Atlanta,' I said softly. 'In that order.'

'Oh,' he said. 'Good.'

I didn't want to look back toward the check-in for the motel because I could hear the cops gathering. I was hoping that the magic words *please*, *thank you*, and *sorry* had done their work with Cheryl. I didn't feel like trying to outrun Georgia cops.

I just headed for the closest room with a car parked in front of it. Because sometimes you get lucky.

I knocked on the door, number seven, as urgently as I could without sounding like I was too much trouble.

Nothing.

'Denny?' I called out in a hoarse whisper. 'The professor from down at the bookstore sent me. Look out your blinds at the check-in. Somebody called the cops on you!'

Nothing.

Then the blinds parted just a little. He could see all the cops congregating around Cheryl.

'Jesus,' said a voice from the room.

'You've got, like, ten seconds to come with me and Sammy,' I said, a little louder. 'After that we disappear behind the building and you go *directly* to jail.'

It was a good bluff. I was certain Denny had done something or other to make him nervous about cops.

And it worked. The door opened.

'Who are you?' he asked.

Denny was five-foot-four with a pockmarked face and blood-shot eyes. His nostrils were rimmed in white powder, and he was wearing a torn pink Hawaiian shirt.

'My name is Foggy Moscowitz,' I said, 'and I'm in from New York.'

I figured he would interpret that however he wanted to, and it would mean something to him, because that's the way a person's brain works. It makes you see patterns even if there aren't any there.

'Oh. Jesus. New York.' He opened the door all the way. 'Lemme get my stuff.'

I peered in. The motel room looked like some sort of perform-ance art installation. 'Den of the Degenerated.' The bed covers had exploded everywhere, both lamps were on their sides, the phone was off the hook, the television was on, but it was only playing jangled static and white noise.

Denny gathered his effects, a plaid cloth valise and a London Fog raincoat, and brushed past me at the door.

'This is Sammy,' I said.

Sammy waved.

'What do we do?' Denny asked, wired, ignoring Sammy altogether.

'Around in back and over there to the Colonnade,' I said like I knew what I was doing.

'The Colonnade?' he snapped. 'That's where all those cops *eat!*'

'We're not going into the restaurant,' I said, headed away from the cops. 'We're going to hide behind the dumpsters in back there.'

I figured that any restaurant would have dumpsters in back. Plus, the cops weren't really after Denny. And it appeared that Cheryl had been true to her word. They weren't looking our way at all. A couple of them were even laughing. Good old Cheryl.

But it was enough for Denny. He picked up his pace, I glanced at Sammy, he shrugged, and off we went.

FIFTEEN

There were, indeed, dumpsters behind the Colonnade. Behind the dumpsters there were trees. In front of the dumpsters there was cratered blacktop. And in the air, something I'd never experienced before.

'What is that *smell*?' I whispered as we got closer to the dumpsters.

'Day-old coleslaw,' Denny answered absently. 'How long do we gotta stay here?'

Sammy produced his Colt once more. 'Just until you give us the money you owe Tree,' Sammy said calmly.

Denny looked at the Colt. Then he looked at me. Then he nodded.

'Right. Tree sent you. Right. OK.' He set down his valise. 'I got it. I got it right here.'

Denny knelt. He zipped open the valise. Only instead of money for Tree, he came out with the meanest looking automatic pistol I'd ever seen. He fired right away, and Sammy went down.

I moved just as the first shots went off. I went to Denny's left, then down. I was on my side on the blacktop and rolling into him. I hit his left shin hard just as the burst from his gun was finishing. He lurched forward, over the valise and nose down on the pavement.

I kept rolling and managed to roll up behind Denny. But he flipped, lying on his back and aimed the pistol at me.

I was close to his valise and I kicked it hard. All kinds of stuff went flying into the air and he was confused. He still shot, but the shot was wild.

I jumped and landed on his leg; kicked him underneath his chin. I heard a crunch and Denny howled, but he was still waving that pistol around.

I kicked again, trying to knock the gun out of his hand, but I lost my balance and ended up on my back right next to him.

He sat up and put the barrel of the gun right on my cheek. I slapped it away just as the shots went off.

He tried to stand, but his leg was wonky. I didn't think I'd broken it, but it couldn't have felt good.

I scrambled up and grabbed the London Fog raincoat he'd dropped beside his case. I whipped it around and slapped his face with it, whirled it around and slapped his hand. Then I tossed it over his head and jumped to my right. He shot once more, wildly, with the raincoat covering his head.

I was standing beside him, waiting for the hail of bullets to stop. When it did, I kicked his left leg out from under him and he went down, still tangled up in the raincoat.

His hand was waving, and I guess he was trying to get off another round, but all I had to do was grab the gun out of his hand. I didn't have to kick him in the side, but it seemed like the right thing to do under the circumstances.

I took a couple of steps back and looked over at Sammy. He was sitting up holding his chest.

'Samuel?' I asked tentatively.

'Vest,' he gasped. 'Hurts. Not shot.'

He was struggling for breath, but there wasn't any blood.

'You're wearing a vest?'

He nodded. 'Tree gave it to me.' Big breath. 'Said Denny might . . . might . . .'

'OK.' I shook my head. 'So, thanks for warning *me* about that.' I looked down at the gun.

'What the hell is this thing?' I went on.

'It's a PM-63 RAK,' Denny said, struggling to get out from under the raincoat. 'I got it in 'Nam.'

Sammy leaned toward me. 'What the hell *is* that thing?' he repeated.

'It's, like, a commando gun,' Denny explained. His jaw was already beginning to swell and turn purple. 'A hand-held automatic. Polish.'

'You got this in Vietnam?' I asked.

Denny nodded. 'I think you broke a rib.'

'You're a vet?' Sammy asked.

'Two years in hell,' he said. 'Look, keep it. Keep the gun. Sell it. You'll get more for it than I owe Tree. Or, you know, see if Tree maybe wants it instead of his money. I used to think I needed it to protect myself. Obviously, that don't work out for me too well.'

'You don't just have the money?' Sammy asked. 'It would be so much simpler.'

'No,' Denny answered, irritated. 'I don't *just have the money.*'

I glanced over at his suitcase and the stuff that used to be inside of it. In addition to the expected socks and underwear, there were three large baggies nearly filled with powdered sugar. Only I knew it wasn't powdered sugar.

'That's a lot of coke,' I said.

'Used to be a lot more.' Denny bit his lip. 'I'm my own best customer.'

'Look,' Sammy said, struggling to his feet. 'I want to sort this all out, but we just fired off an automatic weapon and there's an army of cops about a hundred yards away. In case they're headed our way, shouldn't we . . .?'

I nodded, wrapped Denny's gun in his raincoat, and tucked it under my arm.

Denny was already gathering up the rest of his stuff.

I looked around, scouting out our perfect exit. On the other side of the Colonnade and a quick jaunt down Cheshire Bridge, I could see a couple of massage parlors. Any port in a storm.

We were gone in the next ten seconds, but the smell of rotting coleslaw came with us for a little while.

Half a block down, and we ducked into a storefront called, apparently, 'Girls-Girls-Girls-Massage-Fun!' The reception area was only slightly larger than a closet and the walls had rose wallpaper on them. There was a half-dressed blond Asian woman at a counter and a gigantic, tattooed gentleman sitting in a chair behind her in the corner. He was fully dressed, but he was half asleep. Behind them both was a double doorway with a burgundy curtain in front of it.

'Hey, boys,' the Asian woman said. 'Chaunt?'

All right, then, *she* had the most southern accent I'd ever heard. I had no idea what *chaunt* meant, so I repeated it.

'Chaunt?'

'*What do you want,*' Denny translated, whispering.

'Oh.' I nodded. 'Would you happen to have three . . . um, rooms open at the moment?'

'Salons are twenty-five dollars up front,' she said amiably, 'and the rest depends on what you select from the menu.'

She tapped a laminated piece of paper on the counter in front of her. Just like a menu. Only it was filled with phrases that were written in English but otherwise held no meaning for me whatsoever in the current context. *Half and half* and *Torn* and *Denial* and *Super Happy.*

Sammy was already shelling out seventy-five bucks.

'Let's see where the afternoon takes us,' he said, smiling.

The girl shrugged. The bouncer leaned back and closed his eyes again, and a *hostess* appeared from behind the burgundy curtain. She was barely over four feet tall and if she was eighteen then I was eighty. She was wearing a white bikini and flip-flops, and her hair was cut short, Twiggy short.

'Gentlemen,' she said in a hoarse voice.

We followed her down a short dark hallway until we got to several doors. She stopped, so we did too.

She tapped on the door to her right. It opened. Another teenager with long black hair, dressed in a sheer, short nightgown, stood there looking us over.

After a second, she said, 'Well, *somebody* come in.'

I nudged Denny, he took a step, and I followed.

'Two at once is extra,' the hostess said.

I nodded. 'Understood.'

Sammy stuck out his lower lip. 'I'll be across the hall.'

The hostess tapped on that door, it opened, and Sammy went in.

The room for Denny and me was only a little larger than the reception area. The walls had the same rose wallpaper on them. There was a fairly genuine massage table on one side and two comfortable looking vinyl chairs on the other, and a large, floor-to-ceiling cabinet in one corner. The hostess closed the door behind us, and the long-haired girl moved to take off the top of her nightgown.

'Hold it,' I said. 'We actually just want to sit here and rest for a while.'

She froze. 'Are you two guys cops?'

'No,' I said.

Denny sat down in one of the chairs. 'He works for Tree.'

She relaxed. Almost smiled. 'Oh.'

'Mr Wonderful, here,' I said, inclining my head toward Denny, 'took some money from Tree and my friend and I were sent to retrieve it.'

'Only I don't got the money,' Denny explained. 'And there's cops from the Colonnade over there at the Motor Inn.'

'So we came in here to . . . rest,' I concluded, 'and think about what to do.'

She relaxed all the way, readjusted her nightgown top, and leaned against the table.

'I don't do this all the time, you know,' she said, only a little defensively. 'I go to college. Georgia State.'

I took a seat. 'I never went to school. But I read a lot.'

She almost smiled again. 'I *love* to read. That's my major, which is English.'

'You already speak English pretty well to me,' I cracked.

'Ha-ha,' she said, without a hint of mirth. 'English Literature. I'm reading Chaucer now.'

'*Canterbury Tales*,' I said. 'I read that. Took me forever.'

She boosted herself up to sit on the table, folded her hands in her lap, and said, 'Whan that Aprill with his shoures sote the droghte of Marche hath perced to the rote . . .'

'Stop,' I told her, smiling. 'That right there, that's what slowed me down. Middle English. I had to go back to the library and get the CliffsNotes to figure out . . .'

'It just says, "When April showers drench March roots . . ."' she explained simply.

'Exactly.' I sat back. 'And after I finished the first couple of lines like that, I figured that the guy's point, Chaucer's point, is that after you've been cooped up in the house all winter, you get itchy to get out and take a nice long Spring walk, right?'

'Exactly!' Big smile at last. 'Thanne longen folk to goon on pilgrimages!'

'What the hell?' Denny exploded.

We both looked at him.

'I mean,' he said, a little softer, 'are we gonna get some action here or not?'

'Not,' I said instantly, leaning my head toward the girl. 'My friend and I are trying to talk about literature. That's *it*, get me?'

'But . . . we already *paid*,' he said, lost.

'Doreen,' the girl said.

I turned to her.

'That's my name,' she told me.

'Ah. I'm Foggy.'

She laughed. 'That's your *name*? Lordy.'

I sat up. 'It's actually *Fyvush*, wise guy, but I've been called *Foggy* since I was three, so.'

'Foggy.' She shook her head.

'We already *paid*,' Denny repeated.

I laid the London Fog raincoat in my lap. Denny knew his gun was in it.

'We're just going to sit here, Denny,' I said, 'until I think the coast is clear, and then we're all going to where Sammy is staying, and we're going to wait for Tree.'

'I like Tree,' Doreen volunteered.

'Me too,' I said.

'Tree's a psychopath!' Denny complained.

Before I could respond, there was a knock on the door.

'Cops,' Sammy whispered. 'I can hear them up front in the reception area.'

Doreen hopped down off the table. 'Cabinet.'

I nodded. 'How do you mean?'

She opened the door to let Sammy in. 'This happens all the time. We have several . . . sensitive clients.'

'Sensitive?'

'A state senator and two judges, off the top of my head.' She went to the cabinet and opened it. Then she fussed with something in the cabinet and she stood back.

I peered in. The cabinet had a false back that opened, like another little door, into what looked like a dark narrow hall.

'What's that?' Denny asked. His voice wavered.

'It's the way out,' Doreen answered, a little impatiently. 'Lets you out behind the building. Go across Welbourne Drive and through a couple of trees into Nino's parking lot. Go in. Have a little nice Italian nosh, right?'

I smiled at Doreen. 'You're kind of great, you know.'

She smiled back. 'Anything for a fellow Chaucer lover.'

'Christ,' Denny moaned.

I muscled him in front of me and into the cabinet, then I followed. Sammy followed me. The unlit passageway was barely wide enough. Sammy had to turn sideways. But it was only maybe twenty yards to a dead-end.

Denny panicked. 'We're trapped!'

I reached over his shoulder and shoved on the wall in front of him. It clicked open and swung out. The sun poured in.

'Move.' I gave Denny a little shove.

In seconds, the three of us were outside in the hot sunlight. A few yards away there was a street that ran into Cheshire Bridge. Across that street was a parking lot and Nino's Italian restaurant.

'I could go for a little something Saltimbocca,' Sammy allowed.

'In this humidity?' I shook my head. 'All I want is a gin and tonic.'

Sammy headed for Nino's. 'Maybe they have a bar.'

SIXTEEN

Nino's wasn't open, and the sun was almost gone.

We stood around in the parking lot looking conspicuous in the extreme, even in the dim light. I was about to rail significantly about the lack of cabs on Cheshire Bridge when Sammy started walking toward that very street.

'It's the bus.' He pointed down the street and there it was, lumbering our way.

'I'm not getting on the bus with a gun and a lot of cocaine,' Denny complained.

Sammy looked at him. 'Why not?'

He squirmed. 'I got a weird kind of claustrophobia. Plus, the bus smells bad.'

I shoved him toward the bus stop. 'Couldn't be any worse than that coleslaw smell.'

The bus wheezed and began to slow down. We stood at the stop. Sammy reached into his pocket for a handful of coins. In short order we were headed up Cheshire Bridge toward Piedmont Road before we even sat down. And, in fact, it didn't smell all that bad.

'Where are we going?' Denny whispered, sweating, his valise on his knees.

'If the bus turns left on Piedmont, we're going to my place,' Sammy said. 'If it turns right, we're headed for Buckhead. We can go to Aunt Charley's. Get a drink there. Figure what to do.'

I looked at Sammy's face. Calm and undisturbed.

'You seem to be quite knowledgeable about Atlanta, buses and bars, for a guy who just got here,' I observed.

Sammy sat back. 'Well. That's a story. See, the reason you-know-who sent me here in the first place was that I been here before. Last year.'

I smiled. 'Thanks for not mentioning her name. What's the story?'

'OK.' He squinted. 'OK. See. A few years ago, you left

Brooklyn. You left before you could get involved with your father's associates.'

'No,' I corrected him, 'I was quite involved with them, I just didn't participate in their more nefarious enterprises. I always thought that maybe my father had said something to Red Levine.'

'You mean your father who died protecting Red.' Sammy nodded.

'Yeah, that's the guy. But go on.'

'Well, I *did*.' He folded his arms.

'You did what?' Denny asked, clearly sucked in by Sammy's story, even though he didn't understand it.

'I did get involved in the *more nefarious enterprises*, as Foggy puts it,' Sammy answered. 'In your father's line of work, to be precise.'

I said, 'Somebody sent you down here to paint a house.'

Sammy nodded silently.

Denny twitched. 'You're a house painter? That don't sound so bad.'

Sammy and I turned his way. Denny was obviously not familiar with the vernacular.

'Um, anyway,' Sammy went on, 'there was a certain guy here in Atlanta who was what they call a Grand Dragon of the Ku Klux Klan.'

'They. They call a guy a *Grand Dragon*?' I stammered.

Sammy nodded. 'Imagine the brain that comes up with *that* moniker. But the guy was a real problem, see? For one thing, he made a newspaper that he called *I See the Truth!* With an exclamation point. And he was always spraying swastikas on Temples and burning down Black churches with, like, people *in* them, right? It was too much. So somehow you-know-who got wind of the seriousness of these events and talked to a guy who talked to a guy, if you see what I'm saying.'

'Wait,' Denny said. 'This Nazi guy. I remember this. On the news. Jesus. You did *that*?'

'Pipe down, if you don't mind,' Sammy told him softly.

'You came down here to take care of the swastika guy,' I said, 'on advice from *you-know-who*? Seriously?'

'I'm not sure you know the full extent of her extent,' Sammy said. 'But, yes, that is the story. I was down here for almost a month what with the planning and the research and all. But I got him in the end.'

'You got him in the *eyes*!' Denny snapped, then turned to me. 'The guy, the dragon, he was shot in both eyes!'

'Poetic, the eye thing,' I told him. 'Given the name of his newspaper. I get it.'

'Thanks. I thought it out.'

I smiled. But this put Sammy Two Shoes in a little different light than I'd seen him in before. And in that light, I probably should have had second thoughts about the murder of the actor Emory.

So what else could I say but, 'I'd like to hear the whole story.'

The bus turned left on to Piedmont, headed for midtown and Dickson Place, and Sammy obliged me with a little something called *The Story of Sammy Two Shoes and the Klan Dragon*.

Samuel Cohen arrived in Atlanta on a hot November day. He'd taken the train from Grand Central so he could have time to think. It was a three-day trip, so he had a sleeper.

He got off the train at Peachtree Street without luggage and stood out like the Yankee hoodlum that he was: pale blue suit, dark blue shirt, off-white tie. Almost everyone around him was in short-sleeved shirts and sunglasses.

There was a place called the Coach and Six, a motor inn, not too far down the street going north, and across the street was the Jewish Community Center.

Sammy got a room at the inn and wandered over to the center for no particular reason, except maybe to see what the Georgia Jews looked like. Turned out they looked like anyone else, only better dressed. He made small talk; said he was visiting from Brooklyn. Somebody said they had relatives in Brooklyn and did he know Sylvia and Allen Reingold. He didn't.

He had dinner at the Coach and Six and it wasn't bad. Then he went to his room, took off his suit, and sat on his bed in his underwear cleaning his gun.

The next morning, early, he was up, in the same suit, and asking the check-in clerk about transportation. The clerk said that Sammy could rent a car or take a cab, but the bus stopped right out front of the inn, it only cost a quarter, and if he took it all the way downtown he could get a nice look at Peachtree Street, Atlanta's jugular vein. That's not what the clerk called it; that's how Sammy interpreted it. Which, when Sammy thought about it, was probably a window into his own brain.

So he took the bus. At Pershing Point there was a building that reminded him of the Flatiron. At 15th Street there was an art museum, and at 14th the sad vestiges of what had once been Atlanta's hippie culture. All the way down Peachtree, in fact, there was something to see, and Sammy was glad he'd taken the clerk's advice.

When he arrived downtown, he got off the bus at Davidson's department store. He crossed the street to the Woolworth's and went inside to the lunch counter, even though it was only ten o'clock in the morning. He sat on a swivel stool and ordered a cup of coffee. He had taken a seat so that he could look into the kitchen through the services portal. Because in the kitchen, in a stained apron and a paper hat, with a cigarette dangling from his thin, chapped lips, was the Dragon.

The Grand Dragon of the Ku Klux Klan was a short order cook at a downtown Woolworth's. He was also a primary importer of cocaine from Bogota, a major east coast distributor. The guy had also spray-painted swastikas on the Jewish Community Center, and he had set fire to three churches on Sunday morning in the middle of services. Still, Sammy felt like laughing at him because he looked like a marionette. Skeletal and short with one slow eye and a crewcut that made his head look like a fuzzy penis, he wasn't what Sammy had been expecting at all. In fact, the guy looked so ridiculous that Sammy reconsidered the job entirely. Maybe just give him a talking to, throw a little scare his way. The poor guy looked like he was about to fall apart anyway.

Sammy left a big tip and strolled out on to the street. He wandered around the corner until he found an alley. The alley led to a service entrance at the back of the Woolworth's. It wasn't a particularly revolting alley. It smelled like urine, and there were rats unafraid of sunlight or Sammy, but as alleys went, Sammy had seen worse. He lit a Kool. The menthol tasted good to him. He meditated on the many ways in which life was funny while he watched the rats patrol the back corners of the alley for a crust of bread or some moldy cheese.

He had no idea how long he'd been there when two people came out of the service door. One was the Dragon, the other was a waitress. When they saw Sammy they froze.

'That's the guy with the big tip,' the waitress whispered to the Dragon.

Sammy hadn't really noticed the girl before when she'd been waiting on him, but now that he noticed, he thought she was pretty. Curly blond hair, a little too much eyeliner, her green waitress costume a little too tight in all the right places. Her name was Dee, according to the pin on her apron.

So Sammy said, 'Dee, could you give us a minute? I have a message for your friend.'

'We ain't friends,' the Dragon croaked. 'She's a skank.'

Sammy smiled. 'Is that true, Dee?'

Dee backed through the door, eyes wide, and disappeared.

The Dragon glared at Sammy. He had a copy of his own newspaper, *I See the Truth!*, tucked into the front pocket of his apron. He was shaking ever so slightly.

'What?' the Dragon demanded, leaning forward.

'My name is Samuel Cohen,' Sammy began, 'and I represent some people who don't like you. They don't like what you're doing here. You should stop.'

The Dragon laughed. 'Is that right? Well listen at this, you stump-jumper: I do what I want. Every day of my life.'

And with that the Dragon reached behind him and came back with an FN Barracuda, six-shot revolver. Security forces pistol. Sammy'd seen others just like it.

Sammy moved quickly. With one hand he slapped the Dragon across the face with his palm. His other hand grabbed the Barracuda and took it away from the Dragon. Then he took one step back and put the muzzle of the gun right on the Dragon's left eye.

'Don't say stump-jumper,' Sammy said calmly. 'It's not polite. Plus, I don't know what it means.'

'Kiss my ass, dickwad,' the Dragon growled. 'You can't do a goddam thing to me. This is *Georgia*, boy. We blow y'all *up* down here. Blow 'em up good.'

Sammy shifted his weight. 'Are you talking about the Temple bombing down here in, like, 1959? Because that's some slow shit if that's what you mean. One bombing in fifteen years. I mean, I know it's too hot down here to move *really* fast, but that just seems *lazy.*'

And then Sammy pressed the barrel of the gun on to the Dragon's open eye.

The Dragon wailed, 'Ow!' And then he reached up to push the gun away.

Sammy reacted without thinking. He pulled the trigger. The bullet went into the Dragon's eye, through the brain, what there was of it, and out the back of the skull, into the brick wall close to the service entrance door.

The Dragon fell back on to the dirty alley floor, dead before he hit the ground. Sammy leaned over and shot the Dragon again in the other eye.

Sammy removed the man's sad, crumpled newspaper from his apron, unfolded it so that the banner was full, and laid it over the Dragon's face. He wiped the gun off with the stained apron and then put it into the Dragon's hand.

Then he did what Sammy always did. He took the guy's shoes. It was an ancient superstition that Sammy had somehow found appealing, even though he couldn't remember the meaning of it. He took the guy's shoes and threw them in the dumpster. The rats watched. They didn't scatter. They were intrigued by the show.

Sammy nodded. 'If you want a fresh snack,' he said to the rats, 'take a look under the newspaper.'

With that Sammy left the alley, walked a long way down Peachtree going north, eventually stopped at a bus stop across from a grand old movie house called the Fox and waited. He smoked two more Kools before the bus came. He got on and went to the Coach and Six. He made a point of thanking the desk clerk for the bus recommendation while he was paying his bill.

'You're leaving already?' the clerk asked pleasantly.

'Just a quick trip,' Sammy said. 'Got the job done.'

'Well, I hope you'll stay with us again when you come back,' the clerk said.

Sammy nodded, left, got a cab, went to the airport, and was back in Brooklyn in time for a late dinner.

Sammy concluded his story, staring at Denny, who had become increasingly uneasy as the story went on.

Denny looked at me. 'It was on the news. One of the theories was that the guy, this grand Dragon guy, he shot himself!'

I squinted. 'In both eyes?'

Denny sat back. 'I *know*, but. Jesus.'

I turned to Sammy. 'You shouldn't be back here in Atlanta. This doesn't make sense. Shayna would never send you—'

'There's another guy down here,' he interrupted, 'that I needed to get. It's a connection with the whole porn thing. A couple dozen underaged Jewish girls go to this so-called modeling agency downtown, and they get money for a legit photo shoot, and then one thing leads to another. And then before they know it, it's a whole other thing. If you know what I mean.'

I only had a hint as to what he was talking about. And I didn't want any more information.

'You're actually here in Atlanta,' I said, 'for another job like the Dragon guy.'

He nodded once. 'I am.'

Denny squeaked. 'Jesus! It's not me, is it?'

Sammy laughed. 'We're taking you to Tree. Pay him what you owe him. This is my only interest in you.'

'So there was a plan inside a plan,' I went on to Sammy. 'Shayna set you up to work for Tree, but you were actually here to work for . . .?'

'Justice,' Sammy answered. 'I'm here to work for justice. I'll tell you the rest later. But Shayna didn't send me to work for Tree. She sent me to work for the guy Tree works for sometimes, when he feels like it.'

'You mean this so-called Mike guy,' I said. 'Only Tree seems like the kind of person who does pretty much what he feels like doing all the time.'

'He is,' Denny muttered.

'So *pay* him,' Sammy said.

Denny leaned forward. 'Who's the guy?'

Sammy stared.

'Who's the guy you come to Atlanta to pop?' Denny went on. Foolishly.

Sammy stood up just as the bus was slowing down.

'Our stop,' he said, walking toward the exit.

Somehow the bus had gotten back on Peachtree Street headed toward town, and our stop was at the corner of Peachtree and 11th. We headed down the cracked cement sidewalk toward Dickson Place, illuminated by a surprising number of streetlights. The air was filled with the smell of weed, baking bread, and some kind of cinnamon incense. We didn't talk.

When we were nearly at Dickson, Tree emerged from a screened-in porch across the street where there were candles burning.

'Little Buddy!' he called out happily. 'Look what you did! It's Denny!'

Tree was very lively. Could have been speed, but I was guessing coke.

Denny turned to run. Sammy grabbed him.

'He's got a lot of coke in his bag,' Sammy told Tree, 'and he also had a cool gun.'

I unrolled the London Fog raincoat I'd been carrying and showed Tree the PM-63 RAK.

Tree's eyes got big. 'That *is* cool.'

He took it, examined it, pointed it at Denny, laughed, and then put the gun in his belt. Then he grabbed Denny's bag and opened it; smiled.

'OK, Denny, here's the deal,' Tree announced. 'You're out. You won't be able to get any kind of job in Atlanta ever again. You have to leave town today. And if anybody smells you back here in town, I will find you and I'll cook and eat your liver in front of you while you're still alive. Do you understand that?'

Denny started crying, but Tree had already moved on.

'Right,' Tree said to Sammy. 'What about your *other* job?'

Sammy hesitated. 'You know about that how?'

Tree only cleared his throat.

Sammy nodded. 'Cool. I'll go get my stuff.'

Without another word, Sammy turned and headed up to his apartment. Denny looked between me and Tree for a couple of seconds, and then he just took off running back up 11th toward Peachtree.

Tree looked into my eyes. Really looked. 'I did know that Sammy had another gig here in town,' he whispered. 'I wasn't *supposed* to know, but I did. Mike talks about private stuff when I'm around sometimes and he may have said something about Sammy bumping off his rival, some other porn guy. Mike assumes that because I'm big I'm not very bright.'

'But he's wrong,' I told him. 'I always think it's to your advantage when people think they're smarter than you. Makes them say things and do things they think you don't understand. But then you know more than they do, and suddenly they're transparent.'

'Exactly.' Tree got a funny look in his face. 'I wish you and me could sit down and talk. I think you maybe got *insight*.'

'It would be an interesting conversation,' I said.

But Sammy was already back down from his apartment with what looked like a briefcase.

'You take care of yourself, Tree,' Sammy said as he passed by. 'Come on, Foggy.'

And with that, we were headed back toward Peachtree.

SEVENTEEN

On the flight back to LaGuardia, Sammy was unusually quiet.

I finally said, 'You're a lot more *involved* in my father's world than I thought you were.'

He nodded. He knew what I meant. 'After Red died, a younger crowd filled in the gaps, and it was more like business. Your aunt Shayna was still in demand, though, so her more personal requests were still important.'

'Like icing a Klan chief,' I said, 'or keeping some nice Jewish girls out of the pornography industry.'

'For example,' he acknowledged.

'And when I wanted to get you out of town because you stabbed an actor,' I went on, '*you* suggested calling Shayna.'

'You're just now figuring this out?' he asked. 'I thought you were supposed to be the smart one.'

'So do I have this right: Shayna already scheduled you to head south when the bruhaha at the theatre went down.'

Sammy nodded once.

I sat back. 'I *thought* Shayna pulled your escape together a little too quickly.'

'But the thing is,' Sammy said, '*you* came to get me. When you realized I didn't kill Emory, you just got on a plane – without luggage, I notice – and came to get me. *That's* a pal.'

'More than a pal,' I agreed. 'Legally speaking: an *accessory.*'

'You want to know why there were wheels inside of wheels with this whole deal, right?'

I stared. 'I want to know why you stabbed Emory with a pencil. I mean, at that point I figure she was already dead, right?'

'Right,' Sammy acknowledged.

'What aren't you telling me?' I went on.

'OK, let me start this way: I love Phoebe. A lot. Like, more than anything.'

'Yeah, Sam, I could see that. So, there you go,' I said, like it was a complete explanation of everything.

And because I'm supposed to be the smart one, it only took me about thirty seconds to figure it out.

'You were in the dressing room before anybody,' I whispered. 'You found Emory dead. And for some reason, you thought maybe Phoebe killed Emory, so you popped a pencil in Emory's neck to, like, distract the police.'

'These police,' Sammy said sympathetically, 'they got so many crimes to deal with that they don't really have time to explore the details of any one case. A bleeding neck wound looks pretty much like cause of death, and what with no tox screen and all, case closed right away.'

'Yeah, but Sam,' I objected, 'nobody liked Emory. Could have been anybody that iced her, don't you think?'

'Only Phoebe was the main one getting threatening notes from Emory,' Sammy allowed, 'which everybody knew. The cops would have gone right to Phoebe. That was my thinking on the spur of the moment. I admit it: I wasn't thinking right. Apparently, love does that to a person.'

'And how could you figure on the cops being so lazy that

they'd nab Phoebe because she was the one standing closest to the body when they came on the scene?' I concluded.

'Right,' he told me. 'I mean, I was going out of town anyway, and when you thought that was *your* idea, I also figured you'd pursue the matter while I was gone.'

'Which I did.'

'And Phoebe's out.'

'Not exactly,' I told him. 'I got her lawyer to do a little extra . . . the lawyer got a tox screen. Emory was poisoned, your fingerprints were on the pencil, and now the general consensus, I think, is that you two are *both* guilty of the murder, you and Phoebe.'

He glared. 'So you made things worse.'

I nodded. 'A little.'

'For God's sake, Foggy,' Sammy began.

'I'll fix it,' I said firmly.

'How?'

'I'll find out who really killed Emory.' I looked down at my hands in my lap. 'See, Sammy, Phoebe isn't from your world. She's from a different reality, where people don't just kill each other to take care of a problem. It's my understanding that, in the theatre world, everybody in a play always wants to kill somebody else in the cast. If they don't, you're doing something wrong. The difference is they don't actually do it. They don't kill anybody. And they hug and kiss when the show is over, crying like they're leaving home forever. So my thoughts on the subject are as follows. Phoebe didn't kill Emory because she's not that kind of girl. You didn't kill Emory because Emory was already dead. I also don't think any of the other actors killed Emory because of the aforementioned other world in which they live. So my conclusion is that Emory was mixed up in something outside of the wonderful world of theatre that got her popped. The first thing I have to do is find out what that something was.'

I turned to Sammy for his reaction. He was sound asleep.

We parted ways at LaGuardia. He got a cab to Brooklyn; I found a shuttle that would let me out at the Benjamin. It took a while. I had time to reflect. And that reflection led me to wonder why I ever thought that coming to New York was a good idea. What I *wanted* was to watch a pigeon eat something disgusting on a curb. What I *got* was being an accessory to two murders. My conclusion was that I should have stood in bed.

Still, I figured I had to play the hand I'd been dealt. I had to figure out who killed Emory. And to do that, I had to learn more about her, to find out what she'd been into. And to do *that*, I had to go back to the actors who knew her. At least for the span of rehearsing for *Hamlet*.

Emory played Ophelia. Best I could remember, after a little more reflection, was that Ophelia had the most scenes with Polonius. Then next with Hamlet. Didn't mean that either of those actors would know Emory any better that anyone else, but I had to start somewhere. I always found that any action, even if it's the wrong one, is better than no action at all. And even the wrong action can lead to the right conclusion. If you're lucky.

So after a tossing-and-turning night at the Benjamin, I was up just after noon, headed back to Tisch and the dorm room where I'd talked to Polonius. On the way I pondered why I hadn't bothered to remember the actors' real names and was still thinking of them as their characters' names. That wasn't like me. My conclusion was that it meant something. Something about the play or the characters had to do with why Emory had been killed. Or did it? Was I just grasping at the proverbial straws?

My head still crowded with ideas like that, I found myself at the dorm room door. I tapped.

One of the roommates answered. She was wearing a T-shirt that said *Exonerated* and gold satin gym shorts. I'd seen her at the table when I'd talked to Polonius. I started to say something, but she got there first.

'It's that cop again,' she called out.

Then, leaving the door open, she wandered back into the room. I took a step in. There had been a party. The place looked a little like Denny Bennet's motel room only times ten.

Polonius had been in the kitchen and she waded through the debris toward me with lowered eyelids and a broken gait. She was wrapped in a green terrycloth robe. It was awful. It looked like she'd been attacked by moss.

'I. Have the worst hangover. Ever invented.' Her breathing attested to the honesty of her statement.

'Cool,' I said, 'but I need to talk about Emory.'

'Christ,' she whispered.

She went back to the kitchen, got coffee in a mug nearly the size of her head, and then went to sit at the dining table by the window. I joined her. The other roommates had already split.

'I already told you everything,' she complained, rubbing her forehead.

'Just looking for one more thing,' I assured her. 'What was Emory interested in outside of the theatre?'

She stopped rubbing her head and glared.

'What?' she groaned.

'Would you happen to know what else Emory did beside act in plays and irritate people?'

'I didn't *know* her,' Polonius said, trying to make it clear to me that I was an idiot.

'It's important,' I assured her. 'Anything she talked about or complained about or laughed about outside of the play.'

'All she *did* was complain.' She took a healthy gulp of coffee. 'I did my best to tune her out. She hated me.'

'You said,' I agreed. 'But could you really try to think back for a second?'

'Why?'

'Because I think she was killed because of some nefarious activities not remotely involving theatre.'

She thought. '*Nefarious*. That's bad stuff, right?'

'Yes.' I didn't mean to sigh when I said it, but I did.

'Yeah, I don't know if this qualifies,' Polonius told me, taking another swallow of coffee, 'but she really had some pretty bad fights with her boyfriend. I mean, like, a black eye once, and a big cut on her arm.'

'Happen to know her boyfriend's name?'

She shook her head. 'But Phoebe would know.'

'She would?'

'Phoebe knows everything,' Polonius assured me. 'Look, I'm fairly sure somebody put a squirrel inside my head last night when I wasn't looking. I gotta take, like, fifty aspirins and go back to bed, OK?'

She stood up.

'You know what helps a hangover,' I began.

'Get lost,' she interrupted. 'That'll help *my* hangover.'

'Right.' I stood. 'The thing is, Phoebe's in jail. Hard to get to.'

She groaned. 'Then why don't you just ask Phoebe's boyfriend? You know him, right? He brought you to the theatre. And *he* knew Emory. Better than anybody, I think.'

She stumbled her way toward what I assumed was her bedroom while I stood there with what I assumed was a stupid look on my face.

'Sammy knew Emory?' I asked.

'Emory *introduced* him to Phoebe, Sherlock,' she groaned.

And she was gone.

Sure, I was *supposed* to be the smart one, but clearly the speed of my native intelligence had been dulled by a return to the New York air. Or something. Because it wasn't until that moment that a bigger picture came into focus. And it was a picture I did not care for.

Sammy Two Shoes took me for a ride. How was it possible that I hadn't seen that before? Was it just that I was so hungry for New York that I let New York take advantage of me? Was it just because I missed the old days and the old pals so much that I could let them get away with murder? Literally?

I managed to walk out of the apartment. Even managed to get on to the street and hail a cab. But by the time I was sitting in the back of that cab, all I could do was worry.

'Benjamin,' I muttered. 'East 50th. Make it in under twenty minutes and I double the fare.'

I eased back in the seat just as the driver floored the gas. We were there in twelve.

EIGHTEEN

I sat in my room for about an hour, dazed. Then I ordered room service, a steak and a bottle of Scotch, which you wouldn't believe how much it cost. And when it came, I drank the bottle and stared at the steak. And when the bottle was nearly gone, I started making phone calls. It was still afternoon.

The first call was to the public defender who was supposed to be handling Phoebe's case, Helen Baker. She answered on the second ring.

'What?' That's all she wanted to know.

'It's Foggy Moscowitz,' I told her. 'I have to talk with Phoebe.'

Silence.

'Ms Baker?' I prompted.

'Why?' That was her next question.

'She knew Emory pretty well, I'm told. I need to find out what Emory was up to besides theatre.'

'Why?' Again.

'Because I think Emory was involved in some sort of criminal activity that got her killed.'

'Criminal activity.' She snorted. 'You mean *besides* acting in lesbian *Hamlet*? Which, excuse me, sounds like a felony.'

'It wasn't lesbian *Hamlet*. Look. Nobody liked Emory. She was mean-spirited, kept an offensive journal, and shot up somebody's door in a terrific example of overreaction.'

'Maybe she was just overacting,' Ms Baker interrupted.

'Far as I could tell,' I said right back, 'she wasn't capable of any kind of acting at all, but that's not the point.'

'So what is the point?'

'I'm trying to find Emory's murderer,' I snapped. 'Why are you in a *mood*?'

'A *mood*?' Her voice was three times louder than it had been. 'I'm working on sixteen cases at the moment. Sixteen! And for this *particular* one, there's not much I can *do*! So if you don't mind, fuck off, Mr Jenkins!'

'It's . . . Moscowitz,' I began.

'I know who it is!'

'Wait,' I said slowly. 'There's someone there at your desk with you.'

'Of *course* there is,' she said, maintaining her ire.

'And you can't really talk to me now,' I went on.

'I don't have time for this!'

'OK, but you should know I found Sammy Cohen. And I brought him back with me. He's in Brooklyn as we speak. And also, I found out he knew Emory better than I thought he did. Emory introduced Phoebe to Sammy.'

'I'm hanging up now!'

'Can you meet me at the bar at the Benjamin for a late lunch?' I suggested.

'That's right!' And with that, she slammed down the phone.

So that took care of my lunch date. The next call was to my mother. Or really, to my aunt, and that's who answered the phone.

'Hello,' Shayna said, deliberately sounding weak and timid.

'Shayna, it's me.'

'Ah.' A little more like her normal voice. 'You've been thinking.'

One of the disconcerting things about my aunt Shayna was the speed of her observations. She could tell in three words that I was disconcerted. And like lightning, she knew why.

'Yes.' I wanted to see how much she would tell me. And how much she would withhold.

'This is not something we can talk about in a telephone conversation,' she said.

'Well, I'm not coming over to Brooklyn right now. I have a lunch date.' I was hoping she could tell that I was mad.

'You want to come for dinner?' Like it was a light, casual family thing.

'The current man with two shoes,' I began, a little more harshly than maybe I should have, 'is not the person I left behind several years ago.'

'He is not,' she agreed. 'He was kind of a boy then. He's a man now.'

'Not how I'd put it.'

'How would you put it?' she asked.

'When I left, he was dangling his toes in the kiddie pool,' I said. 'Since then, you threw him in the deep end.'

'Luckily, he's a good swimmer.'

That was it. No denial, no apology.

'Look, he pulled me into this. And you pulled just as hard. What the hell, Shayna? What's going on?'

'What's going on?' Her voice was an octave higher than it had been. 'You took a powder. You went to Florida. You got straight. Now you're supposed to be some kind of a do-gooder. And now, here you are, up from Florida out of the blue, *unannounced*, acting like some kind of bigshot.'

'Hang on,' I interrupted. 'Hang on. You're turning this around. You're putting this on me. I didn't . . . you got me involved in *murder*!'

'Florida made you soft. You would *never* complain about a thing like that if you'd stayed in Brooklyn like you were supposed to.'

I took a beat because I didn't want to explode. And in that beat, I reflected. And that reflection made me realize that Shayna had never in her life talked to me like that. Never. So maybe something was wrong. Really wrong.

'You're scared,' I said after that moment of silence.

And at that, my aunt Shayna burst into tears. Another first. I'd never heard her cry.

'It's Sammy,' she whispered.

'OK.' I let out a breath. 'I have to see this person at this lunch. And then I'll be over, right?'

'Thanks, kiddo,' she sniffled. 'I . . . OK, I love you.'

And she hung up.

I sat in my room for a minute, trying to figure out what the hell was really going on. Then I gave up, took a shower, put on the powder-blue suit, and went downstairs for lunch.

Helen Baker was already there, sitting at the bar.

I approached. She started shaking her head.

'You found Sammy Cohen and you brought him back from *where*?' she demanded.

'Does it matter?' I sat down beside her. 'You asked me to fetch him. Mission accomplished.'

'I asked you to find the real murderer, too,' she mumbled, turning toward her martini.

'But to do that, I really have to talk with Phoebe.'

She roared. 'I made you my official investigator for the case! You can go down to the station and just tell them you want to see her any time you want!'

'I can?' I blinked. 'OK. The thing is, I know your world more from the other side of the bars. I just waltz in there and ask?'

'I wouldn't waltz, but yeah.' She took a healthy swig of her drink. 'What is it you're hoping to find out?'

'I think Emory was into something of a troubling nature.'

'Such as?' She was staring at the lunch menu.

'Cocaine. I'm pretty sure there was coke residue on her mirror in the dressing room. And a person has to be in deep to do lines like that in the middle of a show, don't you think?'

There were extra menus on the bar. I slid one my way.

She nodded. 'It kind of fits. Her weird journal, the whole shooting up somebody's door thing. Now that you mention it, it does sound like coke.'

'Right. I'm having the burger.'

The bartender appeared. 'Burger for the gentleman,' he intoned.

'Caesar Salad for me,' Ms Baker said. 'With grilled chicken.'

'Anything else?' the bartender asked.

'Could you bring me a little soda water and lime?' I asked.

'On the house,' he said, smiling.

'I love this place,' I told him. 'I'm thinking of buying it.'

'I'll alert the staff,' he said, and then he turned to go.

'Better bring me some fries with my salad,' Ms Baker said softly.

'Of course,' the bartender said, and then he was gone.

And when he was gone, Ms Baker said, 'What makes you think Phoebe would know anything about Emory's drug habits, or any other habits for that matter?'

'I've been given to understand that a stage manager, in the world of the theatre,' I explained, 'knows everything. They're not like us, these stage manager types. They're supernatural creatures.'

She only thought about it for a second. 'OK. So, after lunch you'll go with me to the station house where she is, I'll sign you in, because it will be quicker that way, and you'll talk to her, but in my presence.'

'OK, but why?'

'Why what?

'Why do I have to talk with her in your presence?'

'Because,' she said, picking up her martini, 'I have to know everything. Get used to it.'

The bartender brought my soda water, and I drank some of it just to keep from cracking wise with Ms Baker. Because I didn't want to alert her to the fact that I liked her. Sometimes if a person knows you like them, they can take advantage of you. Like Sammy took advantage of me.

So we sat there in silence for a moment.

Then she said, 'You've come to a satisfactory conclusion in a hundred percent of your cases down in Florida. A hundred percent. That's impressive.'

'I guess it depends on what you mean by *a satisfactory conclusion*,' I said.

'You *protected* a kid. It's in the name of your employing organization. You helped. Every time.'

'OK.' I took another conversation-avoiding sip of soda water.

'Don't you want to know why I looked up your record?' she asked.

'Why did you look up my record?' I obliged.

'Because I asked around about you.' She finished her martini. 'You've got a rep that anybody would envy.'

'When the legend becomes fact, print the legend,' I said.

'What?' She swiveled toward me.

'That's a quote from *The Man Who Shot Liberty Valence*,' I explained. 'That movie. I think maybe a lot of what you heard is my legend. Not my fact.'

'Oh. Well. Nevertheless.'

Our food came. We ate it.

Before long we were in a cab headed for the precinct house on West 10th. Once we were there, Ms Baker led the way, and in a shockingly short amount of time, we were in a room sitting across a table from Phoebe Peabody.

'I'll get right to the point,' I began. 'I need to know about Emory's outside interests. Outside of the scope of your play.'

Phoebe stared. 'Where's Sammy?'

'Brooklyn,' I said, glancing sideways at Ms Baker. 'He may have thought you poisoned Phoebe, so he stabbed her in the neck.'

'What?' Her eyes got about as big as they could get.

'He did it so that he would take the rap,' I explained, 'and then he left town to avoid the police. He loves you.'

'I didn't poison Phoebe,' she rasped. 'And Sammy didn't stab her in the neck.'

'He did, in fact,' I assured her. 'He told me so.'

'And his fingerprints are on the pencil,' Ms Baker confirmed. 'So now the district attorney thinks you *both* did it. Killed Phoebe. A *folie à deux*.'

'A *what?*' Phoebe asked.

'Emory was involved in *something*,' I interrupted. 'Something that maybe had to do with Sammy. I mean, Emory introduced you to Sammy, right?'

'She did.' Phoebe sat back. 'But you're *really* asking me about Emory's boyfriend. He was extremely bad news. Sammy knew him. Didn't like him.'

'What's his name?' I asked.

'Sammy always called him *Tanner*,' she told me. 'I guess that's his last name.'

I slumped a little in my chair. It was no wonder that Sammy hadn't mentioned this little detail. If he had, I'd definitely have gone back to Florida and done my best to forget I'd ever come to New York at all.

Ms Baker noticed my concern.

'You know this Tanner?' Ms Baker asked.

I nodded. 'It's not his last name.'

Tanner Brookmeyer was the kind of hood that other hoods were afraid of because he was crazy, coked-up *all* the time, and involved in the darkest part of the underworld of pornography. Everybody knew him. Nobody liked him. My family had always done their best to steer clear. A well-dressed man in his early fifties, *his* legend was deliberately scary. His real first name was Eugene, but he acquired his street name because of how many hides he'd tanned in the process of getting his work done. Usually with a blowtorch. And he regularly beat people and filmed it for entertainment purposes. Sometimes he beat them so bad that they left town. Sometimes in a hearse. And those were his good qualities. In the old days I didn't know anybody who wasn't terrified of him. If he was Emory's boyfriend, no wonder she was edgy all the time.

But the thing was, if Tanner wanted to kill her, he wouldn't put poison in her fancy water bottle. He'd use a belt buckle.

'I didn't know he was still around,' I went on. 'But this verifies my idea that Emory was into coke, as I was telling Ms Baker earlier. I mean, Tanner Brookmeyer is a significantly wrong guy.'

And it occurred to me that maybe Sammy was involved with Tanner. That would be a very troubling association. Though it might help to explain Sammy's transformation from a nice little two-bit hustler to a genuine ice machine.

'So, you know the guy,' Ms Baker confirmed.

'I know *about* him,' I said.

'He's the guy to talk to.' Phoebe stared into my eyes. 'Sammy can be so sweet. He didn't kill Emory any more than I did.'

I took a breath. I didn't want to mess up the kid's delusion.

'OK,' I said. 'So what do you think Tanner and Emory were into?'

'Seemed like coke,' Phoebe said. 'They were both pretty hyped up when they were together. Tanner's older, like fifty, maybe. But Emory was all over him. I mean, it could have been love, but it smelled like coke.'

'The two are easily confused,' I agreed.

'I should have a look for paper on this guy,' Ms Baker said. 'This Tanner guy. What's his last name?'

'Brookmeyer,' I told her, 'but you probably won't find anything on him. He's not the kind to get caught.'

'Is he the kind to kill his girlfriend?' Ms Baker asked.

'Oh, absolutely,' I said.

'OK,' she said. 'Then go get him.'

'Me? No.' I shook my head. 'You should send in, like, Godzilla to get this guy. He's not human. I think he's probably an evil spirit of some sort.'

'Grow up, Nature Boy.' Ms Baker laughed.

'I'm not kidding,' I assured her. 'I can't fetch him.'

'Maybe you and Sammy could do it together?' Phoebe suggested.

I sighed because I could see how things were lining up. I was going to have to go to Brooklyn and see why Sammy made my aunt Shayna cry. And then I was going to have to go to Sammy to see if I could talk him into dying for Phoebe. Because that was what we were both going to do when we went up against Tanner Brookmeyer.

'I should be getting back to Florida,' I announced. 'I probably have a case or maybe even a couple of cases down there. Plus my rent is due, and I don't like to be late. Also, there is this girl who works at the donut shop down there—'

'The thing is,' Ms Baker interrupted, 'as a duly sworn officer of the law, it's my obligation to correct the warrant that's out on you. Fill in the right name. Contact the guys over in Brooklyn. Let them know where you live. In Florida. Fry's Bay, right?'

'You *really* looked me up.' I glared.

'I had to in order to make you my case investigator. Which you are, legally. But it's up to you. Fulfill your obligation to me with regard to this case or go back to Florida and wait for some pissed-off detective from Brooklyn to come and get you. Your choice.'

'Right.' I nodded. 'Some choice.'

'Look,' Phoebe said, 'whatever else Sammy Cohen is, he's in love with me, right? And I'm in love with him. So, you *gotta* help us. It's some kind of law, somewhere.'

Threats from a lawyer and laws about love. The world was an impossibly complicated case, all right.

I stood up.

'Where do you think you're going?' Ms Baker began.

'I'm going to Brooklyn to get Sammy so we can collect Tanner Brookmeyer,' I said. 'Not because you threatened me – I thought we were friends, by the way – and *not* because of some star-crossed love between a hoodlum and a theatre type. I'm going because I love my aunt.'

And without further explanation, I left the room, went to the subway, and got on a train. And all the way to Brooklyn I thought about what a spectacular chump I probably was.

NINETEEN

B rooklyn had become an imaginary place to me during my Florida years, the way a childhood memory makes things bigger and brighter than they were in reality. But walking up the street to my mother's place, even the garbage in the streets and the graffiti on the walls felt like home.

Up the stoop, up the stairs, knock twice on the door, and there was Shayna. Her eyes were rimmed in red, and she was wearing a blue chenille bathrobe.

I stood in the doorway. 'It's a little late in the day for the robe, don't you think?'

She put a finger to her lips, then she motioned me in.

Sammy was sitting on the sofa in the front room. He had his Colt in his hand, but his hand was in his lap.

I looked at Shayna. 'Was he here like this when I called you earlier?'

She nodded.

Sammy looked up, a little lost. 'Oh, hi, Foggy. When did you get here?'

'Just now,' I told him. 'What's up, Sam?'

'I,' he began, and then seemed to lose his train of thought.

'Sammy?' I said softly.

'I've made some . . . mistakes.' He sighed and closed his eyes.

'Yeah.' I stepped into the apartment, but only a little. 'In what regard?'

'Cocaine,' he began, a little philosophically, 'is bad.'

'I agree,' I said. 'All it wants is more of itself. You get a little bump, but the second it drops below a hundred percent, you get desperate for a little more.'

'It don't do your judgment any favors either,' he assured me.

'I recall.' I took one more step into the room. 'So. What's going on now?'

He looked up. 'Now?'

'You're in my mother's apartment with a gun in your hand, Sammy,' I said quickly.

He looked around. 'Oh. Yeah.'

'I talked with Phoebe,' I said, 'and with Phoebe's lawyer. The consensus is that you knew Emory pretty well. She introduced you to Phoebe. And Emory was Tanner Brookmeyer's girlfriend.'

Sammy's face contorted like he'd been shot in the guts. 'I hate him.'

'Yeah,' I said, 'there's a long line for that. What's going on, Sam?'

I edged a little closer to him, glaring at Shayna.

She nodded. 'Want some coffee?'

'Love some,' I snapped.

And Shayna beat it to the kitchen.

'Phoebe wasn't supposed to get in the middle of this,' Sammy said, and he sounded miserable. 'I was trying to get at Tanner.'

One more step. 'Maybe you should start at the beginning.'

And so he did.

Sammy Two Shoes Cohen had always felt lost. As a teenager, he'd wanted to be a folk singer, but everyone made fun of that. His only friends were criminals and his family didn't want him. He wasn't bad looking, though, and he was tall. So he managed to get by on the periphery of his world until he ran afoul of Tanner Brookmeyer. Tanner didn't like Sammy. Maybe it was exactly because Sammy was taller and better looking, or maybe it was because of Emory Brewster.

Emory Brewster was a spoiled kid from the upper east side of Manhattan. Best schools, best clothes, best drugs. She met Tanner at a party with some of her spoiled rich friends, and she didn't like him. She liked Sammy. Sammy had come with the caterer, his uncle, as part of the package: he was the entertainment. He played blues guitar and sang in a voice that he thought sounded like Sonny Boy Williamson. Under the name Spider Cohen. Lots of the girls were impressed, but no one more than Emory. She bought a hundred dollars' worth of coke from Tanner that night and shared it all with Sammy. It made his playing wild. By the end of the evening, Emory and Sammy were making out in the shadows.

Until Emory wanted more coke.

She said she'd be right back and went to find Tanner. An hour later the caterer was cleaning up, most of the guests were gone, and Sammy felt stupid.

Emory had gone home with Tanner. Coke beats the blues every time.

But Tanner held a grudge because Sammy had kissed Emory first. So he went out of his way to hire Sammy for all manner of demeaning, humiliating, and dangerous gigs. And Sammy went along because that's what you did, and because he needed the money.

Emory wasn't entirely heartless. Just mostly. She introduced Phoebe to Sammy. Emory had worked with Phoebe on a couple of shows and had the idea that they'd like each other. Emory did a bit of encouraging, a little matchmaking, and it took. Sammy fell for Phoebe and vice versa.

But Sammy had grown to hate Tanner, hate the jobs that Tanner made Sammy do. So when Sammy was bolstered by love for the first time in his life, he suddenly had the confidence to stand up for himself.

Unfortunately, Sammy's idea of getting even was severely on the gangster side of things. And to make matters worse, he went to Shayna, and Shayna organized things the gangster way.

They started by wrecking Tanner's main contacts in the drug world. Sammy went to Atlanta, for example, and killed Tanner's coke supplier, a little weasel who was also a Grand Dragon of the Ku Klux Klan. And just recently Sammy had gone back to Atlanta to kill a guy in charge of Tanner's Atlanta porn kingdom. So Tanner's livelihood was in trouble.

And in between other such questionable acts of revenge, Sammy may have killed Emory Brewster.

'I didn't mean to ice her,' Sammy concluded softly. 'I just wanted to freak her out.'

I didn't move, because he still had his gun in his hand, and I was severely worried about his state of mind. But I had to clarify.

'What *did* you mean to do?' I asked politely.

'The show she was in before the *Hamlet* thing was this old Agatha Christie. *And Then There Were None.* She played the part of Emily Brent, some religious nut who was mean to her maid. In the play she gets it from cyanide poisoning, this Emily character. The thing is, the cast in *that* show hated Emory too, just like the *Hamlet* guys. Twice somebody in the Christie cast put cyanide in Emory's water bottle. Not enough to kill her, just made her nauseous and confused; she forgot her lines a lot. They all thought it was a good joke. Emory thought it was the coke. Anyway, Emory got fired from that gig. I heard about it from Phoebe because Phoebe was the stage manager for the Christie. She thought it was a good joke too, so when Emory got to be such a pistol in the *Hamlet* thing, I figured to try the gag again. Only maybe Phoebe thought it was funny too, so Phoebe dosed Emory's water and maybe things went too far, and it iced Emory, so I used the pencil bit in a moment of panic, as I may have indicated earlier, maybe.'

Sammy had more to say, but at exactly that moment the door to the apartment busted open and there were two guys with guns.

One of them was Tanner Brookmeyer.

TWENTY

Tanner looked around the room.

'This is Brooklyn?' He shook his head. 'It stinks.'

'This is my mother's place,' I said quickly, 'and it actually smells like lavender.'

He turned my way. 'You've got to be Foggy Moscowitz.'

I nodded. 'Whether I want to be or not.'

Without warning Tanner smiled, pointed his gun, and shot Sammy in the thigh.

Half a second later Shayna appeared in the hallway to the kitchen with a Colt Python in her hand. It was just like Sammy's, only it looked bigger in her hand.

She fired, and the guy who'd come in with Tanner howled. He'd been shot in the foot. I moved the second Shayna's gun went off. Ducking low, I plowed into the guy with the shot-up foot. He went down like he was taking a dive in a prize fight: reluctant but resigned. Hit the floor with a smack and conked his head on the oak leg of a table by the door. After that he didn't move.

At the same time Tanner whirled and fired at Shayna, but she was already gone, zipped back into the kitchen. I was low enough to grab Foot Guy's gun, but I lost my balance and fell on my backside just as Tanner turned his attention to me. I pointed the unfamiliar pistol, but before I could fire, somebody else did, and Tanner twitched backward. He leaned against the wall by the door. Blood began to bloom on his shoulder like he suddenly had a carnation in his lapel. I looked over at Sammy. He'd fired the shot at Tanner, and he was grinning. He thought his troubles were over.

But Tanner had other ideas. He lowered his pistol, pushed off from the wall, came to a solid stand, and sighed.

'OK, OK,' he said. 'We got that out of the way. Everybody got shot. Now. Let's talk.'

'I'm messing up Mrs Moscowitz's sofa,' Sammy said, watching the blood from his thing ooze on to the pale gold fabric.

Tanner looked around. 'Yeah, the whole place is gonna need a good clean. Is Benny OK?'

I took a guess that the guy with the bullet in his foot was Benny, and another guess that the question was addressed to me.

'He's out,' I said, getting to my feet. 'But he's OK. Except, you know, for his foot.'

'Right, right,' Tanner said.

He was eyeing the gun in my hand. I looked down at it, then I set it slowly on the floor. 'Let's not have any more gunplay for the nonce, right? Let's talk. Like you said.'

Tanner nodded and put his gun away. 'Sammy?'

Sammy set his gun down on the coffee table, on top of the fanned-out *Look* magazines.

Shayna's voice, strong, came from the kitchen. 'I'm not putting my gun away, Tanner. This is my house. You shouldn't be here.'

'Well,' Tanner said lazily, 'it's really your sister's *apartment*, but you go ahead. Hold your little gun in your hand if you want.'

'Listen,' I began, 'this is really something between you two boys. My mother's sick and my aunt's very emotional at the moment. Couldn't you both take this somewhere else?'

'Oh no,' Tanner complained. 'You're in this as much as anybody. You're working with that lawyer, you went to Atlanta and helped Sammy kill my guy, and your aunt Shayna has been messing with my enterprises here in this neighborhood for, like, five hundred years. I am *exactly* where I want to be.'

'Well, in the first place,' I began, 'I did not help Sammy kill anybody. And in the second place, I swear to God I had no idea that you and my aunt were at war.'

'Shayna hates me for personal reasons I don't care to discuss at the moment,' Tanner told me.

'So why wouldn't I just come in there and shoot you dead right now?' Shayna called from the kitchen, her voice high and strained.

'You might want to,' Tanner answered, 'but you won't. Because you're not the type. That was your brother-in-law, Foggy's pop. Now *there* was a guy who knew how to do it. Did you know he killed a guy with a toothpick once? Swear to God.'

'What is it you want, Tanner?' I asked, mostly to stop him talking about my father.

'Well, obviously, I want Sammy. He's causing me a lot of trouble business-wise, plus I hear he killed my girlfriend.'

'He didn't,' I began, mostly to keep Tanner from shooting Sammy.

'Doesn't really matter,' Tanner said dismissively. 'Girls come and go. Emory was itchy and I was tired of her anyway. Actors. What are you gonna do? But he did it to get my goat, and I don't stand for that.'

'OK,' I allowed, 'but given what you just said, your goat wasn't really gotten, was it?'

Tanner paused. Maybe he was thinking, but it didn't look like it.

'I don't like you,' Sammy said to Tanner. 'And you don't like me. You made me do some rotten stuff. I messed you up a little. I'd call it even.'

'Even?' Tanner laughed. 'You took out my coke supplier, and then you shot my southern porn guy!'

Sammy shrugged. 'You still got numbers, protection, and hookers.'

'Yeah, but all the real *fun* is in coke and porn,' Tanner complained.

Sammy smiled. 'Not for you anymore.'

With that Sammy lunged for his pistol. Tanner pulled out his gun again and shot Sammy in the shoulder. Sammy shot back, and Tanner bent over.

I dropped to the floor, scooped up the gun, and rolled.

Tanner was trying to steady himself on the wall. I shot twice; hit his gun arm once. His gunshot went wild, into the mantlepiece.

Shayna appeared in the hallway again and fired until her gun was empty, shrieking while she did it. The sound of her voice was terrifying.

Tanner had at least three bullets in him at that point. He was probably beginning to think better of being in a room with Sammy, me, and a crazy woman.

He felt for the door handle, fussed with it, fired in Shayna's direction, and managed to open the door. Sammy had slumped to the floor in between the sofa and the coffee table and was taking aim right for Tanner's head.

Tanner laughed. 'Round one!'

And he was out the door.

I was up and at the door in a flat second.

'Let him go!' Shayna shouted. 'Let him go, Foggy!'

It was a moot point. By the time I got to the doorway, Tanner was halfway down the hall and almost to the staircase.

I was a little puzzled that, with all the gunshots, there was no one in the hallway looking, no other residents peering out their doors.

'Close the door, Foggy!' Shayna commanded, coming into the living room, 'and give me a hand with Sammy.'

Sammy was lying on the floor and his breathing was weird.

'I'm sorry, Shayna,' he was mumbling. 'I messed up your sofa.'

'Not your fault,' she told him, lowering her gun. 'It's that Tanner. He didn't turn out so well.'

'He did not,' Sammy agreed.

I got over to Sammy and helped him back on to the sofa. Shayna disappeared into the kitchen.

Sammy shook his head. 'I'm sorry, Foggy. I'm sorry for all of it.'

He was on the verge of crying.

'Are you sorry enough to tell me the whole story?' I asked him.

He looked up at me. 'The whole story?'

'The story of why you didn't tell me about Tanner, why my aunt hates him, and why I'm involved in all this so much that you have to apologize to me.'

'Oh.' He nodded. 'That story.'

He slumped back and sighed. Shayna went to get stuff to fix Sammy up, and then he told me that story.

Sammy Two Shoes fell in love. It had never happened to him before. He would have done anything for Phoebe. He told her a little about his nefarious life. She didn't care. He said he'd quit the life and get a legit job. She didn't care about that either. Maybe she got a thrill out of dating a criminal, but also maybe she loved Sammy back just a little.

They kept their relationship a secret. He didn't want her exposed to the relative brutality of his life. She didn't want him to know just how vicious the theatre world really was. So they lived in a third world, something they made out of afternoon movies and late suppers and nights in Chelsea in a room that Sammy kept as a hideout.

They lived in that blissful other world until Phoebe made the mistake of agreeing to stage manage the all-female *Hamlet*. She did it because the director was famous and just about to direct some big show Off Broadway. Phoebe had to work on *Hamlet* if she wanted to work on *Oh! Calcutta!* Yes, two exclamation points. And a lot of naked people.

It was all going well enough until Emory started losing it. An excess of coke, too many late hours, and *way* too much Tanner Brookmeyer. The director would have fired her in the first week, except that Tanner paid a visit to the theatre. Nobody knew what was said, but Emory stayed in the show. The show opened. Emory got worse. Phoebe was about to replace her when Sammy heard through a lightning-fast grapevine that his old pal Foggy Moscowitz was in town.

Sammy grabbed Phoebe by the arm and got a cab to Reno Sweeney's. And sure enough, there, at the bar, was the afore-mentioned pal.

'You know the rest,' Sammy said.

'I know the rest?' I railed. 'I don't know anything. Why did you come get me at Reno Sweeney's? What did you think I was going to do?'

Sammy looked surprised by my ire. 'Well, you save little kids, Foggy. And what is an actor but a little kid in an unwieldy adult body? I figured you do your voodoo and set her straight, and everything would be fine. Now everything's a mess.'

I folded my arms. 'Right. This is all my fault.'

He looked down. 'I should have just let you alone. I know that. I just . . . your rep is really righteous, and when I heard

you were in town, it seemed like some kind of sign, you know?
Like God wanted me to see you.'

'Don't bring God into this mess,' I snapped.

Shayna came back from the kitchen with a tray. But it wasn't
tea and sandwiches. It was alcohol, gauze, tweezers, and a sewing
kit. Shayna was going to take the bullets out of Sammy. And
none too soon. His breathing was weird, and his eyes were beginning to glaze.

'I'm not talking to you,' I told Shayna. 'You're the one who
made this mess.'

Shayna shot me a look. 'Don't you worry about that. I'll take
care of that. You go talk to your mother. I'm sure she's worried
about the gunshots.'

I nodded once, and then I went to see my mother.

TWENTY-ONE

The sudden appearance and equally sudden disappearance
of Tanner Brookmeyer seemed surreal to me. I was trying
to think what to say about it to my mother as I went into
her darkened room.

She was sitting up, squinting.

'How's the migraine?' I asked.

'Well,' she told me, 'all the shooting didn't help.'

'I guess not.'

'We haven't had guns going off in this apartment in almost
seven years,' she lamented. 'I thought all that was behind us. But
then your aunt started associating with that Sammy Cohen. She
won't tell me what that's all about. She thinks I'm too sick to
handle it. But I guess Sammy would be the one that started the
shooting.'

'It was Tanner Brookmeyer, actually,' I told her.

'Him? He's still around?' She shook her head. 'I figured
somebody would have taken him out by now.'

I looked at my mother's face then. Her hair, long-since white,
was frizzed around her head so that it looked like a kind of light

was around her face. Her skin was smooth, and her eyes were bright. You could still see the beautiful teenaged girl in the middle-aged widow. I'd forgotten how pretty she was. Or how calmly she could accept gunplay in the living room.

'How're you doing, Ma?' It was all I could think of to say.

She closed her eyes. 'You figure it out.'

'It's not just a migraine,' I surmised. 'I never even heard of your staying in bed so much.'

'I got a bigger problem,' she said.

I nodded. 'OK. How bad?'

'Bad enough that I have a last request,' she said softly.

'A last request? Seriously?' I shook my head. 'That's not really your style either.'

'My style?' She sat up a little. 'How would you know anything about *my style?*'

'What's the last request, then?' I asked.

'Figure out how we can get rid of Tanner Brookmeyer,' she said, her voice stronger. 'If you do that, then Sammy gets back to his old self. Once that happens, you can figure out how to get his girlfriend out of jail. Then he lives happily ever after. And *then* I'll have an easier time talking you into moving back to Brooklyn. There. That's my agenda. In a nutshell.'

I had to smile. 'You've given this as much thought as Sammy gave to getting me involved in his personal problems in the first place.'

'That sounds a little like an insult,' she said, but she didn't sound insulted. She was laughing.

'Well, as it happens, I was planning on getting Sammy's girlfriend out of jail anyway,' I told her. 'After that, all bets are off. Sammy's not the happily-ever-after type, and in Florida I've got an apartment with an ocean view and a donut shop waitress who likes me.'

'A girl?' She sat up even more. 'What's her name?'

'Bibi,' I told her, 'but let's not get distracted. Why are you so interested in getting rid of Tanner Brookmeyer?'

She looked away. 'I don't like what he's doing to Sammy.'

It only took me a second before I got it. She liked Sammy. She had more motherly feelings toward him than she did for me. I could see that very clearly at that moment. Lots of reasons for it, probably. He was around; I wasn't. He was still in the life; I'd gone straight. He needed her; I didn't. The only thing odder than that realization was the way I *felt* about it. I didn't care. My feelings weren't hurt or some Freudian crap like that. I genuinely understood their bond, and I thought it was righteous.

Then I had the strangest sensation that the only real reason I'd come to the city at all was to save Sammy Cohen. Blossom and Dorough, that was just a bonus. God or the Universe or some psychic motivation from my mother had delivered me to Manhattan.

'OK,' I told my mother. 'I'll figure this out. Sammy's going to be fine.'

She looked at me then. 'Promise?'

'I promise,' I said. 'But what's the real reason for all this?'

'What do you mean?'

'You know what I mean.' I folded my arms. 'All of a sudden Sammy Cohen is somebody I'm supposed to watch over?'

'Two things,' she said. 'Two things I probably should have told you a long time ago, but first one thing then another, and then you're gone. To *Florida*, for God's sake. So here it is with both barrels. See, your father had a roving eye. I didn't care because he was a good provider and a kind person. I didn't love him, so that helped. And he was always honest about it. The point is: Sammy's his kid. Your father's son. He's your half-brother. There, I said it. Now you know.'

She looked down at her hands.

I stood there like I was made out of stone. Two sensations at once. On the one hand, I was knocked over and down the block and into the water under the Brooklyn Bridge. But on the other hand, it made a very sudden kind of sense. Me and Sammy. Brothers.

'Does he know?' I asked after about five hours.

'Yup.' She wouldn't look up at me.

'Sammy knows?'

'Always has.' She still wouldn't look up. 'Always thought of you as a big brother.'

'And why, *exactly*, has this always been a secret?' I could hear the ire in my voice.

'*Exactly?*' She sighed. 'I was embarrassed? I couldn't find the right moment to tell you? I thought it would change your opinion of your father? Or of me? I mean, take your pick, kiddo. Plus, you and me? We never really did have that kind of sit-down-and-talk relationship.'

'We didn't *what*?' My ire was all the way to the surface now.

'Are you going to help him or not?' she demanded, finally snapping into eye contact.

'You said *two things*,' I snapped. 'So Sammy's supposed to be my brother. What's the other thing?'

'Oh. Well, the other thing.' She closed her eyes. 'You're right, this isn't a migraine I'm having right now. I got Lymphoma. Blood cancer. So. *That's* the other thing.'

I had around five hundred things I should have said to her. I didn't say any of them.

Instead, the phone in the living room rang.

Shayna answered it, and she called out, 'Foggy, it's for you. Says she's a lawyer.'

My mother had closed her eyes and slumped down in the bed. I went into the other room and picked up the phone.

'Moscowitz!' Ms Baker said before I even had the phone to my ear. 'Where is Sammy Cohen?'

'How did you get this number?' I asked, a little dazed.

'You said you were going to Brooklyn to get Sammy and, subsequently, Tanner Brookmeyer,' she snapped.

'Well,' I began slowly.

'Just thought you'd want to know that the police have issued an APB for Sammy,' she interrupted. 'He's wanted for the murder of Emory Brewster.'

'Um,' I ventured.

'As a co-conspirator with Phoebe Peabody. Both their prints were on the water bottle with the fatal poison. They both did it.'

'Both . . . both of them?' I stammered.

'Right. So if you can lay your hand to Sammy, don't let go. You have to bring him in.'

I looked over at Sammy. He was barely conscious, and Shayna was stitching him up.

'I don't have my hands on him at this exact moment,' I said unsteadily.

'You find him, or the police will,' she said, cold. 'And they're probably coming to your mother's place.'

'What? Why?'

'You have to know that your mother's apartment is one of Sammy's known addresses,' she said.

'Yeah.' I nodded. 'I guess it probably is at that. OK. Give me an hour. I'll get hold of him and bring him over to Manhattan.'

I hung up without saying anything else. I didn't even have to think twice.

'Sammy,' I said softly. 'Come on. We have to go.'

TWENTY-TWO

S hayna stood up. 'He's not going anywhere. I just took two bullets out of him.'

'We have to go,' I said to Sammy, ignoring my aunt.

It was clear that Sammy was in a bad way, but he managed to get to his feet anyway. He pulled his shirt together and buttoned it as best he could, mess that it was. He picked up his suit coat, struggled, and got it on. He looked down at the rip in his pants leg and shrugged. Then he patted Shayna's shoulder.

'Like it's the first time I ever had a bullet dug out of me,' he told her, smiling.

'You're not leaving,' Shayna said firmly. 'Either of you.'

'That phone call I just got,' I explained, 'was from Phoebe's lawyer. The cops are coming after Sammy and they know this is one of his addresses. If he stays here, they'll get him.'

Simple enough.

'OK,' Shayna said, 'but he could stay across the hall at Mrs Feldman's. She owes me, like, a dozen favors.'

'Right,' I answered. 'The cops would never think to look across the hall.'

Shayna looked down. 'OK, let me think.'

'Remember how you didn't want me to know exactly where Sammy was when he went to Atlanta?' I asked her. 'So when I told the cops I didn't know where he was, it would be the truth? How about if you let me return the favor?'

'Foggy's right,' Sammy intervened. 'It's better if you don't know. Come on, Foggy.'

And he headed for the door.

You had to give it to the guy. Two bullets, a truckload of trouble, his girl in jail, and his second-best suit all shot up, he was pretty much the same old Sammy. Only a little slower getting to the door.

'He's gonna bleed,' Shayna warned.

'Maybe a towel or something?' Sammy suggested.

Shayna sighed and went into the hallway bathroom. She came back right away with a thin towel that had horses on it, like for a kid. I'd never seen it before. She handed it to Sammy, and he put it under his suit coat on his shoulder wound.

'What are you going to do about Benny?' I asked her.

'Who?'

I inclined my head in the direction of the lump of clothes on the floor, the one with the bleeding foot.

'Oh, him.' She stared at the guy. 'I guess I'll patch him up too, before I send him on his way.'

She was made entirely out of iron.

I sighed. 'I had a little talk with my mother.'

She stared back. 'Really.'

'Maybe you should look in on her,' I suggested.

Our weird psychic connection, strained as it was, seemed to be mostly intact. She understood at least a little of what transpired between me and my mother. Or anyway I thought I could see that on her face.

Sammy had his hand on the front doorknob. 'Let's take it a little slow down the stairs, OK?'

And he was out the door.

Shayna shook her head. 'You know what this means, kiddo. You gotta shift into high gear. This is getting messy.'

'Have you ever driven a car?' I asked her, cold.

'No, but . . .' she began.

'Then what would you know about shifting gears?'

With that, I closed the door and followed Sammy down the hallway.

'Where are we going?' he asked without turning around.

'The cops have it that you and Phoebe conspired to kill Emory,' I began. 'So they're after you.'

'Right,' he said, making it to the top of the stairs. 'I got a little place in Chelsea that I keep for just such emergencies.'

'This is the place where you and Phoebe used to hole up?' I asked. 'You don't worry that maybe the cops know about that at this point?'

He paused. 'What did you have in mind?'

'I'm of two minds,' I said, catching up with him at the top of the stairs. 'One: you come back with me to the Benjamin and rest up there while I go to Helen Baker's office and lie to her. Two: you come with me to Helen Baker's office and we figure how you can turn yourself in and get a little hospital attention. Do you have a preference?'

'Well, to tell the truth,' he said, his voice lowered, 'your Aunt Shayna is really good at first aid, but I'm in kind of a bad way, here. But I can't say I like either one of those options, Foggy, truth be told.'

He could barely move, his pants leg was soaked in blood, and his face was pale. I realized that he'd have a hard time making it down the stairs, let alone making it all the way to the Benjamin.

So when we got to the street, Sammy sat on the stoop and I managed to get a cab.

I helped Sammy in and told the driver, 'Greenpoint YMCA, thanks.'

Sammy looked at me. 'That's unexpected.'

'Yeah. I picked option three.'

And we didn't talk again until we were getting out of the cab at the Y.

'Do they let guys like us stay at the YMCA?' he mumbled.

'I guess we'll see,' I told him.

Turns out that if you had the bread, anybody could stay. As long as you were a man. The *young* and the *Christian* part never entered into the conversation I had with the guy at the check-in office. I got us a room with twin beds. The check-in guy told me to have a blessed night. I said I'd try.

Up one flight of stairs, I got Sammy settled in. Small room. No windows. Very plain. Sammy collapsed on to one of the beds in his suit and his shoes. I managed to get his shoes off and a cover over him, but he was out.

There was a desk and chair in the room too, and the desk had a notepad, a pencil, and a Bible in the drawer.

I left Sammy a note. I told him to stay put, that I'd be back to change his bandages and bring him some food, and I was off.

Around an hour later, I showed up at Helen Baker's office. It was a jumbled and lively place. Maybe twelve people talking at once and phones ringing and someone at one of the desks had her face in her hands, crying.

I spotted Helen before she saw me and motored on over to her desk.

She looked up from a huge file in front of her.

'Where's Sammy?' she asked.

'He got shot,' I told her. 'Tanner Brookmeyer paid us a visit at my mother's place.'

What the hell, I thought. If the cops really were going to my mother's apartment, they'd see the evidence, and Shayna would probably tell them that Tanner had been there.

'Is he dead?' she asked coldly.

'No.'

'Then why isn't he here?'

'He's resting,' I said. 'I just wanted you to know that I've got him holed up safe and I want to talk with Phoebe again. I have an inkling of a theory.'

She sighed and shook her head. 'No, you don't.'

'Well, you say I'm your investigator,' I said, 'and my investigation has brought me to several weird conclusions that I would like to verify, so I have to talk to Phoebe.'

I stared.

She stared back.

Then she closed the file in front of her and stood up very suddenly.

'Going to the jail again,' she announced.

No one seemed to pay any attention, and we were off.

On the way to the lockup, she tried to get me to tell her about my theory, but I began to regale her with the story of Tanner Brookmeyer busting into an apartment in Brooklyn, shooting things up, getting shot, with a large dose of the feisty aunt character. That kept her occupied until Phoebe showed up in the little room where they let you talk to criminals.

Phoebe sat down. 'What's happening with Sammy?'

I smiled. She really did like him.

'He got shot, but he's OK,' I said.

'Shot?' She nearly stood up.

'Tanner,' I told her.

She nodded like it made sense.

'But I need to ask you something, and you have to be honest or it won't work, right?' I locked eyes with her.

'OK,' she said, not blinking.

'Sammy told me about the gag where somebody put cyanide in Emory's fancy water,' I said, 'when she was in the Agatha Christie show that you stage managed. Small doses, just to mess her up, not to kill her.'

Phoebe looked at Helen Baker. Helen Baker was looking at me.

'So Sammy did the same thing to Emory in the *Hamlet* show,' I went on. 'After you told him about it. He thought it was a pretty neat way of making her so wacky that she'd get fired.'

Phoebe's face lost all color. She sat back and she was having a little trouble breathing. Which told me what I wanted to know, but I needed her to say it out loud.

'The problem is,' I prompted, 'that you had the same idea.'

Phoebe closed her eyes. 'She was just such a problem. And after she shot up Nan's apartment, I thought I had to do something about it. So.'

'So you *did* put cyanide in Emory's water,' Helen whispered.

'Not enough to kill her,' Phoebe said. 'Just.'

'The problem was, as it turned out, that Sammy did it too. Same amount, not enough to kill her. Only . . .'

'Oh my God,' Helen said, shaking her head, 'you *did* both kill her.'

'But it's *accidental homicide*,' I said, 'which, correct me if I'm wrong, might not merit jail time.'

'If we can prove that there was no intent to kill,' Helen said, thinking as she talked, 'and Sammy and Phoebe both confess to what they did, *and* we can prove that neither had knowledge of what the other was doing . . .'

'And maybe get actors from the Agatha Christie to testify

that the same gag had been pulled on Emory in *that* show,' I suggested.

'It won't be easy,' Helen said, sitting back. 'But maybe. Just maybe.'

Phoebe sat forward very earnestly. 'We really, really, really didn't mean to kill her.'

I turned to Helen. 'Maybe things have changed since the last time I was in front of a judge, but the *really-really-really* defense doesn't work that well, right?

Helen glared. 'What else have you got?'

'So about the tox screen,' I went on, smiling back at Helen. 'You asked them to check for cyanide specifically, or did they do a general?'

Helen shook her head. 'Just cyanide.'

Helen was clearly irritated. Didn't seem situational. I figured she was always a little irritated.

'Then you should ask them to look for strychnine,' I told her.

'Strychnine?' There was that glare again.

'It's the main chemical in certain kinds of rat poison,' I told her, 'but a lot of people use it to cut cocaine. People like Emory's boyfriend Tanner Brookmeyer, for instance. The same Tanner Brookmeyer who just told me, like an hour ago, that he was tired of Emory. That she was itchy.'

'What does *that* mean?' Helen complained.

'It means that Tanner Brookmeyer killed Emory,' I said. 'I think it also means that Tanner knew about Sammy's dosing Emory.'

'How in the hell would he know that?' Helen roared.

'What you don't understand about Tanner is that he's got eyes and ears all over Manhattan. And actors gossip more than any other single profession on the planet. Tanner got wind of the cyanide gag somehow and thought to use it to get rid of Emory.'

'Wait, that would mean . . .' Phoebe began.

'That Tanner orchestrated things in a kind of brilliant way,' I concluded, 'so that Sammy would take the fall, because he figured that only Sammy would have enough criminal in him to pull the gag. I think that Phoebe was just caught in the middle of gangster games.'

'Which means that this poor kid, Emory, was poisoned *three* times,' Helen interjected.

'She was *not* well-liked,' I said.

'This is just the kind of thing that Sammy was worried about,' Phoebe said earnestly. 'He didn't want me to get mixed up in his world. This is why.'

'This is *bullshit*, Phoebe,' Helen snapped. 'This is a story that Moscowitz is making up in order to get you off the hook.'

'No, I think that's what really happened,' I assured her. 'I think Tanner's smarter than I ever gave him credit for.'

'Now *Tanner* killed Emory?' Helen stood up.

I stood up too so I could look her in the eye.

'Check and see about the strychnine,' I said.

She could see I meant it, so she nodded.

'What are you going to do?' she asked me.

'I guess I'm going to have to shift into high gear,' I sighed, 'like my aunt told me to do.'

TWENTY-THREE

The first thing I did was go to Pete's, my favorite pawn shop. It was close to Times Square. I guess Times Square used to be a great place: sophisticated swells in top hats and swishing socialites in emerald gowns. But 1976 was *not* being kind to the area, what with all the X-rated movie houses and the guaranteed muggings. It was a Disco Sewer, and then some.

But Pete's was a reliable place to pick up a cheap gun and I felt I needed more than the .44 I'd brought with me from Florida if I was *really* going after Tanner Brookmeyer. Which, if I'd stopped to think about it, I would have run back to Florida *so* fast that my feet would have burned asphalt.

Pete's was non-descript on purpose. Nothing to draw anyone's attention to the fact that the place fenced about a quarter of all the stolen items in that part of Manhattan. It had been years since I'd been in the place, but there it was, squeezed in between a shoe shop and an X-rated bookstore. A red neon OPEN sign buzzed loud enough to be heard on the noisy street. There was a flugelhorn in the window and beside it was a sign that said: *Formerly owned by Chuck Mangione!* Right.

There was a bell on the front door, and it announced my presence like an alarm. The place was packed and stacked floor to ceiling in narrow little aisles. I made my way to the back, past the electric guitars and rolltop desks and television sets and large power tools and cement statues.

At the back there was a cage and, inside the cage, where Pete should have been, sat a teenaged girl with a shag haircut and purple eyeshadow. She was wearing a white button-down man's shirt with a loud 1940s tie.

She looked up from the book she was reading. 'Help you?'

'Where's Pete?' I asked her.

She gave me the once-over from my leather-weave shoes to the shoulders of my sharkskin suit.

'You ain't been here in a while, I guess.' She sighed. 'Pete's dead. The diabetes. It's what you get from sitting in this chair for forty years eating pizza.'

I nodded. 'Last time I saw him he had to weigh in at three hundred.'

'Oh,' she said, 'you mean the *lean* years. He was near five hundred in his casket.'

'You inherited the place?' I asked.

She shook her head. 'Pete was my uncle twice removed. I just work here to get through Sarah Lawrence.'

'That's a college, right?' I smiled.

'That's what they tell me,' she said, putting down her book. 'You in the market for a flugelhorn?'

'Deadly small gun,' I said softly.

Without missing a beat she said, 'You want a SIG Sauer P220. Semi-automatic, just came out, designed in, like, Switzerland or something. You gotta see this thing. It's beautiful.'

She hopped off her chair, rummaged for seconds, and came back with a pretty little gun about one and a half inches wide and five and a half inches tall. She held it up in front of my face.

'And you have ammo for it,' I assumed.

'All you want,' she confirmed.

'I have to be sure it works,' I began.

Before I could finish my sentence, she began breaking the gun down, and had it apart in under sixty seconds. It was like watching ballet.

'Sarah Lawrence must be some school,' I said.

She laughed. 'Guns I know from Pete. Christmas at his place was a trip. This gun is in great shape.'

'How much?'

'I'd like to see Mr Franklin.'

'A hundred dollars?' I snapped. 'Is it made out of gold?'

'No,' she said. 'It's made out of the regular gun stuff, but it's also untraceable and comes without any questions attached. Questions like "Do you have a license?" and "What's your name?" You know, nuisance stuff.'

'Ah.' I smiled. 'That's good old Pete talking.'

'I loved that fat bastard.' She sighed.

'Throw in a bit of ammo?' I asked.

'You're not very good at this,' she said amiably. 'You're supposed to haggle more. You could have had it for seventy-five at least.'

I nodded. 'I'm in kind of a hurry. Why don't you say you sold it for seventy-five and use the extra for Sarah Lawrence? What's your major?'

'Pot.' She shrugged. 'Minor in coke. But I have time to read here in the store.'

She held up the book she was reading. It was *The Magic Mountain* by Thomas Mann.

I smiled. 'Tolerance becomes a crime when applied to evil.'

'What?' She stared.

'That's a quote from your book,' I told her. 'My aunt Shayna used to say it all the time when she had been drinking and thinking about the Holocaust.'

'Oh.' She thought about it. 'Right. Tolerating evil *is* a crime.'

'Yes.'

'Is that what this gun is for?' she asked.

'Yes,' I said quickly. 'I'm battling evil.'

I hauled a bunch of twenties out of my wallet and slid them to her through the opening in the fence. She put the gun back together in no time and gave it to me, then went into some drawer for the bullets.

As she was sliding the shells my way, she stopped. 'Got something else for you.'

And she fell silent.

'What is it?' I asked her.

'In battle,' she said, 'there are not more than two methods of attack: the direct and the indirect; yet these two in combination give rise to an endless series of maneuvers.'

I blinked. I stared. I said, 'OK. Where did that come from?'

'Sun Tzu's *Art of War*,' she answered. 'I'm reading it for one of my classes. Thought it might help.'

'It might,' I admitted.

She passed me my bullets then.

'Hope it does.' She smiled sweetly, like a kid. 'Good luck battling evil.'

'Thanks,' I told her, shoving the gun and the bullets into my outside suitcoat pockets. 'Good luck battling college.'

And I was out the door.

So, .44 in my shoulder holster, SIG in my pocket, I headed for my next stop, a little diner down 42nd Street.

It used to be called Mickey's Diner when I lived in New York, but the sign only said *EAT* in its contemporary iteration. It was almost empty. I had no idea what time it was, and I was even a little hazy on the day. But it was very reassuring to look through the serving portal into the kitchen and see the reason I'd come into the place. I hadn't seen him in more than ten years, but I knew it was him.

'Lonnie!' I called out.

The old man looked up from the grill. He was wearing a crinkled paper hat and he had an unfiltered Camel in his mouth. The face was made out of creases, and his eyebrows were so white they were almost invisible.

He squinted in my direction for a minute.

'Is that little Foggy Moscowitz all grown up?' he croaked. 'I heard you were dead.'

'I went to Florida.'

He shrugged. 'Same thing. What's new?'

'Out back?' I suggested.

He nodded and headed for a back door in the kitchen. I went back outside and around the edge of the building to an alley. I couldn't help but think about Sammy's alleyway in Atlanta with the Klan Dragon and the rats. Except Lonnie was a good guy and, as far as I could tell, there weren't any rats around.

Lonnie was waiting for me.

'What's it been?' he asked. 'Ten years since I saw you?'

'Maybe more.' I got close to him. 'I need a specialty.'

He didn't say anything.

'I'm going after Tanner Brookmeyer,' I went on, 'and I'm going to need a big distraction just off Columbus Avenue.'

He dropped his cigarette and turned to go back inside.

'I know where Tanner lives,' he mumbled. 'But I'm not gonna help you kill yourself.'

'Tanner shot up my mother's apartment,' I said calmly, 'and threw a few bullets at Shayna.'

That stopped him. Lonnie and Shayna went way back. Like, to the Fifties, when New York was really New York.

He didn't turn around to face me. 'Is that why you want to get him?'

'No.' I took another step his way. 'Tanner killed his girlfriend and wants Sammy Two Shoes to go down for it.'

Lonnie turned around. 'I like Sammy.'

'Me too. He's the reason for my involvement in a big mess that has to do with a dead actor and a person named Phoebe Peabody.'

'So, you're doing this for Sammy.'

'That's how it started,' I admitted, 'but it seems to have gotten a little personal. Plus, you know, Tanner Brookmeyer is a menace to all decent citizens.'

'Agreed. All right. Let's assume that I could pull off a specialty like you want. How soon would you want it; what's the timing?'

'I'm pretty stirred up right now,' I told him. 'Could you pull it off tonight?'

He shook his head. 'What I got in mind takes twenty guys or more. I couldn't possibly pull it off until around ten tomorrow morning.'

'Twenty guys.' I took a breath. 'I'm not sure I've got the cabbage for twenty guys.'

'For Sammy and Shayna,' he told me, 'and against Tanner Brookmeyer? It's gratis. And I mean I'm going to have to *narrow it down* to twenty. Not to mention that it's for you, the semi-famous Foggy Moscowitz, salvation of troubled children in the far-off land of Florida. Any idea how many people would do this just to say they did something with you? Hundreds.'

'I find that hard to believe.'

'The thing about a rep like yours is that you've got nothing to do with it at this point. A rep like yours has got a life of its own. I think now it has less to do with you, the actual person, and more to do with you, the *mythology*. See?'

'No,' I told him, 'I don't see. But if it helps me to do what I have to do, then OK by me and thanks very much.'

'Where're you staying? At your mother's?'

I shook my head. 'The Benjamin on East 50th.'

'Oh.' He waggled his head. 'Fancy.'

'Can you do it or not, Lonnie?'

'How do you feel about ten tomorrow morning, like I said?'

I smiled. 'It's an unusual time for a thing like this. What have you got in mind?'

'Leave that to me. You just be there and ready before ten, OK?'

'What am I going to do to thank you, Lonnie?' I asked him.

'*Thank* me?' He laughed, but it sounded more like coughing. 'Chances are you won't make it out the other side of this to thank anybody. Your legend will be huge . . .'

I got his drift. 'But I'll be gone, you're saying.'

'Gone but not forgotten,' he said, and he went back inside.

Right. I had the guns. I had a scheme. All that was left was one piece of equipment. For that, I headed to Ralph's on West 76th, about a block off Columbus. There wasn't a sign or anything, but Ralph's was one of the hidden delights of the city, in my opinion. It was a kind of secret recording studio. A bunch of the folk singers in the early 1960s used to record their more subversive material there. I'd heard an amazing stolen copy of a tape during Sammy's folksinger phase. It was a Dave Van Ronk duet with Phil Ochs in which they allegedly outed FBI spies in the Harlem Black Panther Party, weaving the names of the informants into the lyrics of the song. How they got the names was a mystery, but Ralph's studio was raided, the place ransacked, Ochs and Van Ronk 'unofficially detained' and all the copies of the song were destroyed. Except for the copies that were already circulating in the folk underground at the time. Hot stuff for somebody like Sammy, a young man looking for a reason to be righteously indignant, and then to sing about it. Sammy recorded a few tunes at Ralph's while I sat on a busted sofa in the next room listening. Golden days.

The point being that Ralph was disposed to helping me. At least I hoped he was. I needed a special something for my encounter with Tanner, and I knew that Ralph had one.

The building looked the same as it always had, a three-story brick with a thick iron entrance door. The street was like a hundred other blocks in Manhattan, a little garbage, a few parked cars, a ninety-year-old woman in a mink stole and short shorts walking her Pekinese.

I looked at the buzzers. They were different from the last time I'd visited. There were three. One was unmarked, one was for the Shapiro family, and the last one only had a picture of a mandolin. I figured Ralph for a mandolin player.

The second I buzzed an angry voice roared out of the speaker. 'What?'

'It's Foggy Moscowitz, Ralph.'

There was a moment of silence.

'Spider Cohen's friend?' Ralph wanted to know.

'The same,' I said.

The door clicked, and I was in. Down an unlit hallway, all the way to the back, to the door marked BEWARE OF FROG! It opened just as I got to it, and there was Ralph.

He looked about the same as he always had. He was wearing baggy Bermuda shorts and a T-shirt with a picture of Che Guevara on it. His goatee had more white hair than blond in it, and his hairline was a little further back on his head than it used to be. But his eyes hadn't changed. They still looked like he knew a secret that was about to make him laugh.

'Foggy.' He grabbed my arms, pulled me in, and hugged me.

I had no idea what to do. I stood there while he squeezed me, then let me go. He took a few steps back and nodded.

'You look just like yourself,' he proclaimed, and then he turned around and was off into the recesses of his sanctum.

What could I do but follow?

The studio was more cluttered than I remembered, and it didn't look exactly in the peak of use. He must have noticed my observation.

'Phil Ochs killed himself this past April,' he said softly. 'Did you hear? Hung himself in his sister Sunny's home.'

I told him I hadn't heard. Truth be told, I didn't know much about Phil Ochs, except that I liked a couple of his songs back in the old days. The days that Dave Van Ronk used to refer to as 'the great folk scare of the early sixties.' But for some reason, maybe the melancholy in Ralph's voice, I was struck through with some kind of sadness that took hold.

'Sorry,' I told Ralph.

'I haven't recorded anything in here since.' He looked around. 'I don't know if I ever will.'

'Ever?' I didn't know what else to say.

'I had a band booked for this summer. Kids from Georgia, call themselves the *B-52s* if you can believe it. Supposed to be playing at CBGB sometime. But.'

Without further explication, he plonked down in an over-stuffed chair beside one of three drum kits in the room.

'Look,' I began.

'You're not here to record something,' he interrupted. 'And Spider Cohen hasn't played a gig in forever. So. What is it? Because I hear that Cohen is something of a criminal at this point. And not the good kind. And from the look on your face, I'm guessing that you've got something serious in mind. But if it has anything to do with the kind of crap Cohen's into now, I'm *completely* not interested.'

'I want to help Sammy,' I said quickly. 'He's in trouble, and I'm his friend. I'm going to take down a guy named Tanner Brookmeyer.'

Ralph's eyes widened and he sat back in his chair.

'I see that you know the guy,' I said.

He shook his head. 'I don't. But I know who he is. I know guys who know guys who get their coke from him.'

'Right. And Tanner used some of that coke to kill his girlfriend, an actor by the name of Emory Brewster. Only the cops think Sammy did it, so I have to get him out from under, right? That's the story. Most of it.'

He looked away. 'I don't want to hear the rest. And I don't know what I could do . . .'

'I need a tape recorder,' I said. 'Like, a spy tape recorder, something that I could put in my suit coat pocket. And the last time I was here . . .'

He jumped up. 'I showed you the Mohawk Midgetape 44. Model BR-1. This one was made in 1957 and uses a metal tape cartridge. Got three subminiature tubes and a built-in hand crank for manual rewind.'

He was already at a large desk in the corner by the time he finished his last sentence. He tore through the drawers like crazy and came up with a little golden thing.

'I love this.' He beamed. 'It's so *cool*. So, like, James Bond.'

'Just as I remembered it,' I told him.

'You think you can get Tanner Brookmeyer to talk into this and confess his evil deeds?' he asked, grinning. 'That, my friend, is hilarious. How am I supposed to get this back when you're dead and in the East River?'

'I could buy it from you,' I suggested.

'Not for sale.' He held it aloft for a moment. 'But.'

Ralph went back to ransacking his desk drawers. After a few moments he produced a cigar box.

'Really?' I asked him.

'No, come here,' he said, motioning me over. 'Look.'

I went to the desk and he demonstrated. He opened the cigar box and there was a nice row of very real looking Cubans. He picked one up, and there were others underneath. Or so I thought. Ralph worked some kind of magic and all the cigars came out to reveal a secret compartment in the box just coincidentally the size of the tape recorder.

'You're kidding me,' I mumbled.

'This box,' he began, energized considerably, 'with that tape recorder in it, was sitting on this desk when these FBI thugs came in here and arrested Dave Van Ronk. I recorded everything. I still have the tapes in a safe deposit box. That's why I'm still in business. Because every single thing the Feds did and said in my house was *way* beyond illegal. So, you know. Don't tell *me* this shit doesn't work.'

'I wouldn't dream of it,' I said. 'So . . .'

'When you go to Brookmeyer,' Ralph continued, 'you tell him you brought a present, like a peace offering or whatever. You set this on the desk, have your little talk and he says what you want him to say. Then, when he gets mad, because he will, you grab the box and say if he's going to be that way about it, you're taking your cigars back!'

'Then I get out,' I said.

'Maybe. Or maybe he shoots you in, like, fifty places. Could go either way.'

And there it was: the reality of my situation. I suddenly felt a little like David going up against the big Philistine with nothing but a slingshot and a song in my heart.

TWENTY-FOUR

I t only took me a second after walking out of Ralph's before I realized how close I was to Tap-A-Keg, the local hangout of Nan the understudy. Which was not far from her apartment. Which meant that Nan lived within a couple of blocks of Tanner Brookmeyer.

Probably didn't mean anything. Tanner lived in a building that he owned, on the top floor. The whole top floor. Nan lived in a closet with a bathroom. I'd forgotten that Manhattan could be like that, a penthouse could be right around the corner from a gaggle of hovels.

Carrying the box of cigars under my arm, a little heavy thanks to the tape recorder inside, I took the brisk stroll up the street and around the next block to good old Tap-A Keg. But I stopped short of going in even before I thought to switch on the tape recorder. Because a sudden revelation popped me in the head.

Those guys at Tap-A-Keg had been covering for Nan; I'd known that when I was talking with them. I'd kind of forgotten it with all the ensuing adventures. And to tell the truth, I hadn't really thought it was important anyway. Nan didn't kill Emory.

Or did she? Did she maybe have a hand in it?

Nan had been awfully jittery when I'd spoken with her. I'd put it down to nerves, her place being shot up, her fellow cast member being murdered.

But Nan had actually exhibited a bit of cocaine behavior. *That* was the revelation that hit me in the head. And I felt a little stupid for not putting it together until that moment, a little like a rube from Florida.

Nan had *not* been at Tap-A-Keg when she'd said she was. That's what her pals in the bar were covering. Which meant that she'd lied to me, that she had done something she didn't want me to know about. And what if that something had to do with extra-strychnine coke?

Then I wondered why I would even think that. Was the whole scene screwing with my perceptions? A flight to Atlanta, a couple of gun incidents, a tussle with Tanner, and the revelation that Sammy Two Shoes was my little brother? It was all too much.

And, because the Universe thinks it's got a really good sense of humor, that was the moment I saw Nan coming out of her local bar.

She was a little unsteady, like one martini too many. She was dressed in shorts and flip-flops with some kind of disco blouse, all sequins and swirls.

She didn't see me, or she didn't remember me. She just balanced herself against the doorframe of the bar, got her bearings and her balance, and launched off toward her home.

I watched her walk away, as best she could, and wondered if her lifestyle meant anything to Emory Brewster's murder. What was it one of the other actors had told me? That she was more a professional understudy than an actual actor? Most of the pay with none of the work. I guess it was a nice gig if your goals were hanging out at your local saloon and bumping lines of coke when you felt like it. Some people drift. Some people can be happy like that.

A couple more seconds and I decided that I should live and let live. I *was* a buttinsky. And I didn't need to be on Nan's case, did I? I already had three people on the hook for Emory's murder. What was I doing looking for a fourth?

So I hoisted my box of cigars a bit, stepped off the curb, and hailed a cab for the Benjamin.

I usually underestimate the value of sleep. I often forget that when I don't have it, I don't work right, and when I do have enough of it, I'm pretty much a ball of fire.

But when I woke up in my hotel room, I was feeling I might have slept for a couple of weeks. I was having a hard time remembering anything after seeing Nan on the street. I knew I got in a cab. I knew I made it to the bar in the Benjamin. I knew I had complimented the bartender several times on what a spectacular negroni she made. She finally told me that she made it with Amaro. I told her that it wasn't a negroni, then. She asked me if I'd just had a baby or else why was I holding tight to a box of cigars. I told her that the cigars were a gift from a friend. She asked me if she could have one. I said yes.

And then I woke up in my hotel room. I sat up. The box of cigars was on the nightstand. I opened it. There was one missing. I broke into the secret compartment. Tape recorder still there. I put the package back together. I lay back down.

I never gave drinking advice to anyone in my life, but if I were so disposed, I would tell everyone who would listen that after seven negronis you might as well just pound a nail into your forehead. It would be about the same sensation either way.

The clock on the nightstand said it was nearly eight o'clock in the morning. Which would have meant that I'd slept for almost nine hours, and it was time for me to get up, get showered, and get going over to Tanner Brookmeyer's penthouse apartment. Where he would kill me and put me out of my misery. Which was, if I remembered *Hamlet* correctly, a consummation devoutly to be wished.

So I dragged myself out of my bed, stumbled into the shower, spent a delightful twenty minutes there relaxing the negroni knots in the back of my neck, and managed to get dressed, all before nine.

Guns in place, cigars in hand, I launched my leaky little ship out of the room and into the elevator.

The good old Benjamin had a coffee service in the lobby,

thank God, and I took advantage of it like I'd never see coffee again. Which was, I had to admit, a possibility.

Three large cups of coffee and two trips to the gents' room later, I was on the street getting a cab. I could have walked, but it was already a little hot, and I wanted to make certain I was in place early, as per Lonnie's instructions.

Lonnie, I reminisced on the cab ride over to Columbus, was not a bad short order cook, but he was among the greatest grifter-planners in history. World class. He once orchestrated a complex ballet of seventy people in order to boost the entire set of the Broadway musical *Cabaret* just so he could set it up in his cousin's warehouse by the docks for a party. Swear to God. After a matinee on Sunday, the whole thing was taken apart, moved to the warehouse, set up for a party all day Monday and back in the theatre in time for the show on Tuesday night. I couldn't remember the occasion, but I'd been there at the party as a teen-ager. There was a lot of acid around in those days, so the details remained a little hazy. And the ensuing years had probably exaggerated the story a little. But I'd seen it with my own eyes. And it had been done with such stealth and grace that it never even made the papers. After that, Lonnie was a legend.

So while I didn't know what Lonnie had in mind, I had confidence in the guy. Sometimes you just had to trust other people. The gag would be to get all or most of Tanner's goons and guards away from Tanner's penthouse long enough for me to get in, get what I wanted, and get out.

So at 9:45 there I stood, corner of Columbus and Something, waiting. It was a normal day. Students, cops, panhandlers, hookers, businesspeople, flies, and garbage all shared the street amiably enough. The sky seemed a little overcast, but in the canyons of the city it was hard to see the sun even when it was out in full. The smell was ridiculous, but familiar. The noise was something like a big waterfall, constant and blank. A lot of nothing happened for a while. I shifted from leg to leg, I scratched an itch. I felt my shoulder holster about a hundred times. I tried to calm myself down by remembering what the ocean looked like at sunset.

And then Hell erupted all over the Avenue.

Sirens, a fire engine, two cop cars, then a swarm of activity, and the smell of gas was everywhere.

People started moving really fast. Some even ran. Even though I was sure Lonnie was responsible for the chaos, I still had half a mind to run too.

Then I saw Lonnie and two other guys in gas company uniforms talking with the cops. I didn't hear the entire conversation, but the gist involved a serious gas leak and a major evacuation of the entire building. The building that Tanner Brookmeyer owned. The one where he lived.

Things started happening really fast after that.

Lonnie and the two other guys went into the building with a bunch of cops. A guy from the fire truck got on a bullhorn and started yelling orders. The police were beginning to cordon off the block.

I backed away, got to the corner, found my way to the adjacent alley, and hurried toward the back door of Tanner's building just ahead of the oncoming cops.

I didn't want to risk the elevators, so I ran up the back staircase, all five floors.

The door at the top of the stairs was locked, but that was no problem. I popped it in under five seconds. It swung open on to a lush hallway. There was a thick blue and white Asian rug on the hardwood floors. The walls were decked in original paintings. And there were healthy live plants, big ferns in ornate pots. At the end of the hall was a grand arch and half-open double doors. The elevator was right next to them. And there was an alarm going off to wake the dead, a real skull-crusher.

I broke the lock on the hallway door and slammed it shut so that one could get through it without a sledgehammer.

I walked down the hall as calmly as I could, reached into the cigar box and turned on the tiny spy tape recorder, then knocked on the double doors, even though I could have just gone in.

There was no answer.

'Tanner?' I called out. 'It's Foggy Moscowitz. I brought you a peace offering.'

The alarm cut off. You could still hear the helter-skelter of the other floors in the building, people yelling, cops ordering, doors pounding. But the bone-rattling noise on Tanner's floor was gone.

A second later I could hear footsteps approaching from inside the penthouse. I took three steps back and held out my hands.

One of them had the box of cigars in it, the other one was open and empty.

Two guys stormed through the doors. They both had guns and the guns were pointed at me.

'Cigars!' I said, waving the box. 'For Tanner!'

I held the box out in their direction.

They stared, frozen.

Then, without fanfare, Tanner breezed in between the two guys, no gun, and sauntered up to me, smiling. He was wearing a burgundy silk robe, the kind a rich society swell might have worn, if it had been 1941.

'Did you do all this?' he asked.

'All the chaos and noise outside?' I nodded. 'There's a gas leak. Can't you tell?'

'You mean that smell? Sure, most of my guys went down to see what's happening. But I always, *always* keep a couple of guys with me. So.'

'Well, good,' I told him. 'I want witnesses to the fact that I came bearing gifts.'

I waggled the box of cigars.

'Are those Cubans?' he asked, eyeing the box.

'You used to really go for these.' I nodded.

'Yeah.' He sighed. 'I quit. Gave up smoking. It's supposed to be bad for your health.'

'Really.' I stared at the box. 'These are all natural. You know. Hand rolled.'

'Why are you here?' he demanded.

'Why would I bring you such a nice gift, you mean?' I nodded. 'That's a fair question.'

'Especially after I shot up your mother's home, threatened your favorite aunt, and put a couple of bullets in your old pal Sammy Two Shoes.'

'Yeah, that's the point,' I insisted. 'I don't want any more of that kind of thing. My mother is sick, see. She's got the cancer. And my aunt Shayna, I mean, you *know* she's nuts, right?'

'How do you mean, *nuts*?' he asked.

'I mean she's not right in the head,' I said. 'Flip City. Got all these conspiracy theories in her head. She's ten minutes away from the loony bin, no kidding, Tanner.'

'And your mom's got cancer?'

'Lymphoma,' I said.

'What's that?'

'I don't know.' I shrugged. 'Some kind of blood cancer, she says. I want her to live out what's left of her life in peace.'

'With your crazy aunt taking care of her.'

'Right.' I held the cigars aloft. 'And this is what I brought so you'd at least listen to what I have to say.'

Tanner shook his head and sighed. 'Check him,' he told one of his guys.

The guy moved so fast that I dropped the box of cigars. It hit the floor and opened and several of the stogies rolled out.

Tanner's goon patted me down and took the .44 out of my shoulder holster but missed the SIG Sauer tucked snugly into my ankle holster.

Tanner turned and walked back into the darkness of his lair.

'Come on in,' he called over his shoulder. 'Let's talk.'

I swooped up the cigar box, collecting the errant smokes, and followed. The goons followed me.

Tanner's palace was not what I'd expected. The ceilings were at least twenty feet high. There were wildly expensive rugs on the floors, the kind you'd find in an English manor house. In fact, the whole place looked like that: antiques and fine old furniture everywhere, a Gainsborough and two Turners on the wall, and that was just in the foyer. I expected a butler to come and try to take the cigars.

Tanner wafted into another room, maybe a parlor or a living room, it was hard to tell with the dazzle of finery. I noticed then that Tanner wasn't wearing shoes. He had on fancy slippers. It seemed hilarious to me that a homicidal maniac would wear such dainty footwear, but I kept the laughs in check.

He sat in a huge leather armchair and pointed to the place he wanted me, one of two upholstered seats, what they called a Queen Anne, high back with wings, overstuffed arms. I sat in the one closest to Tanner. It was unbelievably comfortable.

'I have to say,' I began, 'this is some place.'

Tanner looked around like he was seeing with new eyes. 'Yeah, it is. I guess I get kind of used to it.'

'Who did this, all this decorating and collecting?' I asked, my eyes roaming over beautiful paintings and polished desks and marble statues. 'Is that an actual Rodin?'

He turned.

'Camille Claudel,' he told me. 'She was a student of Rodin's. Do you like it?'

'It's remarkable,' I said. 'But about Sammy.'

'Right to business.' He leaned forward and called out. 'Howard, would you bring us some tea?'

From another room in the place a voice rang out, 'Immediately, sir.'

So there *was* a butler. And he was going to bring us tea. The strangeness of it all was just beginning to seep into me.

'Sammy was sore because you always handed him the crap jobs,' I said quickly, 'and you can kind of understand that. He's got a sensitive soul. You know, being a musician.'

'Sammy Cohen was a dick with a guitar,' Tanner snapped. 'All the girls thought he was something but look at him now. He's not as smart or as rich as I am, not even close. He's in that same old salt and pepper suit and I'm in handmade Italian. And his girlfriend works in the *theatre*. I mean, come on. She's not even an actress.'

I could tell he was heating up. What was it about Sammy that made Tanner so mad? It couldn't have been about Emory, not a burn that hot.

'What did Sammy ever do to you?' I asked innocently.

'What did he do?' Tanner's voice was almost an octave higher.

Without warning a man in a tailored suit appeared with a tray. There was a tea service on the tray that would have done all right for the Queen, in keeping with the general atmosphere of the place.

'I took the liberty of croissants,' said the man with the tray. 'It's too late for breakfast rolls and, of course, far too early for a traditional tea cake.'

Tanner turned toward the man and I thought he was about to take the guy's head off, but instead he let out a long breath.

'Thank you, Howard. A perfect idea. And Earl Grey?'

'Of course.' Howard set the tray down on the table nearest Tanner.

'Do you like Earl Grey?' Tanner asked me.

'Who doesn't?' I answered.

It was about then that the extremely surreal aspect of my situation finally kicked in completely. I had a sudden fear that maybe I was still asleep at the Benjamin, that it was the middle of the night and I was dreaming about my encounter with Tanner. All I could do was stare while Howard poured tea. The tray also had a silver butter dish and a basket with a white linen cloth that held, I assumed, croissants.

Howard looked at me then. 'Sugar, sir? Milk?'

'Both, thanks,' I mumbled, still staring.

'I see you have an eye on the croissants,' Howard said to me, smiling. 'I made them myself this morning.'

'It's the morning after the night before for me,' I admitted, 'and all I've had for it is coffee. So a croissant sounds just like the ticket.'

'Hangover?' Tanner commiserated. 'I thought you looked a little blurry-eyed.'

'This will help,' Howard said.

He unwrapped the basket, pulled out a pastry, steam rising, and placed it on the whitest plate I'd ever seen. A knife and a third of a stick of butter added, and he handed it to me before the tea.

I took the plate and absently set down the cigar box on the side table. A mistake.

'Shall I take these cigars to your humidor, Mr Brookmeyer?' Howard suggested, reaching for the box.

My reaction was stupid and clumsy. I dropped my white croissant plate and lunged, grabbed the box and clutched it to my chest. Before I was finished, I regretted every move I'd made.

I tried to cover. 'Mr Brookmeyer tells me he's given up smoking. I wouldn't want these beauties to waste away in some unused humidor. I'll take them back to Florida, I guess. I have a friend there who would appreciate them. He's a Seminole elder.'

But Tanner cut me off. 'Hand them over.'

He held out his mitt. Howard was already cleaning up my mess and dealing with the plate on the carpet. I thought about it for a second, but what could I do? I gave the box to Tanner.

His bodyguards appeared in the double door frame. Only one of them had his gun in his hand.

Tanner sat back in his leather chair, sighed, and opened the box. He picked out a cigar. He rolled it in his fingers, then he sniffed it, and then he closed his eyes.

'These actually are Cubans,' he said softly. 'You can smell the rum and revolution.'

'I was serious about making a peace offering,' I said. 'I only wanted the best.'

But he wasn't finished. He rummaged around in the box and took out all the cigars. He put them on the tea tray. It only took him a few more seconds to figure out the false bottom and discover the nifty spy tape recorder. And when he did, it made him smile.

'There we are,' he said, delighted. 'I knew it had to be something. I didn't figure it to be something this stupid. Have a look, Howard. I think Mr Moscowitz here was going to tape record me saying something incriminating. And then?'

He looked at me.

'And then,' I obliged, 'I would take the tape to Helen Baker, the lawyer for Phoebe Peabody, and let the law handle the rest of it.'

'Who's Phoebe Peabody?' Tanner asked.

'Sammy's girl. The stage manager.'

'Right, right,' he said quickly. 'And what were you hoping I'd say, just out of curiosity?'

Howard had frozen in place. His face was a mask, something blank and implacable.

'I was going to get you to admit that you killed Emory,' I told him. 'And that would get Sam and Phoebe off the hook.'

Tanner squinted. 'Huh. That would have been tough to pull off.'

I shook my head. 'I can be really persuasive,' I said. 'I could probably have gotten you to say something that would have—'

'No,' he interrupted, 'I mean it would have been tough because I didn't do it. I didn't pop Emory. I mean, I was tired of her, and I knew she mostly liked me because I gave her free coke, but why would I kill her? I'd just break it off, you know, like a *person*. You have a very low opinion of me, Foggy, and frankly, that hurts my feelings a little.'

Tanner set the tape recorder down on the side table next to his chair.

I sat back. 'You didn't do it.'

'I didn't do it,' he repeated. 'From what I hear, Sammy and Phoebe did it. Cyanide in her water. Which, if you ask me, was kind of a corny way to do it. It's just like that play Emory was in with everybody dying right and left. I know Sammy's not all that bright, but seriously, he couldn't come up with anything better than *that*?'

I looked at Howard. 'Your boss didn't kill Emory Brewster.'

'No. Sir.' Howard was polite about it; he was also firm in his belief.

I held up both my hands. 'OK. OK. I've obviously made a big mistake here. Bonehead mistake. So here's my thinking: you shot up my mother's apartment; I stirred up a lot of mayhem around your home. I think we're even.'

Tanner smiled. 'You think we're even.' He looked at Howard. 'He thinks we're even.'

'Yes. Sir.' Howard was still frozen in place.

'I'd like to take another crack at that croissant,' I forged ahead, 'and maybe sip a little Earl Grey and then be on my way.'

'The thing is,' Tanner said, his voice gone harsh, 'Emory only liked me because I gave her free coke, as I said, and when I wasn't around, she two-timed me with half the out-of-work actors in Manhattan. And then your friend Sammy started working overtime to ruin my operation. So, see, I had to do something.'

Howard thawed just enough to swoop up the tea tray and exit the way he'd come in. Tanner's goons took several steps into the room very suddenly. And Tanner pulled a pistol out of his fancy robe.

'What did you do, Tanner?' I asked, staring at his gun.

'Did you meet Nan?' His voice was ice.

'The understudy?' I nodded.

'It was easy.' Tanner laughed. 'Everybody hated Emory. I guess you found that out. It wasn't a secret. But Nan . . .'

He trailed off, and things fell into place for me.

'Nan is one of your distributors,' I guessed. 'She was your way into the lower echelon of the theatrical community. She knew a lot of actors. She's got a good-sized coke habit of her own, so you were able to suss her out, maybe give her a deal. So when it came time to get rid of Emory, all you had to do was give Nan a special baggie of extra-strychnine cocaine to give to

Emory. I'm also assuming that it wasn't the first time Nan delivered coke to Emory, and maybe other actors, at the theatre. Like, before a show.'

'Your reputation is really well-deserved,' Tanner said. 'You're a lot smarter than I figured.'

'All true?' I goaded.

'All true,' he confirmed.

'And the thing is,' I went on, shaking my head, 'I actually gave you a helping hand. The night that Emory died.'

'What?' Tanner cocked his head like a dog.

'I broke Emory's hand mirror.'

I let it sink in to see if he'd get it. He didn't. So I thought maybe if I explained it to him, it might give me time to figure out what to do next.

'Emory tried to Mace me in the dressing room that night,' I explained, 'and I knocked the can out of her hand. It broke her mirror. The mirror, incidentally, upon which she did her lines of coke. Anyway, actors freaked out. Phoebe cleaned up. Evidence of the bad coke was gone since, as I said, that's what she used the mirror for. And Sammy helped you out too. He stuck a pencil in Emory's neck, right in the jugular, so that the cops wouldn't look at the poisoned water bottle, but it also kept them from running a toxicology screen on Emory's body. Because my guess is that Emory was already almost dead at that point thanks to a couple of lines she bumped up before the show started. She was pretty wired when she came into the dressing room.'

'Let me stop you there,' Tanner growled. 'I don't care. I gave bad coke to Nan to give to Emory. Nan was one of my little elfin helpers. She delivered coke to lots of actors. There. It doesn't matter. Emory is yesterday's news. And, by the way, so are you.'

With that he raised his gun and took aim.

My response was easy. I fell out of the Queen Anne, rolled, and came up behind the other Queen Anne with the SIG in my hand.

Tanner fired right into the chair and the bullet barely missed me coming out the other side. I fired back but Tanner was already headed out the door where Howard had gone. The two bodyguards were roaring my way.

They both fired, but I was already on the floor, almost flat. I shot one guy through his shin bone from under the chair. He howled and went crashing down. The other guy was nearly on top of me. I was lying on my back looking up at the ceiling when I saw him lumber over the coffee table, so I fired wildly. It didn't do anything but put holes in Tanner's ceiling. The bodyguard's gun was ten inches from my face. I swatted it out of instinct, and the gun went off, plugging the Queen Anne again.

I rolled, came up on one knee, and fired once right into the bodyguard's belly. He paused for a second, looked down at the blood that was already there, and shook his head.

He took aim and fired. He would have popped me good if I hadn't just fallen down again. The bullet zinged past me and into the wall somewhere left of the marble fireplace.

I tried to aim from my position on the floor, but it wasn't easy. I got off two shots that didn't do any good and the guy was suddenly standing over me, grinning.

He pointed his gun at my forehead. I pulled the trigger of the SIG, but it just clicked. It wasn't out of bullets; it just wouldn't fire. So I did the only thing I could think of. I bopped the guy in his crotch, hard as I could, with the barrel of the SIG. He made a sound like a train coming to a halt on worn-out tracks, dropped his gun, and then went down himself.

I didn't hesitate. I jumped up, grabbed the tape recorder, shoved it into my pocket, and ran for the exit into the hallway. Just as I got out, something came crashing through the door at the other end of the hall, the door I'd broken so nobody could get in.

A second later there were cops and firemen swarming in. I still had the SIG in my hand. I dropped it instantly and was about to start a very earnest explanation when a guy in a gas mask and a gas company uniform pushed past the cops and grabbed my arm.

'He's one of ours!' he yelled. 'He's an inspector!'

I nodded. 'I think the leak is coming from that penthouse,' I shouted, pointing to the double doors. 'Some kind of drug ring. They all have guns!'

Cops ran past me. Firemen began checking something in the hallway ceiling, and the guy in the gas company uniform led me to the stairway and down the stairs.

One flight down and we were alone.

'Lonnie?' I asked softly.

He nodded. 'We gotta vacate.'

That was all. He raced me down the rest of the stairs and out to the alley behind the building. There was a gas company van waiting. We got in and sat on the padded benches that lined the walls.

The van backed out of the alley and headed around the corner and down Columbus. We were five blocks away from the uproar before Lonnie took off his mask.

'So?' Big smile.

'I don't know what to say,' I confessed. 'That was astonishing.'

'Did it work?'

I pulled out the tape recorder. It was still running.

'This is an amazing piece of equipment,' I said, staring down at it. 'Do you know Ralph? Ralph's recording studio?'

Lonnie shook his head. 'But you got what you wanted?'

'How did you do all that?' I asked him.

He reached under the bench where he was sitting and produced a blank spray can. One pump and the van smelled like rotten eggs.

'This is the smell they put in the gas to let you know there's a leak,' he explained. 'Because natural gas doesn't actually have a smell, so if the gas was on you wouldn't know it. That's why they put in the smell, see? It's called *mercaptan*.'

'Gas doesn't smell?'

He shook his head. 'They added it after some school in Texas blew up in 1937. And I got a big supply in aerosol cans. You spray a couple of cans like this around, and everybody panics.'

'So how many of the guys I just saw outside Tanner's building were yours?'

He sat back. 'That's the beauty. Me and ten other guys pulled this off. The rest were legit cops and firefighters. Once you get a panic about a gas leak, it kind of takes on a life of its own.'

'Funny.' I sat back. 'That seems to be the story of my visit to the city in general: kind of taken on a life of its own.'

'You haven't answered my question,' Lonnie insisted. 'Did our gag work out for you or not?'

I stared at the tape recorder. 'The thing is, we're up to four people now. Four people who killed Emory Brewster. And only one of them meant to do it. The other three didn't really know what they were doing.'

'I don't understand.' Lonnie sighed.

'I don't either, Lonnie,' I admitted. 'What am I supposed to do now?'

TWENTY-FIVE

I took the tape recorder back to Ralph. He was surprised to see me.

'You didn't die!' he said.

'Not for lack of trying,' I answered. 'Can you transfer what's on the tape to a cassette? Without listening to it.'

I was standing in his doorway. He was dressed in a tux. A red tux with a pale pink shirt and bow tie. I was just too tired to ask him about it.

He leaned close to me. 'Is there something dirty on it?'

'I don't want you to be an accessory,' I said wearily. 'In case the cops ask.'

'Oh,' he said quickly. 'Right. Well. Come on in. I've only got about twenty minutes before I have to go, but I think I can pull this off if the tape's not too long.'

'It's not.'

He took the recorder out of my hand. I followed him into his place. It looked a little tidied up since the previous visit. Again, I didn't care to ask.

He busied himself at a console of some kind. I sat down on a piano bench and leaned my back against the wall.

After a couple of minutes he piped up.

'OK. I'll have a cassette in a jiffy. High-speed dupe. You're not going to ask me about this ridiculous monkey suit?'

'That suit is an insult to monkeys *everywhere*,' I assured him. 'And isn't it kind of hot for a tux? I don't remember New York being this hot.'

'It's summer.' He shrugged. 'I got opening night tickets for *Godspell* at the Broadhurst! That's what the suit is for.'

'What is *Godspell*?' I asked.

'What's *Godspell*?' He seemed insulted. 'It's only the best musical about Jesus *ever*. I saw the original production in 'seventy-one at La Mama. But this is *Broadway*, baby. Broadway tonight!'

My knowledge of musicals about Jesus was slim, so I was disinclined to comment.

'Aren't you going to ask me how I got tickets to a Broadway opening?' he went on.

I sipped a breath. 'How did you get tickets to a Broadway opening, Ralph?'

'I know the stage manager!' he was delighted to tell me.

I took a second. Then, 'Stage manager. Really.'

'You know, the stage manager runs the whole thing,' he told me absently, fussing with his console. 'Knows everything that goes on in the show. Like, *everything*. You would not believe the gossip.'

'Gossip.'

'You know.' He clicked something and the console went quiet. 'Who's dating who, who hates who, who's got the best coke.'

I sat up. 'Right. I heard that about stage managers. They know everything.'

'Oh, they do.' He leaned forward and plucked a cassette tape from in front of him; held it out to me. 'Here you go.'

'Maybe you should erase the original,' I suggested, 'and hide your spy tape recorder away for a while. Just in case.'

'This is the Tanner Brookmeyer thing? Is he on this tape?'

I nodded.

Ralph went right to work. 'I'll erase the tape and then burn it.'

I turned toward the door. 'You know, I heard Phil Ochs at Newport. I think it was 1963. He was fantastic.'

'Tell Spider I said hello, right?'

I put the tape in my pocket and nodded. 'Have fun at *Godspell*.'

He didn't answer me because he had already dished up a quarter of a teaspoonful of coke and was just about to enjoy it.

Helen Baker listened three times in a row to the cassette I'd brought her. Without comment. Because I didn't want anyone else in her crowded office to hear, I'd told her to listen to it with headphones. It took half an hour to find some. My hangover hadn't gotten any better, and I was just starting to realize that I needed food.

I was sitting in an uncomfortable metal chair beside her desk, distracted by all kinds of activity in the office. She finally took off the phones.

'"I gave bad coke to Nan to give to Emory." That's all he says.' She bit her upper lip. 'I mean, I can certainly bring the guy in for questioning, but there's more on this tape to incriminate *you* than Tanner.'

'Me?'

'You confess to destroying the very evidence that would substantiate Tanner's culpability.'

'You mean I broke Emory's mirror,' I said, 'and then it got thrown away.'

'Yes.' She shook her head. 'I can't go to a judge with this.'

'Did you check Emory's body for strychnine?'

She nodded. 'I haven't heard back yet.'

'The strychnine was in the coke,' I told her. 'Get a really smart doctor to prove that it was the strychnine that killed her, not the cyanide or the pencil in her neck.'

'That might not be the case, Sherlock,' Helen demurred. 'Might have been a ridiculous combination of everything. I mean, just how many people wanted to kill this Emory?'

'All of them,' I said. 'Far as I can tell.'

'OK.' She slumped down in her chair; she was exhausted. 'You still have to bring in Sammy. Where is he now? Because I know he's not at your mother's apartment.'

'The cops went there,' I surmised.

'Yes.'

'But they didn't find anything.' I was sure of that. 'Not even blood or bullet holes.'

'Right,' she agreed. 'How did they manage that, your mother and your aunt?'

'Practice.' I stood up. 'So are you telling me I risked my life *and* pulled in a huge favor to get that tape, and it doesn't do any good?'

'I don't know how *evidence* works in Florida,' she snapped. 'But here in the big city . . .'

She trailed off because she saw the look on my face.

'OK, OK,' I said. 'I have to eat. Then I'll go get Sammy. Then I'll decide what I want to do next.'

I knew she wanted to say something else; I could tell from her expression. But I got out of her office before she could verbalize. And before I lost my temper.

Sure, I thought to myself when I was out on the sidewalk, the concept of *evidence* in the strictest courtroom sense might have been a little fuzzier in Fry's Bay, Florida than it was in New York City. But I'd just about cooked my bacon to get the goods on Tanner, and in my opinion, the goods were gotten.

And, sure, I was hungover, hungry, and hapless, so my opinion might not have been completely informed. But the idea that I'd busted into the lion's den – nearly got killed, and narrowly escaped – for nothing, it didn't sit well. It didn't sit well at all.

I knew that I should go back to the YMCA and check on Sammy. Having bullets taken out of you is no joke. But I also knew that if I didn't get something in my stomach and start to think straight, the rest of the day was going to go about as well as my visit to Helen Baker's office.

So I looked up and down the block. Two diners, an Italian place, and a hot dog cart in the street. For me, penne with vodka was the perfect hangover cure, so I headed for Vittorio's, which described itself on the sign as *real* Italian food. I had to tip the waiter a ridiculous amount of money to talk the chef into penne with vodka, but when it came it was worth it. And it was gone in less time than it took to ask for it.

Now, the secret to really good penne with vodka, to me, was always in the tomato sauce. Can't be from a can. You have to make it with fresh tomatoes, fresh basil, a little Chianti, and a lot of garlic. The vodka's essential, but not the star. The star was the sauce. And that was exactly how the chef had made it.

In short, I tipped again, bigger than before, and left Vittorio's singing. Actually humming under my breath. I was thinking of the old Glenn Miller number 'Elmer's Tune' and I didn't know why. 'What makes a gander meander in search of a goose?' That's what they wanted to know in the version of the song that was playing in my head.

I was stepping off the curb to flag a cab when I realized that the B part of the song was, 'Listen, listen, there's a lot you're liable to be missin'.'

The cab stopped in front of me about the time I realized that the song was a telegram from my subconscious. But what had I missed?

I settled into the cab and mumbled something about the Greenpoint YMCA. Then I spent the rest of the trip trying to remember everything about my conversation with Tanner. I got stuck on the moment when Tanner was really agitated about Sammy and just on the verge of telling me why he was so irate when Howard the butler had come in with the croissants I never got to taste.

Was that what I was missing? Something about Tanner's rage toward Sammy?

If Tanner had been telling the truth about not really wanting to kill Emory, not really caring about her at all, then why had he given the poisoned coke to Nan to give to Emory? And was that connected to his feelings about Sammy? Was Sammy still hiding something from me?

But the cab was in Brooklyn by the time it came to me that I could ask Sammy about that.

The room at the Y was dark. I didn't want to disturb Sammy's sleep, so I came in quietly and didn't turn on the lights. I only took two steps into the little room before I heard a very distinct clicking sound. Like, maybe, somebody clicking the safety off a gun.

Then the lamp by the bed came on, and there was Sammy, sitting up, wincing, and pointing his Colt at me.

He blinked, then sat back. 'Oh.'

'How're you feeling?' I asked him.

'Like somebody took to my chest with a jack hammer,' he told me. 'But the bleeding seems to have stopped for the most part.'

'That's good news.' I sat down at the desk. The note I'd left for Sammy was undisturbed.

'Where you been?' he asked me softly.

'I had a whole thing,' I hedged. 'Then I went to see Phoebe's lawyer.'

He was having trouble keeping his eyes open. 'Is she out of jail?'

'Not yet,' I had to say. 'But can you talk for just a minute?
'Sure.' But the eyes closed.

Sammy was on his side. His suit was significantly the worse
for wear. His face was contorted. I knew he was in pain.

The bed was one of those metal jobs. The headboard and foot
were the same, and a bare mattress, we hadn't bothered with the
sheets. As a kid I'd been in jail cells that were jollier.

'Why does Tanner hate you, Sam?' I asked.

That opened his eyes. 'There's a question.'

'You've got an answer?'

A long breath and a bit of adjustment on the bed, and he told
me the story. 'Why Tanner Brookmeyer Hated Sammy Two-Shoes.'

Sammy had spent a lot of his life feeling lost. He loved music,
but it didn't love him back, not in the way he thought it should.
He wanted a record deal, but nobody was interested in the kind
of folk blues he sang in the era of disco. He thought he loved
Emory Brewster, but she only loved cocaine and the theatre. In
that order. Then, when one of his best friends left New York to
go live in Florida, he didn't know what to do with himself, so
he meandered into the family business, which was, in general,
being a hoodlum. He'd never been sure which of his aunts was
really his mother, and he'd only heard rumors about his father,
a much-loved and more-feared hit man of great renown. And a
man who already had a family somewhere else.

But thanks to a friend of his aunt, a woman named Shayna,
he acquired a moral compass of sorts. Sammy learned from
her that killing children was wrong. Killing victims of abuse
was wrong. On the other hand, killing Nazis, fascists, bigots,
rapists and child molesters was not only right, it was required.
Sammy took to that philosophy. He believed it was his spiritual
calling.

Then one day, after he'd been working for Tanner for a while,
Tanner asked Sammy a question. It was a question about Shayna.
Tanner asked Sammy if Shayna was *available*. Tanner said he
had always admired her, and they were about the same age, in
the same business, and went to the same Temple, when they
went. Tanner said it would be a nice change from the teenagers
he was used to dating.

But Sammy's reaction was not a good one. He shoved Tanner. Then he hit Tanner. Then he went over to Shayna's apartment where she lived with her sister and he told Shayna that Tanner was after her, but he had syphilis. Shayna said that she was afraid of Tanner, and rightly so, because Tanner was crazy.

So Sammy and Shayna planned a hit on Tanner's primary supplier of cocaine, a little man in Atlanta who was a racist, an anti-Semite, and a Grand Dragon in the KKK.

Sammy went to Atlanta and killed the little man. When Sammy came back from Atlanta, Shayna and her sister sat Sammy down and told him that he and Foggy Moscowitz, the friend who'd gone to Florida, were half-brothers. Same father. They said that's why Shayna had taken him under her wing. Sammy liked the idea, because he and Foggy had been brothers in arms anyway, so why shouldn't they be brothers in fact?

But the important part of the story was that word got around: Sammy was actually the son of the famous hitman, now deceased. Word also got around that Sammy had ruined Tanner's chances with Shayna, and that Sammy was beginning to dismantle Tanner's network bit by bit. The problem for Tanner was that he couldn't move against Sammy directly, because the legend of Sammy's real father loomed large, as they say, and half the hoods in Brooklyn were suddenly watching out for Sammy the way they used to watch out for this Foggy Moscowitz in the older days.

But Tanner wasn't the kind to let things go.

'For what it's worth,' I told Sammy softly, 'I just found out, like, hours ago that we're brothers. I never knew.'

'I know.' He sighed. 'Your mother didn't want you to think less of your father. You know, what with his cavorting.'

'*Cavorting*,' I repeated. 'The thing is, I never thought much about my father one way or another. I knew the legend. I never knew the person. So, not really an issue. But you and me . . .'

'I don't want it to change anything between us,' he complained. 'I like things the way they are. You like me. I like you. We got into scrapes when we were kids. You're helping me now. I don't see any percentage in singing "Michael Row the Fucking Boat Ashore" at this point, do you?'

'I hate that song,' I admitted.

'Who doesn't?'

'You don't even want to talk about it a little?' I asked.

'Maybe after we get Phoebe out of jail,' he said. Then he added, 'And if we are somehow able to avoid being killed by Tanner Brookmeyer. Which I wouldn't give us odds, at this point.'

'Yeah.'

I told Sammy what I'd done, all about going over to Tanner's place. How I'd taken a big risk and fallen on my ass, at least according to Helen Baker.

He took it all in silently.

'OK, yes,' he said at length, 'that *is* going to make it harder for us to stay alive. I mean, it sounds to me like it was a good idea, but Tanner tried to shoot you before it really got where you wanted it to get, right?'

'I don't know what that means, exactly,' I said. 'What I do know is that we have to get Tanner before he gets us. Because he's coming for us.'

'Oh, he's coming for us,' he agreed.

And with that he swiveled and shifted and groaned and, when he was done, he was on his feet.

'What the hell do you think you're doing?' I asked him. 'You're, like, barely alive.'

'I'm going to get Tanner Brookmeyer,' he answered, wincing. 'Are you coming with me or not?'

'Do I have a choice?'

'You could always run away to Florida again,' he mumbled, heading for the door.

TWENTY-SIX

The thing about going to war with someone like Tanner Brookmeyer is that you had to know there was no chance of winning. Not in any obvious way. Once you realized that, the next thing you had to figure out was how to keep *him* from winning. And *winning* for Tanner, in this particular instance, meant killing Sammy and me.

Sammy explained that he had been working overtime to erode Tanner's foundation, but that was only a nuisance. Tanner could always find another coke supplier, another porn king, another rich girl. To him, one was pretty much like another.

Sammy's real idea had been to keep Tanner busy plugging holes, distracted, so he could hit from the blindside, something Tanner would never see coming.

We were in a cab going back to Manhattan before Sammy revealed that part of his scheme.

'Like a lot of miscreants, Tanner doesn't like banks,' he said softly. 'He keeps almost all of his money in that fancy penthouse where you went. In a safe built like Fort Knox, a whole room-sized number, all the walls lined with three feet of iron. Joshua could blow his horn and the whole building could fall down but the safe would still be locked.'

I sat back in my seat. There was no point in interrupting Sammy. He'd get to the point eventually. Because I was certain it didn't involve going to Tanner's penthouse to crack his safe.

'The thing is,' Sammy went on, 'I know a plumber.'

He took a heavy breath. I could tell he was in pain. And his shirt was wet, so he was bleeding through his bandage.

'Plumber?' I said after too long a silence.

He nodded. 'Arnie. He's, like, eighty at this point, but in the younger days he installed the copper pipes in that building before it was Tanner's, back in the thirties when it was built.'

'Uh huh.' I had no idea where he was going.

'So when Tanner bought the building and did the new build of the top floor, he needed a plumber to move some pipes so he could turn one of the walk-in closets on the top floor into his safe. He found out that Arnie did the original work, highly recommended, and so Arnie was summoned.'

'You know all this *how*?' I asked.

Sammy turned to me with a whisper of a smile on his face. 'Arnie Cohen, New York's finest plumber, is my uncle twice removed. See? God gave me that. God wants me to get Tanner.'

'I'm very uncomfortable with the way you keep bringing up God,' I confessed. 'But it is a nice coincidence, the plumbing thing. I assume that Arnie gave you some inside scoop about the safe, if I may cut to the punchline.'

'Right.' Sammy nodded and sat back. 'Right. So in order to get Tanner's sauna and his indoor pool set up, the main water line had to be redone for the whole floor. Tanner's penthouse floor.'

'He's got an indoor pool?'

'Not the point,' Sammy snapped. 'Arnie had to run a water main underneath the floor. Which meant he had to put most of that plumbing in from the ceilings of the apartments below Tanner's floor, get it?'

'OK.' Still waiting.

'That's how he discovered that the *floor* of Tanner's safe wasn't three feet of iron. It was three inches of subflooring, just like any other room, with a thin layer of metal on top to make it look like the rest of the walls in the safe.'

'I'm not sure I understand,' I said. 'Arnie figured this out *how*, exactly?'

There was Sammy's smile again. 'The guy who installed the safe had a daughter.'

I waited while Sammy took a couple of deep, painful breaths.

'The daughter had just gotten married,' Sammy went on. 'The safe guy asked Tanner for an apartment in the building instead of pay for the work.'

'In a building owned by Tanner Brookmeyer?' I asked.

'What could be more secure?' Sammy sniffed. 'Tanner paid off all the cops, and no hood is going to mess with the building. The apartment would be as safe as the safe, get it?'

'OK.' I sighed. 'And?'

'And Tanner said yes, the happy couple could have an apartment right below the penthouse. But the safe guy, don't remember his name, realized that three feet of iron would make his daughter's ceiling height less than six feet. And her new husband? Six foot five. So the safe guy, he adjusted. He changed three feet of iron into three inches of iron. And get this: it's less than that along the line where Tanner's water main is, to make room for the pipes.'

'Arnie the plumber knew the safe guy,' I assumed, 'and gave you all this information.'

'Arnie's a loveable guy,' Sammy said. 'He got to know everybody working on Tanner's penthouse. I have a couple of stories

about Tanner's butler, Howard, that you wouldn't believe. You
met Howard, right?'

'I almost got to taste one of his croissants.'

'There you go.' Sammy nodded. 'So, to the point. The safe
guy's daughter and her husband moved in, happy as clams. But
they go to Florida every year about this time. They're gone for,
like, the whole month.'

'Wait.' I sat up. 'Wait *just* a minute. You're not suggesting that
we bust into Tanner Brookmeyer's safe from the apartment below.'

Sammy leaned on his side and fished a set of keys out of his
pants.

'These get us into the apartment below. I made some calls from
the YMCA. We're meeting a group of guys at Tanner's building.
I been planning on this for quite some time. The fact that you
caused such a ruckus around the building just recently is a nice
coincidence. I think that might even make things easier for us.'

I leaned forward fast. 'Stop the cab.'

'Don't stop the cab,' Sammy told the driver.

The driver didn't even slow down.

'We're only three blocks from the place, Fog,' Sammy went
on. 'Come on.'

'I'm not going to break into Tanner Brookmeyer's safe,
Sammy,' I insisted. 'When the cab stops, I walk.'

'Walk where?' he wanted to know. 'Where are you gonna go?'

'I'll go to a bar called Tap-A-Keg,' I said. 'It's close by. I'll
have a hair of the dog, because my hangover is threatening to
kill me worse than Tanner is.'

Sammy looked at me lengthwise. 'You do look a little off
color.'

'Are you familiar with the negroni?' I asked him.

He nodded. 'I told you one of my uncles is a caterer. I used
to tend bar for him sometimes. I can build you a negroni like
you never had. My secret is that I burn the orange peel before I
put it in the drink. It brings out the essential oil.'

I stared at him. 'I'm not going to break into Tanner Brookmeyer's
safe,' I repeated. 'It would only make him want to kill me more.'

Sammy shook his head. 'I don't think that's true. I don't think
he could want to kill you more than he does now. You got into
his house. You shot at him, for God's sake.'

'He shot first,' I answered, a little weakly.

'Yeah.' Sammy laughed. 'Like that makes a difference to him. I mean, you gotta face the fact that you *already* broke into Tanner's home. And you shot at him. I wasn't planning on doing that. I just want to ruin his life.'

I sat back and watched the sidewalk roll by as the cab sped along. 'The thing is, Sammy, that what you're doing is a little sample of what's wrong with the world in general, if you don't mind a little philosophy here.'

He shrugged. 'Why would I mind? Go on.'

'Take a look at this. Tanner hit you so you hit Tanner. But the thing is, when you hit him, he just hits back. Then you hit back. Where does it end? All over the world people say, like I just did, "He started it." And it keeps going, see? He hit me so I hit him so he hits me. Where does it end?'

'Well, in this particular instance,' Sammy answered, 'it ends with Tanner destitute and out of luck: no friends, no money, no life. After that I walk away. Because after that, Tanner Brookmeyer can't do bad stuff anymore.'

'Yeah, but that's what everybody thinks. Once I put this guy down, he won't get up again. That's what the world thought about Germany after the First World War. And how did that work out?'

Tanner leaned toward the cab driver and said, 'This is it right here, thanks.'

The cab slowed; Sammy handed the driver a fifty.

'No,' the guy said, irritated. 'I can't break this.'

'You misunderstand,' Sammy said sweetly. 'It's all for you.'

The driver stared at the bill. 'It is?'

'Maybe you're so overwhelmed by the generosity of this particular tip,' Sammy answered, 'that you can't remember anything else about us.'

The driver nodded. 'My memory's not so good even without the incentive.'

I sighed and got out of the cab. We were a block away from Tanner's building, and not far from Tap-A-Keg. I stood on the sidewalk in silence for a minute or two, and Sammy stood beside me, his hands folded in front of him like a pall bearer waiting to pick up the casket.

On the one hand, I could go to Tap-A-Keg and have a drink, talk to the regulars, find out a little more about Nan the understudy. Then I could go to Nan's place and get her to admit that Tanner instructed her to give Emory the poisoned coke that killed her. And then I could flap my arms and fly to the moon, which was just as likely to happen as a confession from Nan, I realized.

Or I could say goodbye to Sammy, take a pleasant walk back to the Benjamin, maybe grab a nap for my hangover, then pile into my T-Bird and point it south. I could be back at the donut shop by breakfast, joke around with Bibi there, maybe finally ask her out on a date.

Or I could go on a suicide mission with my newly discovered little brother.

Sammy read my thoughts. 'Made up your mind yet?' he asked me. 'Are you coming with me or not?'

'All I wanted was to come to New York, see Bob Dorough, have a slice of Ray's, and then go on back home to Florida,' I began softly.

'And then I happened,' Sammy commiserated. 'Sorry.'

I took a good long look at Sammy then. His lapels were dotted with blood and food, the dark circles under his eyes had nearly turned purple. He was leaning over like a hundred-year-old man, gasping every third breath. And the smile on his face said that he didn't have a care in the world. That's the kind of *happy* you get when you know what you're doing in this world. It was the same smile I'd seen in photographs at my mother's place; photographs of my father.

'You know what, Sam?' I concluded. 'I think I came to New York to find out about you. So I don't really have a choice. I have to come with you.'

'Yes!' he shouted. 'God made you come to New York to do this with me!'

'There's God again,' I mumbled.

And off we went.

TWENTY-SEVEN

The ruckus around Tanner's building had not completely subsided. People who had been evacuated because of the gas leak were still complaining. There were cops and firemen milling around. You could even still smell the gas on the street. Sammy was right: it did make it easier for us. We just walked into the building, right through the open security door. The elevators were taped off, so we had to use the stairs, which was a little rough for Sammy. But we made it to the floor underneath the top floor. There were seven or eight people milling about there, too, but when Sammy made his appearance, everyone looked his way.

Sammy took in all the faces, checking to make sure he knew everyone. Then he introduced me. 'This,' he said, pointing, 'is none other than Foggy Moscowitz.'

There was an audible collective response. Sammy cut it short.

'He's here to help,' he went on. 'In fact, he's the reason for all the confusion on the street around here. The gas leak is bogus. He's the reason Tanner's not in his place right now. We don't even have to use the fire alarm gag that Dickie Sunshine set up.'

Lots of nodding.

'So!' Sammy announced.

Everyone scrambled. We were in the apartment within seconds. An A-frame ladder appeared, and a guy was up to the ceiling with a reciprocal saw hacking into the sheetrock. The saw was almost silent, had some kind of hood over it. The guy sawed a rectangle about three feet long by a little more than a foot wide, right inside the ceiling studs. The sheetrock was handed down and the saw dug into the subflooring underneath the room above. Took less than two minutes to hand down that rectangle of wood, and the guy with the saw was down the ladder. Another guy with a blowtorch was up. The blowtorch was quiet too, and the guy operating it was faster than the guy with the saw. Down came a rectangle of iron. But the guy with the blowtorch lifted his protective visor and sighed.

'There's something else up there,' he complained softly. 'Another layer of something. Feels soft but it makes me nervous.'

Silence.

Then it occurred to me. 'It's a rug. A fancy Persian rug.'

Everybody stared.

'The entire place up there has expensive rugs, every floor surface I saw in Tanner's place. My guess is that he's got a nice one in his safe too.'

The guy with the blowtorch reached up and gingerly tested my theory. He poked, he nudged, and finally he flipped the corner of the rug back to reveal the interior of the darkened safe.

There was another demonstration of affirmative nodding in my direction, and the blowtorch guy came down off the ladder.

Up the ladder was a little guy I mistook for a kid at first. He couldn't have been more than five feet tall, and skinny as a rail. He was very dark, like maybe Southern Italian, and he was wearing a T-shirt and skintight jeans, no shoes. In a couple of seconds he had pulled himself up into the safe. Somebody else went up the ladder and handed him a flashlight and some kind of bulky bag that turned out to be a construction chute. In no time, the chute had been deployed and stuff started barreling down it and on to the floor.

First there were large bricks of coke, maybe twenty of them. These were hustled into official mail bags, and a couple of guys dressed as mailmen shouldered them and were out the door, all without a single word.

Next came cash, bundles of twenties and fifties and hundreds, they just kept coming. These were neatly stacked against a short wall in the apartment next to a hallway. The bundles were laid side by side in layers and stacked until they almost reached the ceiling, the last ones had to be carefully put in place with another ladder.

Then, out of nowhere, two-by-fours appeared, and a quick frame was put together over the stacked bills. Out came sheetrock, tape, mud, and in five minutes two guys were painting the new wall that hid Tanner's cash. I couldn't have guessed at how much was being hidden in the new false wall, but it would have been seven or eight million dollars at least.

Finally down the chute and a little louder than anything previous: a good number of firearms.

These were immediately set upon and taken apart. All the guns were dismantled and hidden in dozens of toolboxes, covered up with screwdrivers and hammers and packs of nails.

I finally turned to Sammy. 'This is incredible, this organization, man.'

He smiled. 'Phoebe.'

'What?' I asked him.

'Phoebe planned all this. I mean, I told her the idea when they were still rehearsing the play. I been planning something like this in my head for a while, but Phoebe took off with it. She made a playbook, assigned parts; we rehearsed it a bunch of times at that dinky theatre where they did *Hamlet*. You know, during the day when there wasn't anybody there. It's something, huh?'

'I think I'm stunned,' I confessed. 'Phoebe's, like, a genius.'

He beamed. 'I know.'

The little guy dropped the chute, then managed his way out of the safe and down the ladder. The guy with the blowtorch winked at me.

'Good call on the rug thing,' he told me. 'And it makes it easier on me; welding the iron flooring back into place ain't gotta be so neat, see? Because it's covered up with a rug! I just gotta be careful when I'm doing it since we obviously gotta flip the rug down first, then weld the iron. OK.'

And he was up the ladder with his blowtorch and the rectangle of iron he'd cut away. Another guy went up behind him to help, and I turned my attention to Sammy once more.

'Where's all that coke going?' I wanted to know.

'Most of it's being sold,' he told me, 'to pay these guys, pay Phoebe's bail, invest in a couple of Broadway shows. Um. A bit of it's going for your mother's medical care. That kind of thing. Some, I guess, will be more of a personal use kind of thing, but there you are.'

'And the money?'

He shrugged. 'Seems like it'll make good insulation for the apartment, don't you think?'

'You didn't take any of it,' I said.

'I'm not a thief, Foggy,' he said, a little hurt. 'I just wanted to take it away from Tanner. I probably won't ever tell anyone it's there. It'll just be, you know, hidden forever. See? I took down Tanner's primary sources of income, and now all his money's gone. He's got no friends; he's got no juice. He's finished. For good.'

I'd never really seen anyone in my life smiling the way Sammy was smiling then.

Everybody was packing up. The blowtorch guy was done. Sheetrock guys were replacing the subflooring and ceiling sheetrock. The entire enterprise took about thirty minutes. It was one of the most efficient capers I'd ever witnessed.

Everyone was packing up when the little guy who'd been able to fit through the opening and actually get into the safe sidled up to Sammy. He had something in his hands.

'Thought these might be interesting,' he said in a surprisingly deep voice.

He handed Sammy three ledgers. They were each about the size of a copy of the *New Yorker*.

Sammy opened one. 'These are Tanner's books.' Sammy looked up at me. 'These are Tanner's main accounts. Money, people . . .'

'The last one is just for people Tanner has on his payroll,' the little guy said. 'It's cops and judges and politicians. In addition to the more obvious criminal element, obviously.'

With that, the little guy nodded and was out the door. Two more minutes and everyone had scattered. The apartment looked like no one had been there.

Sammy and I were the last ones in the place before he handed me Tanner's books.

'Maybe you should take these,' he said.

'What am I supposed to do with them?' I asked him.

'I don't know. You're the one who's on the right side of law and order now. Give them to Phoebe's lawyer?'

I shook my head. 'She's not a prosecutor. But OK. Let me think.'

I didn't want to be carrying the things around out in the open, not with all the people around Tanner's building. So I stuffed them down the back of my pants just so I could get clear of the neighborhood with them, and out the door we went. Down the stairs, out into the back alley. There was still one fire truck there, and a couple of cops, but no one gave us a second look.

TWENTY-EIGHT

We were out on the street and I steered us in the direction of Tap-A-Keg before Sammy and I resumed our conversation.

'Wouldn't you refer to what we've just done as a *caper*?' he asked me, half-seriously. 'You know, when you tell people about it.'

'I think I'd call it more of an *operation*,' I said. 'It was so well organized.'

'You want something run right,' he said, 'get a stage manager.'

I didn't disagree. I just kept walking. And we ended up just where I wanted to: in front of Tap-A-Keg.

'Buy you a drink?' I asked Sammy.

'I thought you had a hangover,' he said.

'Hair of the dog, Sammy,' I said. 'Or maybe you know the great old blues song "What's the Use of Getting Sober If You're Just Gonna Get Drunk Again."'

He nodded. 'I know it well. Sang it once or twice in a club in Brooklyn. Man, they *hated* me.'

I opened the door to the bar. 'I'm sure they didn't hate you.'

But when Sammy and I stepped into the bar we were greeted with something like our worst nightmare.

There, at the bar, with Nan the understudy, sat Tanner Brookmeyer. Otherwise, the place was deserted.

Tanner had a gun in his hand, and that hand was on the bar. And on that bar, in front of Nan, there were ten or twelve long lines of cocaine. Nan was crying. Tanner was wild.

'Hey!' he greeted us. 'Look who it is!'

Nan looked at us and sobbed.

'We're playing cocaine roulette!' Tanner shouted. 'Two of these lines are from the batch that Nan gave to Emory. The rest are clean. Relatively clean. I mean, sure, there's baby laxative and maybe a little talcum, but it's cleaner than a lot of the stuff you get on the street. My point is two of the lines are *unbelievably bad* news. And to tell you the truth, I don't exactly remember which ones. But Nan, here, is gonna play our game, aren't you, Nan?'

He waved the gun in front of Nan's face.

'Tanner.' Sammy shook his head. 'What are you doing? Look at the poor kid.'

Tanner didn't look. He just went right on talking.

'The *poor kid* has acquired quite the drug habit.' He grinned; it wasn't a pretty sight.

'Whose fault is that?' Sammy asked, inching his way toward the unhappy couple.

'Fault?' Tanner exploded. '*Fault?* She's made a career out of *not* working, hanging out in this toilet, and snorting my coke!'

He looked around the bar, shaking his head, obviously disgusted by his surroundings.

'Where are your friends?' I asked Nan. 'The regulars.'

'Oh, I got rid of them,' Tanner said. 'And the bartender. Gave them the day off. Which brings us to the sixty-four-thousand-dollar question: what the hell are *you* two doing here? Did you follow me, Foggy? I mean, I'm not complaining. I get a kind of a two birds/one stone situation, I guess. A little bit of good luck, right?'

I was moving toward the bar like Sammy was, barely perceptibly.

'I've been here before,' I said. 'I just came in to buy Sammy a drink. He's still recovering from the last time you shot him. Remember that?'

'Oh, that's not the last time I'm going to shoot Sammy Cohen,' he said, and he stood up.

He stood up so fast, in fact, that his bar stool went flying out behind him and Nan screamed.

That made Sammy grab his gun; it made me duck.

'You don't kill easy,' Tanner shouted, 'but I know you can get all the way dead *somehow*!'

And he fired a three-shot burst.

I was below the line of fire, hidden behind the side of the bar. Sammy just stood there firing his Python. Nan was on some kind of loop, screaming and gasping and screaming again.

I edged my way around the corner of the bar, pulled my ankle pistol and shot at Tanner's legs. One bullet ripped through his calf and he howled.

Nan took that moment to run. Still screaming, she headed for the door.

Tanner shot at her. She kept running. I couldn't tell if she'd been hit, but she fell silent. Maybe she saw salvation just outside the door and had a moment of focus.

It didn't matter. Tanner fired again and she tumbled forward on to the floor, two feet from the door, groaning, out of steam, and probably bleeding.

'Tanner!' I yelled. 'What are you doing?'

'I'm settling every score!' he told me, top volume. 'Soon as I'm done here, I'm headed for Brooklyn; finish it with Shayna!'

I could actually hear the cocaine in his voice: high-pitched, frantic, insensate.

When a demon like that has a hold of a person, reason goes out the window. It was clear that Tanner would not be swayed by words, and it was possible that bullets wouldn't work either.

Sammy had come to the same conclusion and was edging toward Tanner with his gun firing shot after shot.

I knew a couple of the bullets hit Tanner; I could hear him grunt when they did. But they didn't seem to stop him.

'He's wearing a vest, Sammy,' I announced.

'That's right!' Tanner laughed. 'I've got a vest!'

'But he's not wearing it around his head,' I suggested. 'And I already got him in the leg.'

I saw Sammy take aim out of the corner of my eye. He fired, but Tanner was bobbing and weaving like a fighter, and the bullets zipped by his head.

Tanner was backing away, then, toward what looked like the storage room of the bar.

'Hang on, Sammy,' I said. 'Where's Tanner gonna go at this point? And we have to look after Nan.'

Sammy glanced backward, saw Nan on the floor. She wasn't moving.

Tanner picked up his pace and made it to the storage-room door at the back corner of the bar.

Sammy reloaded in a split-second and kept firing.

I got over to Nan. She was breathing funny.

'The storage room lets out on a loading dock in the alley out back of here,' she said weakly.

'Alley?' Sammy panicked. 'He's getting away!'

'No, Sammy. Think about this!'

What I meant was that Sammy had already taken all of Tanner's support out from under him, and we could just leave him to rot. But Sammy got a different message.

'Right!' He headed for the door. 'Get him out in the alley. Less conspicuous. Good thinking.'

And he was gone.

'I think I got shot,' Nan mumbled. 'In my side.'

I didn't see blood. What I saw was a contorted flip-flop.

'You have a pain in your side?' I began.

'Like a knife,' she moaned.

'Could it be a cramp or something?' I went on. 'Because I think you tripped on your flip-flop and fell over.'

She rolled and stared up at me. 'You're that guy.'

'Yes,' I said, 'I'm that guy. And aside from having the crap scared out of you, I think you're OK. Maybe you should consider laying off the coke for a while, though.'

'Oh.' She thought about it. 'Yeah. Probably so. Good idea.'

I got her to her feet.

'If I'm not shot,' she said vaguely, 'I'd like to go home.'

'How did you and Tanner come to be here?' I asked. 'It's a very odd coincidence.'

'He came to my apartment,' she said. 'He was wild. He said he had some free coke for me. But he scared me, so I told him there were people waiting for me here, at the bar. I said they'd come looking for me if I didn't show. So he dragged me out of my place, and we came here. But he was just as scary to everyone here as he was to me. They objected to everything about him. The bartender picked up the phone. Tanner shot the phone. Most of the guys ran out then. Tanner told the bartender to take off and shot at him. To tell you the truth, I don't believe Tanner was thinking straight.'

'Yeah, you're not all that coherent yourself,' I told her. 'Don't go home. Go somewhere else, somewhere Tanner wouldn't know about. Just in case Sammy and I don't catch up with him, OK?'

She seemed to understand. She nodded, anyway.

And then she limped out the door without another word.

TWENTY-NINE

S o, Tanner was crazy. A product of his own product. Because one of the things about coke is that you *think* you're thinking, but you're not. You're just crazy. What that meant to me was that I should get as far away from him as possible. What that meant to Sammy? I had no idea. But I thought I should check the back alley.

And then it occurred to me how much of my recent life had happened in a back alley.

And then it occurred to me, once again, that if I had any brains, I would go get my car, fill up the tank, and see how fast I could make it back to Florida. Because I thought Florida might be just about far enough away from Tanner Brookmeyer.

And by the time I was finished thinking *that*, I was standing at the entrance to the alley.

It was like any other alley in most ways. Narrow with high brick walls on either side, a couple of dumpsters, a smell that would have killed a lesser man. What made it unique was the odd ballet that was playing out fifteen yards away from me, at the far dead end.

Tanner and Sammy were circling each other like semi-professional wrestlers. Neither one had a gun in hand. They were stepping in garbage and sludge and questionable liquids. They were growling like some kind of mutant bears.

In short, I didn't remotely understand what I was seeing.

'Hey!' I yelled. 'What the hell are you guys doing?'

They both looked my way. I could see that Sammy's bleeding was worse. Maybe he'd torn his stitches.

'He says he wants to kill me with his bare hands,' Sammy answered. 'And my gun was empty.'

Tanner added a low-pitched howl to the conversation.

'Tanner's out of his mind,' I yelled to Sammy. 'You should come over here. You're bleeding.'

Sammy's suit was wet with blood. But Tanner's face was flushed. His hands were jerky. Even far away as I was, I could see that his nostrils were raw, and rimmed in white.

'He's going to want another bump in a minute,' I went on, louder, aiming my words at Tanner. 'He's going to start to get nervous about it, then itchy, then desperate. Am I right, Tanner? Don't you need another little bump about now? Isn't there a little voice in your head that wants just one little bump before you kill Sammy with your bare hands?'

Tanner made a noise like a water buffalo.

'Is that right?' Sammy asked Tanner. 'Would you like to take a break for just a second to have a little pop? I don't mind. You can kill me just as dead five minutes from now, right?'

Tanner paused in his strange circling movements. He seemed to be considering what had been said. Or maybe he just momentarily forgot what he was doing.

Then, without warning, he shoved his hand into his coat pocket and came back with a large baggie almost filled with white powder, maybe ten thousand dollars' worth of coke.

'OK.' Sammy smiled and started backing away from Tanner.

Tanner popped open the baggie and took a big pinch of coke between his thumb and first finger. Sammy continued to move toward me, keeping his eyes on Tanner. Tanner snorted what he'd gotten from the baggie and went right back into it again. Six times.

By then Sammy was next to me at the mouth of the alley.

'A person who does that much coke,' I whispered, 'is going to have some kind of heart attack.'

Tanner was closing up his baggie when he suddenly realized that Sammy had disappeared. He looked around like he'd dropped his wallet, searching the bricks all around him. He didn't even look our way.

'Come on, Sammy,' I said. 'You shouldn't be out and about. You should go to my room at the Benjamin, have a lie down.

Because it doesn't look to me like you can kill Tanner right this minute. It would take a tank.'

He nodded. 'To tell the truth, that sounds about right. But what about you? You only got one bed in that room, and I'm betting you wouldn't mind a little break too.'

'Yeah,' I said, headed for the street, 'but I guess I have to go see Helen Baker, the lawyer; talk with her about these books we got from Tanner's safe.'

'I thought you said she wasn't the one to talk to about that.'

'I keep forgetting that I'm her official investigator. I should at least show her what my *investigation* brought me to: all of Tanner Brookmeyer's illegal activities. I think she'll know what to do with them.'

Sammy laughed a little more heartily than he should have, because it made him cough, and the coughing hurt his bullet wounds.

But he managed to say, 'Can you imagine what'll happen when that poor guy sees his empty safe? I'd give anything to be a fly on the wall.'

He was still laughing and coughing when the cab stopped. We dropped him at the Benjamin with my key, and I went on to Helen Baker's office.

Her office wasn't quite as noisy or busy as it had been the last time. She seemed surprised to see me. She was dressed in a brown suit with a skirt below the knee, and her hair was up in a bun. In other words: courtroom fashion.

'I was just on the way out,' she said. 'And you're a mess. What've you been doing?'

'You're going to want to see what I've been doing.' I unbuttoned my coat, reached around, and came back with Tanner's books.

She stared at them. 'What am I looking at?'

'Everything Tanner Brookmeyer's done wrong,' I told her. 'Including, in that red book, all the cops and judges and politicians he's paid over the years. I thought that would interest you.'

She stared at the red book.

'I already checked to see if you're in it,' I went on. 'You're not.'

'Good to know,' she said, giving me a particularly dirty look.

'I figure you can put all this to good use,' I told her, 'and also bolster the case against Tanner, you know, what with the tape recording you already have. That I gave you. You said you needed more. I got you more, right?'

She was thumbing through the books like crazy, stopping every third page or so, eyes wide.

'This listing here is for the judge I'm going to see right now!'

'About Phoebe's case?' I asked.

She shook her head, 'Different judge.'

'Too bad.'

'Oh, no, the judge for Phoebe's case is in here too. Jesus Monkey Christ, Moscowitz. If these books are really what you say they are . . .'

She found something in one of the books that made her stop talking.

Then she looked up at me.

'What?' I asked.

'Lee Alexander is in here.' Her face was whiter than it ordinarily was.

'Who?'

'The . . . the Mayor of Syracuse,' she stammered. 'He's a friend of mine.'

'OK, you can do whatever you want with all the information in these books,' I said. 'All I care about is getting Phoebe Peabody out of jail and out of trouble. She is, I recently discovered, a more remarkable person than I originally thought.'

Helen seemed to come back to herself and nodded. 'Right. Good. OK.'

She shoved Tanner's books into her briefcase, then took them out and put them in her desk, then took them out and handed them back to me.

'You have to keep these,' she whispered. 'I can't have them on me. You're my investigator. You have to keep them.'

She held them out but all I did was stare at them.

'No,' I said. 'I brought them to you so you could do something good with them.'

'I . . .' She blinked. 'Yes. Of course. So, I have to figure this out. And I'm late for court right now. Could you *please* just take

these for a little while and, and when I get done in court, I'll
call you at the Benjamin. Please.'

I didn't want to, but I took the books back. 'Do you have a
large envelope or something that I could carry them in?'

She reached into her desk and pulled out a large blue folder.
It had a flap and a big stretchy thing that wrapped around it. All
three of Tanner's books fit into it neatly, and the stretchy thing
kept it closed. I couldn't decide if that was better or worse than
just carrying the loose books around. But it didn't matter; Helen
Baker was racing away, and I was standing around her desk like
a chump.

And even when I got back to my room at the Benjamin, that
chump-like feeling was still with me. The room was dark, and I
didn't turn on the lights because I figured Sammy was asleep.

I eased my way in and set the blue folder down on the little
kitchenette ledge right by the door, where the coffee machine
was.

I took off my coat. Then I remembered that I'd sent my other
suit, the seersucker, out for cleaning. I wondered about it. I
opened the closet and there it was, in a clear plastic bag. Looked
good.

And it was about that time that my eyes began to adjust to
the dim light in the room.

Someone was sitting on the bed and it wasn't Sammy. Sammy
was lying there, a little too quiet and still.

I took a quick sidestep into the bathroom beside the kitchenette
and flipped on the room light as I went.

Tanner looked like the creature from the black lagoon, that
movie monster. He was drenched in sweat, his hair was matted
and smeared across his face, and he was shaking like St Vitus.
He had his pistol in one hand and a rolled-up bill in the other.
There was a mountain of coke on the bedside table.

'Your suit came back from the cleaners,' he said, lightning
fast. 'The guy let me in. He thought I was you! Or I told him I
was you. I can't remember which. Still. Nice suit!'

'Seersucker,' I told him. 'Very cooling.'

'It's gonna be a hot summer,' he commiserated.

'How'd you find me?'

'There is a network of bellboys and housekeepers in this town like you wouldn't believe,' he snapped. 'Lot of them work for me. You know, arranging for hookers, drugs, downtown entertainments for the out-of-town mentality.'

Before I could respond, Tanner threw one of the pillows from the bed. It came flying toward my head at the same time as Tanner started shooting. His gun didn't have a silencer, and it was unbelievably loud in the small hotel room.

I flipped off the room light and ducked back all the way into the bathroom. I locked the door and got up on the sink to the right of the door. It was the only place Tanner couldn't shoot me unless his bullets made a U-turn.

But he tried anyway. He fired five more shots through the bathroom door. The bullets went into tiles mostly, but the door had a big hole in it, near the knob.

Tanner reached his hand in to unlock the door, but I kicked his hand hard and he howled. My thinking was that he'd made enough noise that somebody would call the cops or at least the front desk, and some kind of help would show up.

I was trying not to think about Sammy. He hadn't moved since I'd come in, and I was afraid Tanner had done the worst.

Tanner started kicking the door with his foot then, and he snarled like a rabid dog. I slinked down from the sink and grabbed a bath towel.

Tanner's foot came through a panel of the bathroom door. I zipped over, tied one end of the towel around his ankle, and pulled hard. He went down, firing his gun as he fell.

I pulled hard on his leg and most of it came through the hole in the door. It tore his pants and wood splinters raked his shin. He started bleeding and he was struggling to stand, but he couldn't.

I managed to tie the other end of the towel to the faucet in the sink. I knew it wouldn't hold for long, but I was hoping it would do for a few seconds.

I backed away as far as I could in the little bathroom, and then I launched myself as hard as I could at the bathroom door.

It gave way; really hurt my left shoulder. But I came flying out of the bathroom and landed, along with big hunks of door, right on top of Tanner.

He flailed, trying to bring the barrel of the gun up to my face, but a lot of my weight was on his gun arm. He tried to use his other hand to grab my tie, hoping to get a choke hold.

But I was up, standing over him. I kicked his gun hand five times before he let go of the gun. It only dropped a few inches away, but at least he couldn't shoot it.

I kicked again, going for his head, but he grabbed my foot and I lost my balance. I went crashing down, knocking over the Mr Coffee machine in the kitchenette.

Tanner sat up as best he could, trying to figure out what was happening to his leg and why he was stuck.

I scrambled for the gun and got it. I stood, took a few steps back, and aimed for his skull.

'Hey!' I shouted so he'd look at the gun pointed at him.

He looked, but it didn't settle him down at all.

'Empty!' he snapped. 'Besides, you wouldn't pull. I know your rep. You're St Fyvush of Florida! He don't shoot to kill!'

'Really?' I asked reasonably.

And then I aimed right between his eyes and pulled the trigger.

Unfortunately, Tanner was right: the gun was empty.

While I took the merest second to realize that fact, Tanner somehow disentangled himself from the towel and scrambled to his feet. The look on his face was not remotely human. He was standing with his back to the room door, panting.

I tossed his gun away and it clattered to the floor somewhere behind me. I went for my ankle holster.

That was a mistake. When I bent over, Tanner jumped, flew through the air and tackled me like we were playing football. I went down hard on the carpeted floor with Tanner on top of me. He was bellowing and thrashing. I was nothing but scared.

He got his hands around my throat and leaned in with all his weight. He was drooling and breathing hard. His eyes were mostly red. His face was bone white and covered in sweat.

He was going to kill me. I knew that. I felt his grip tighten and I was light-headed, about to pass out.

The next thing I knew, Tanner was sitting back. He'd let go of my throat and he was quiet. It took me a second to catch my breath, and another to clear my eyes.

There was Sammy, face covered in blood, standing behind

Tanner with his tie around Tanner's throat. Tanner's eyes were wide and bulging a little. Sammy was straining and holding his breath, pulling the tie tight. Tanner just looked surprised. He wasn't flailing or panicked, he just couldn't quite comprehend what was happening to him.

I got to my feet about the time Tanner passed out.

'Let go, Sammy,' I said.

'Nuh uh,' Sammy answered.

'I don't want you to kill him in my hotel room,' I insisted. 'I like the Benjamin. I might want to come back here one day.'

'Some hotel,' Sammy said, pulling harder on the tie. 'All this racket and not one phone call, no hotel security coming to check on you. Why would you want to come back here?'

And just at that moment there was a knock on the door.

'Hotel security!' said a very commanding voice. 'Open up!'

I smiled at Sammy. 'Now will you let him go?'

Sammy took a deep breath, unhanded his tie, and Tanner slumped to the floor, unconscious. I looked around, got his empty gun, put it in his hand, and then flew to the door.

'Oh, thank God you're here!' I said as I opened the door. 'Get the police. This maniac got into my room when the hotel delivered my dry-cleaning. And he shot my friend! Look!'

I stepped back.

There sat Sammy on the bed with his face covered in blood, and there was Tanner on the floor, gun in hand, twitching.

Two guys in weird uniforms burst in at the same time as I flipped on the room light. The place was a mess, but the physical evidence supported my story to the hotel dicks.

'I'm an investigator working for the attorney Helen Baker,' I went on, pulling out the card Helen Baker had given me to prove what I was saying. 'This man is Tanner Brookmeyer, the subject of my investigation. We need to call the police now.'

The hotel guys were surprisingly cogent. They looked around. They assessed. One put Tanner in handcuffs while the other called the cops, and then the hotel's on-call doctor.

I sidled up to Sammy.

'He shot you in the head,' I whispered.

Sammy managed a smile.

'Tanner came in with the dry-cleaning,' he whispered. 'He

was surprised to see me. I sat up. He landed on the bed, shoved me down, and put his gun to my temple. The thing is, he was just too loaded. I rolled. He shot. Grazed my sideburn and made the pillow explode. It did *look* like he'd blasted my brains out, but it was really just bloody pillow feathers. See?'

I looked. He was right. Bloody pillow all over my nice bed.

'He was also abusing cocaine while he waited for Mr Moscowitz,' Sammy told the hotel guys, pointing to the coke on the bedside table.

Then they started asking questions. None of them mattered, really. I showed my Florida ID, Sammy showed his driver's license. They checked Tanner's. The cops showed up. It was a tedious couple of hours.

But in the end, Sammy was patched up, Tanner was off to jail, and I was relatively happy.

THIRTY

I called Helen Baker when everyone had gone from my room. She was surprised to hear that Tanner Brookmeyer was in jail because of me.

'I thought you said it would take King Kong to bring the guy in,' she said.

'I said Godzilla, actually.'

'What's the difference?' She let out a deep breath. 'Man, have I had a weird day.'

'*You've* had a weird day?' I repeated. 'I've been chased around Manhattan by a guy who scares everybody on the planet. And he ended up in my hotel bed!'

'In your bed?' Her voice went soft. 'That's a part of the story you didn't tell me.'

'Not in my bed like . . . Sammy was napping in my bed and Tanner shot him in the head – or thought he did – and then waited for me to come back.'

'You left out a whole lot of the more entertaining details of this thing,' she told me, 'but the short of it is that I'm glad you're OK. So. All we need is this Nan character to verify what you've told me about the poisoned coke, and Phoebe Peabody is out of jail and back at work managing ill-conceived theatrical productions.'

'Nan?' I asked.

'The one Tanner mentioned on the tape you played me.'

'I thought you said the tape was no good,' I hedged.

'By itself,' she confirmed. 'But now we have Tanner creating mayhem at this bar and in your hotel room.'

'And he nearly killed Nan,' I added.

'Put them all together, they spell *conviction*.'

'But can't we leave poor Nan out of it?' I said again. 'She's had a pretty rough time lately.'

'She is the proximate cause of Emory Brewster's death. Accessory to murder, pal. She's actually the one who gets Phoebe out of jail.'

'So now I have to bring you the poor little understudy?'

'Yes.'

'I don't like working for you.'

'Nobody does,' she said. 'That's why I have to pay so well. Go get Nan. Bring her in.'

I didn't say goodbye, I just hung up the phone. I looked around at the chaos of my hotel room. It seemed an appropriate metaphor. It looked like the rest of my life at that moment.

So, first things first, I called the front desk to get another room. Turns out that was already in the works. The good old Benjamin.

Second, I roused Sammy. He was lying down in my bloody bed.

'Sam?' I nudged his leg.

'I heard,' he mumbled. 'We gotta go get Nan.'

'No,' I corrected. '*I* have to go get Nan. You have to keep lying down. You've been shot twice.'

He sat up. 'Yeah, I've had worse. Besides, you're getting another room and I have to get up and move anyway, right?'

'Well,' I began.

'So let's just go over to Nan's and get her. I can rest after that.'

'No, Sammy . . .'

'You went all the way to Atlanta to help me track down that

Denny guy for Tree,' he said, standing. 'I can go to Columbus Avenue with you. It's the least I can do.'

'I didn't go to Atlanta to help you,' I began.

But Sammy was already headed for the door.

New York hadn't always had an X-rated bookstore on every corner, but they were certainly everywhere Sammy and I went to get to Columbus Avenue: painted flat black, no windows, no names, no self-respect. I could still remember the New York of the fifties. I was just a kid, but it was a world of chic sophistication, Miles Davis, beatniks, Moondog on the corner of something and 42nd Street. And all in black and white. That's how I remembered it.

That's the thing about living in a town, any town, for a while, since you were a kid. You're not just walking down a particular street in the present; you're also walking down that same street in a hundred different pasts. That corner over there is where I saw DiMaggio, waiting for the light to change, in 1964. Right after he married Marilyn. And that place there used to sell the best bagels in the western hemisphere. It was a laundromat now.

Everything changes.

Sammy and I arrived at Nan's building just as the sky started clouding up. That made the entrance hall dark and it took me a minute to remember which door was Nan's, but when I got there, I realized that the bullet holes would have been my best clue. They hadn't been repaired.

I knocked and called out at the same time. 'Nan?'

Nothing.

I knocked again, but silence reigned. I tested the door and it opened. It looked like the bullets had damaged the lock.

And there was Nan, on the floor of her sad little one-room apartment, absolutely motionless. I couldn't tell if she was breathing or not. I got to her first, but Sammy was right there. She had a pulse, but there was no snapping her out of it. She was down for the count.

Sammy was patting her face and tried mouth to mouth while I got to her phone and called for an ambulance. I told them that she was unconscious from an allergic reaction. It wasn't exactly a lie. She was probably allergic to the coke Tanner had made her snort. But the response time for an allergic reaction was a lot faster than for a drug overdose. I knew that from experience.

Still, it took nearly forty minutes for the medical types to arrive. Nan was still breathing, but she couldn't be revived.

'What was it?' one of the guys asked. 'What's she allergic to?'

'Plum sauce,' I said right away. 'Came with the Chinese takeout. She's allergic to plums, but she didn't know it was in the sauce.'

That was a bit of improvisational theatre. I happened to see the takeout containers brimming over in the garbage can in the kitchen area of the apartment. And it just so happened that aunt Shayna was deadly allergic to plums. They almost killed her twice.

'How did you happen to find her like this?' he went on.

I hauled out the official looking card from Helen Baker.

'She's part of an ongoing investigation,' I said. 'We suspect that she was given the sauce on purpose. To keep her from testifying. I really can't say any more.'

He nodded. 'She's going to Mount Sinai West.'

And that was it. Nan was off. I called Helen Baker from her apartment.

'So Tanner's in jail,' I began as soon as she picked up the phone, 'and Nan's at Mount Sinai. What more do you want from me?'

'Who is this?' But she was kidding. 'And why is Nan in the hospital?'

'Tanner's coke,' I reminded her. 'Apparently she got a little bit of the bad stuff.'

'OK, OK.' She shuffled some papers around. 'I guess all you have to do now is bring me those ledgers, the ones you showed me. I can use them now.'

I caught my breath. 'Right. The ledgers. See you in a little while, then.'

And I hung up.

'I left Tanner's ledgers in my hotel room,' I said as I grabbed Sammy's arm. 'Come on.'

'I thought you gave them to the lawyer,' Sammy complained as we hustled out of Nan's little apartment.

'She wouldn't take them,' I told him, 'until we had something more.'

'And now we have Tanner in jail and Nan in the hospital.' He nodded. 'But maybe we don't have the ledgers, because somebody forgot about them and left them in a hotel room.'

'I was a little distracted,' I said, 'what with Tanner killing you and trying to kill me.'

'I'm not *completely* dead,' Sammy mumbled.

We were out on the street trying to catch a cab when I realized what bad shape Sammy was in. Shot up, running all over town, worried about Phoebe, it was a wonder he could walk. He was wheezing like a pump organ, limping, and making little involuntary pain noises.

But I thought it would be better to get him to my hotel room than to send him back to the YMCA or to a hospital where they'd ask a lot of questions.

So we stumbled into the cab when we got one and made it to the Benjamin. I was so concerned about Sammy that I didn't think to check at the desk, I just went to my room. Which, of course, was being cleaned. By three housekeepers.

Sammy leaned against the wall in the hallway and I went in.

'Sorry,' I said to one of the housekeepers, 'this was my room and I left some stuff in it, just came to retrieve it.'

She looked at me and squinted. I knew I looked like a wreck. Before she said a thing, I could see that the ledgers weren't on the counter where I'd left them. And the closet doors were open. All my stuff was gone.

'They put everything in your new room, sir,' the housekeeper said.

'Right,' I said. 'Which room was that?'

'Oh.' She looked at the other two housekeepers. 'They'll have that information at the front desk.'

'Of course,' I told her. 'Thanks.'

I turned to leave.

'Mr Moscowitz?' she said to my back.

I stopped. 'Yes?'

'Tanner Brookmeyer is already out on bail.'

I turned in a flash. 'What?'

My sudden move startled her. She took a few steps back away from me.

'I . . . I thought you should know,' she stammered.

'How did *you* know?' I asked her.

She looked at the other two women, and all three of them remained silent.

But then I remembered that Tanner told me he was hooked into a network of bellboys and housekeepers. Apparently, they weren't all loyal to him.

'Thanks for the heads up,' I told her.

And I was out in the hallway in a flash.

'I have to go down to the front desk to get my new room key,' I told Sammy. 'Do you want to wait here or come with me?'

'I'll come with,' he groaned.

And we were back in the elevator, down to the lobby, and leaning on the front desk in under two minutes.

'Ah, Mr Moscowitz,' said the young woman there. 'We've given you a free upgrade, a corner suite. I think you'll find it quite acceptable.'

'Sounds great,' I said. 'And thanks. All my stuff got moved there?'

'Of course,' she assured me. 'All your clothes are in your new suite.'

'And my books?' I asked. 'I had a couple of ledgers.'

'Yes, about those,' she said, suddenly nervous. 'Your assistant came by for them.'

I froze. I think I stopped breathing. 'My assistant?'

'He said his name was Howard, I think?' she said, like it was a question.

'Howard.' It only took me another second to remember that Tanner's butler was named Howard. 'When was that? When did he come to get them?'

'About fifteen minutes ago?' Another question. 'Not long before you got here, anyway. But. I'm afraid that without your authorization we didn't feel comfortable giving them to him. I hope that wasn't a problem.'

I started breathing again.

'So the books are actually *where*?' I asked her.

'Oh. In our safe, the hotel safe. Shall I get them for you?'

'No,' I said, exhaling slowly. 'I think they're perfect where they are, and thanks for not giving them out to anyone. Let's keep it that way, right?'

'Of course, sir.' Then she produced a key. 'Your corner suite, third floor.'

'Right.' I glanced at Sammy. 'My friend Mr Cohen here is a little the worse for wear. I'll just get him settled in. He's the one who got shot in my room.'

'Of course,' she told me. 'Does he need anything?'

'Just a moment's rest, thanks to your house doctor.'

She smiled. 'Good, just let us know if there's anything else we can do.'

'Actually,' I told her, 'would you mind keeping my new room a secret? Given what happened up there in the old room, I'd really rather that no one knew where I was, at least for a while, right?'

'Oh, sir,' she assured me, 'we would never divulge that information.'

I nodded, then back into the elevator and up to the third floor.

The suite was a nice surprise. The kitchenette was large, and there was a living room sort of thing in addition to the bedroom. And windows all around. Sammy made it as far as the sofa and collapsed.

'I'm just going to rest my eyes for a second, and then . . .' he began, but he fell asleep before he could finish his sentence.

I checked my closet, and all my clothes had been moved in, along with my suitcase and my shoes.

Then I sat down in the chair next to the unconscious Sammy Two Shoes and tried to think what to do next.

I figured Tanner had seen his ledgers in my old room when he'd come in and tried to kill Sammy, before I got there. And he certainly would have taken them away with him if he hadn't been arrested. But he made bail, called Howard, told him to fetch them from the Benjamin. But the Benjamin wouldn't hand them over. Good old Benjamin.

So what would Tanner do next? Where would he go?

He'd be looking for the books. He'd be looking for me. And he'd still want to kill Sammy.

Even in his coked-up state I didn't think he'd be crazy enough to come back to the Benjamin, not after fighting with hotel security and being arrested there. But he might be waiting outside, on the street, maybe, or in a car. I'd walk out of the hotel and he'd just pop me in the open and wander away.

I wouldn't say that I was generally prone to paranoia, but like they say, you're not paranoid if they really *are* after you. And I was absolutely certain that Tanner Brookmeyer was after me.

So my decision was to go down to the bar in the Benjamin, take a window seat, have a beverage, and scope out the street. When in doubt: drink and wait.

Sammy took no notice of my departure. He was out cold.

Down the elevator and into the bar. I was happy to see a crowd because I didn't want to be a conspicuous individual. I got a table at the corner so I could see down East 50th and Lexington at the same time, at least a little.

The waiter convinced me that I was hungry, and he assured me that the club sandwich would go well with my double martini. Fifteen minutes later, the sandwich was crumbs, the glass was empty, and there was no sign of Tanner.

Just as I was about to venture forth, Helen Baker appeared, busting through the door off Lex like she owned the place, business suit, briefcase, and all.

'I thought I might find you here,' she said, loud, motoring my way. 'What are you doing? Where are my ledgers?'

I stood. 'Hello, Ms Baker.'

'Yeah, hello,' she snapped. 'Where are the books?'

'Safe and sound.' I sat back down. 'You should try the club sandwich in this place. I'm not usually a fan, but . . .'

'What are you *doing*?' she growled. 'I've been trying to call you here at the hotel, but they told me you weren't in. Tanner Brookmeyer is out on bail, which I don't know how that happened. And it's a good bet he's looking for you.'

'That's why I'm sitting here in the corner,' I said calmly. 'I'm apprehending the situation.'

'Oh, really. Well apprehend this: I'm on the hot seat. I broke it to the D.A. that I have the goods on Tanner, and he actually salivated. He's been trying to nail the guy for ten years.'

'And how does that put you on the hot seat, exactly?'

'You saw the books!' she railed. 'It's full of my colleagues! People I work with every day! Cops and lawyers and politicians and judges and . . .'

'Also hookers and bellboys,' I interrupted. 'Don't forget the hookers and bellboys.'

'What are you talking about?' She was clearly upset, and her voice was nearly an octave higher. 'Get up. Get the books. Come to the D.A.'s office with me!'

My martini was taking hold, and I was very calm.

'Let's just leave the books where they are at the moment,' I said. 'But what about if we go talk with Nan the understudy? She's probably willing to rat out Tanner now, since he tried to kill her. That seems like it would go a long way to nailing Tanner.'

'Christ. OK. She's where? Sinai West you said?'

'Right.' I reached into my coat and produced a wadded-up bar napkin. 'Also this will help.'

She glared. 'What is it?'

'It's a sample of the coke I think Tanner used to kill Emory and try to kill Nan. I scooped it up off the bar at Tap-A-Keg before I went out to the alley to watch Tanner and Sammy try to kill each other. It's laced with a lot of strychnine, some of it is. It's the kind of thing a person like you might call evidence, don't you think?'

'Wadded up in a napkin?' She shook her head.

I caught the waiter's eye. He came over. I gave him twice what the bill came to, told him to keep it all if he could manage to get me a baggie. He could, and he did.

Minutes later, still a little nervous to be out on the street with Tanner loose in the world, I joined Ms Baker on Lexington, hailing a cab. Took us longer than I wanted it to, and even longer for us to get to Sinai. Lots of traffic. Maybe it was rush hour, I'd lost all sense of time.

But I started relaxing once we got into the hospital. Seemed safe. A little jazz with the head nurse at the desk, tossing around phrases like 'key suspect' and 'murder investigation' and we got permission to go into Nan's room.

It was down at the end of a long hall, and the smell of the place was making me nervous, a combination of bleach and isopropyl alcohol and low-level dread. But the hallway was unclut-tered and quiet. Room 327, on the right. Everything was fine.

Ms Baker got to the door first, and she was on the verge of barging in, but I interceded, stepped in front of her, and eased the door open gently.

Unfortunately, I was slapped in the face by déjà vu.

There was Tanner Brookmeyer, dressed in a white orderly's coat, standing over Nan the understudy. Only instead of forcing her head down on to lines of cocaine, he'd reverted to a more conventional ethos. He had a gun with a silencer pressed against her temple. He'd also thrown a pillow over the gun and his hand, so you could only see the silencer sticking out. He was just standing there, staring at her. She was unconscious.

He looked up when we came into the room, but he didn't seem surprised to see us. In fact, he smiled. His eyes were droopy, and his face was a little ashen. He'd crashed.

'OK, this'll save me a trip,' he mumbled to us. 'Have a seat, I'll be right with you.'

'Tanner,' I began.

But he didn't hear me. He was talking to Nan. It was clear he didn't realize she was unconscious.

'I always had a little thing for you, as I was saying,' he told her. 'I mean, maybe it was a father/daughter thing, but anyway. And I'm sorry I got you involved in this. You were a good kid. Also sorry for being so crazy at your apartment, and at that bar. I'll go by there later and apologize, OK?'

'Tanner,' I tried again.

'Sh,' he told me without looking at me. 'I'm talking to Nan. I'm saying goodbye.'

I glanced at Ms Baker. She was a lot quieter than usual, and nearly frozen. The only way you could tell she wasn't a statue was the labored breathing and the faint smell of panic.

I took a step toward Tanner. He raised his gun and fired. A bullet tore through my arm. Baker started screaming and ran out of the room and down the hospital hallway. I dropped to the floor and flew forward. I grabbed a leg of Nan's bed and shoved it hard toward Tanner. He fired the gun again, but he did it while he was falling backward.

I looked around. There was a silver bedpan on the metal hospital chair next to Nan's bed. Empty, thank God. I grabbed it, steadied myself, and jumped. Up on the bed, then so high that I hit my head on the ceiling, but I came crashing down on Tanner, slamming the bedpan against the side of his face so hard that something cracked, maybe a cheekbone.

Tanner howled and fell all the way back on to the hospital

floor. And I came down on top of him. My knee landed in his stomach and knocked the breath out of him. He gasped. I slammed the bedpan down on his face again and he dropped his gun.

My arm was bleeding and it felt like it was on fire. I was about to hit Tanner again when he looked up at me. His face was like a little kid's.

'Why doesn't Shayna like me, Foggy?' he asked softly. 'I'm basically the same guy as your father, and you know she had a thing for *him*, Shayna did. I don't get it. I'm just like him. You might as well just pick up my gun and shoot me in the head now. I think I'm done.'

It was such a sad and unexpected speech that I was momentarily stunned.

'I'm not going to shoot you, Tanner,' I finally said.

'Why not?' He was just about to cry.

I dropped the bedpan. It clattered on to the hard hospital floor. I stood up and kicked the gun away. It glided under Nan's bed and almost out the door.

'Because I'm not my father,' I answered him.

The second I said it there was a cascade of images in my brain that would have rivaled any Fellini film. The stoop in front of our apartment in Brooklyn when I was ten years old. Red Levine patting me on the head. Aunt Shayna laughing. My mother singing 'Lush Life' at the top of her lungs. Me and Sammy pitching pennies. Me and Sammy smoking in the graveyard. Me and Sammy stealing cars. It wasn't exactly my life flashing before my eyes, but it was a certain part of my childhood in Brooklyn.

I barely noticed when the cops came into Nan's hospital room. I had no idea where they came from. I didn't even realize at first that Tanner had managed to shoot Nan after he shot me. I didn't feel the bullet wound in my arm anymore. I stood there silent, watching people tend to Nan, tend to me, arrest Tanner. Again.

I don't think I snapped out of it until I heard Helen Baker say, loud, 'Could we please get Mr Moscowitz into an emergency room bed! He's my best investigator!'

I turned to her and smiled.

That's the last thing I remembered.

THIRTY-ONE

I woke up in a hospital bed. Everything was cloudy. The light through the blinds was white and stark. The overhead florescent was off.

A couple of blinks, a bit of coughing, and things were a little clearer. Helen Baker was sitting by my bed, reading. A nurse was on the other side of the bed hanging up some sort of IV. The nurse noticed me first.

'Well,' she said brightly. 'Look who's up.'

Baker lifted her head from her book. 'Oh, good, you're not dead.'

'Not for lack of trying,' I assured her. 'How's Nan?'

'Intensive care,' Baker said. 'But she'll pull through. Look what I got.'

She held up one of Tanner's ledgers.

'How did you get that?' I asked. 'The guys at the Benjamin . . .'

'Court order,' she interrupted. 'I even had a cop with me.'

'So, how are they?' I wanted to know. 'Tanner's books.'

'Illuminating beyond belief.' She lowered the one in her hands. 'If I can prove half of the stuff that's in this, it would go a long way to cleaning up a nice little part of Manhattan.'

'You?' I smiled. 'I thought you were a Public Defender.'

'Screw that,' she said. 'I'm working with the District Attorney on this. It's too big.'

'Plus,' I added, 'you can make a name for yourself.'

She nodded. 'They're already talking about running me for office.'

I settled in. 'I need to call Sammy. See how he's doing.'

She closed Tanner's ledger. 'About Sammy. He came to get Phoebe Peabody when I got the D.A. to drop the charges against her. You should have been there. It was like a scene out of *Romeo and Juliet*.'

'Sammy's in love.' I shrugged.

'Yeah.' She nodded. 'Looked to me like the feeling was

mutual. Anyway, I was there, and Sammy gave me a message for you.'

'Message? Why doesn't he just come and see me?'

'Well, you realize he's still facing charges,' she said. 'He did stab a person in the neck with a mechanical pencil.'

'After she was dead!' I objected.

'Nevertheless.' She slipped the ledger into her briefcase and crossed her legs. 'The message is that he went to see a tree.'

I waited for the rest of it, but Baker shrugged and fell silent.

'He went to see a *tree*?' I asked.

She nodded. 'That was it.'

Two more seconds and I realized something. 'Could he just have said that he was going to see *Tree*?'

'Huh.' That's all she said.

'Did he say how long he might be?'

She shook her head. 'I told him that I wouldn't say anything about him to anyone until tomorrow.'

Sammy had gone to hide out for a while. In Atlanta, on a dead-end street. So at least I knew he was safe.

'What about Phoebe?' I asked.

'What about her? She's off the hook.'

'Do you have her contact information?' I asked. 'I'd like to see her before I leave town.'

'OK, about that.' She gave out with a heavy sigh. 'If I'm going to be the first black female District Attorney of New York, I'm going to need the best help I can get. That includes the best investigator. Meaning I'm hiring you. Right now. On the spot. Big money, prestige, a *badge*.'

I sat up. 'No. I'm going back to Florida just as soon as I get out of this bed.'

'Florida?' She made a face. 'What's in Florida?'

'I have friends there,' I told her. 'And there's this girl at the donut shop.'

'You have *Seminole* friends,' she said, 'many of whom are wanted by the federal authorities. And that girl in the donut shop, Bibi, is dating two other guys at the moment.'

I looked up at the nurse. 'How long have I been out?'

She smiled. 'You were in surgery day before yesterday. And now it's afternoon *today*.'

I looked back at Baker.

She raised her eyebrows. 'What do you want from me? I did my research. I also know that your mother has leukemia. That alone is a good reason for you to stay in the city.'

'What good does it do my mother if I stay?' I began.

'You can give her your bone marrow, knucklehead,' she interrupted. 'You can save her life.'

'Did you just call me *knucklehead*?'

'It's a perfectly good word,' she insisted.

'I disagree. But more than that: I *disagree*. With, like, everything you just said. One of my friends, John Horse, is a mystic. He might be two hundred years old. And Bibi? She's not dating. She's just going out.'

'The distinction is lost on me,' she said, 'but it's your life. Such as it is in *Florida*.'

She made the word sound like a disease.

The nurse finished up her ministrations and split. I closed my eyes.

'Do you really think you can nail Tanner Brookmeyer?' I asked. 'He's been bad for more than twenty years, and he's never gone down for it.'

'These books,' she began, 'which, by the way, I will never ask you how you got, but anyway these ledger thingamajigs? In combination with Nan's statement, which is a doozy, and your tape? I think we've got the bastard.'

I opened my eyes. 'You just used the words *thingamajig*, *doozy*, and *bastard* in the same paragraph. *That's* a compelling argument for staying in New York and working for Helen Baker.'

She stood up very suddenly, briefcase in hand. 'I'm a character. What can I say?'

She headed for the door.

'I'll let you know,' I called out.

She didn't turn around. 'I've already put in the paperwork.'

And she was gone.

So, that was that. In the matter of the murder of Emory Brewster, the cops charged Nan and Tanner both. Nan's defense was that she didn't know the coke she'd given to Emory was loaded. Tanner's defense was that he didn't do anything. The general thinking was that Nan was a credible innocent and Tanner was a career criminal, one who was about to get his just deserts.

Sure, they found Sammy's fingerprints on a part of the pencil he hadn't wiped. They found a tiny bit of fabric from his suit in Emory's hair. They just couldn't find Sammy.

Phoebe tracked me down at the bar in the Benjamin on the day I got out of the hospital. I still had one more night there and I intended to enjoy my suite.

She told me that Helen Baker let her know where I could be found. Phoebe was wearing a forties dress and a hat with a net in front like they used to have. She took the time to admire my seersucker, fresh from the dry-cleaner. We got the niceties out of the way. I asked her how she was doing. She told me she was freaked out, and still scared, and staggeringly relieved, all at the same time.

Then she showed me a letter from Sammy. She said he'd taped it to her apartment door. He'd copied a couple of lines from *Hamlet*. 'Doubt thou the stars are fire; Doubt that the sun doth move; Doubt truth to be a liar; But never doubt I love.' She said she was going to carry it around in her pocket every day of her life until Sammy came back to her. Which I knew he would.

We sat in the bar at the Benjamin for a long time, had a bottle of champagne to celebrate a couple of things. First, a toast to her getting out of jail. Second, a toast to the long arm of the law finally nabbing Tanner Brookmeyer. And then Phoebe told me she got a new gig, a hot new show on Broadway, assistant stage manager. That *Godspell* show Ralph had been so excited about. So we drank to that, even though it sounded terrible.

About the time the bottle was empty, she asked me if I was going right back to Florida. I told her about Helen Baker's New York offer.

'Interesting,' she said, only a little drunk. 'Sammy told me you were out of New York for good, even though he wished you'd come back. But you don't seem that much like a Florida guy to me.'

'My apartment is on the beach,' I argued, 'I know a two-hundred-year-old Seminole shaman, *and* a girl named Bibi likes me.'

'On the other hand.' She held up a hand and started counting things off. 'Broadway, Radio City, Ray's pizza, Delmonico's, the Waldorf Astoria, Birdland, the Village, the Met, MOMA, The

Village Vanguard, Moondog on 42nd street dressed like a Viking, for God's sake!'

She went on like that for another five minutes before I stopped her.

'It's not a fair choice,' I told her softly. 'Because Fry's Bay, Florida, exists in a different reality than this city. This isn't a decision between two different cities at all, in fact. It's not two roads diverging in a yellow wood, like the poet says. This is about who I *am*. Or, really, who I'm going to be. It's not a choice at all, really. It's an existential crossroad.'

She nodded and finished her glass.

'Sounds like a pretty big decision, Foggy,' she said. 'What are you going to do?'

Tell Foggy what to do at www.phillipdepoy.com

ACKNOWLEDGMENTS

For some of the people and events of this novel, acknowledgment must be made:

To the anthology *Ellen Hart Presents Malice Domestic 15: Mystery Most Theatrical* in which a short story of a small portion of this novel appears.

Also to Dean Ford in whose New York apartment I lived for a short while in the early 1970s when I encountered many of the places and versions of the people in this book.

Also to Bob Dorough, whom I met at Reno Sweeney's in the 1970s and whose music continues to influence me.

Also to Hal Peller who showed me around Brooklyn, where some of this novel takes place, in the late 1970s and introduced me to my first egg cream.

Also to every stage manager with whom I have worked over the course of fifty years in the theatre world. Any one of them could plan an excellent heist *and* get away with it.

And finally to the ghost of Benetta McKinnon in whose duplex I lived on Dickson Place in Atlanta in the early 1970s. She had just died when I moved in, and I saw evidence of her several times. Once she left me a bouquet of dried flowers. Also there were junkies living downstairs. It was an odd time.